Bleeding Hearts

Stories of Love and Murder

Sharon Michalove

"Aegean Persuasion" was first published in *Tales of the Golden State of Mind*, 2023.

A Hotel in Istanbul was first published in *The Love Archives*, 2024.

"Chasing Donatello" was first published in *Taking Flight,* Blackbird Writers, revised edition 2024.

"Leaving Cleveland," was first published in *Provoked*, Blackbird Writers, 2024.

ISBN: ISBN: c (Paperback)

ISBN: 978-1-960919-00-7 (E-book)

FOREWORD

Some of these stories first appeared in anthologies, others were available on my website.

First up are two stories connected to my Global Security Unlimited series. Max Grant and Cress Taylor are on their way to Venice on the Orient Express as an epilogue to *At the Crossroads*. In "t's Just a Guise,"they compare Halloween in the US and Max's home, Scotland.

"Aegean Persuasion," first published in *Tales from the Golden State of Mind*, does have a connection to the forthcoming *Murder at the Great Jane Austen Cook Off*. It's a romance, but Lady Agatha Carstairs, who sees herself the Miss Marple, does have a little mystery to solve.

"Sylvie and Alice" is a longer version of "Sylvie Green," first published in the anthology, *A Reason to Be Here*. It is the bittersweet story about a young, newly published author, who meets an admired author near the end of her life.

If you want a heartwarming Christmas romance, "Grace and Favor" might be just your cup of tea. Two widowers meet at a historic hotel in Rye over the holidays. Will they find love—or are they too wary to connect?

"Chasing Donatello," is kind of a caper story about art, theft, and murder in Florence. I might find another story or two for Raine Sheffield.

The last two stories are set in Ohio and Michigan. "Leaving Cleveland" is connected to *Dead in the Alley* and explains how and why Greg's partner, Detective Lane Fairchild, ended up in Sherburne, Michigan. In "Vanishing Trees," newlyweds Greg and Bay have to figure out why their newly planted trees are disappearing and is another story connected to the Murder in the North Country series.

A little added value are the illustrations that accompany some of stories. I produced them using Canva.

Hope you enjoy the blend of mystery, mayhem, murder, and the magic of love in this collection.

GELATO AND GONDOLAS

Gelato and Gondolas is an epilogue to *At the Crossroads*, the second book in the Global Security Unlimited series, a finalist in the 2024 Chanticleer International Book Awards series category. At the end of that book, after a hair-raising climax, Max and Cress are on their way from Paris to Venice on the Orient Express. This is the story of what happened in Venice.

If you haven't read *At the Crossroads*, it's available on Amazon, as is the are the other books in the series, in the series, *At First Sight* and *At the Ready*.

Epigraphs

"I spent the next couple of hours either walking around with a gelato in my hand or on my knees in church asking to be forgiven for the sin of gluttony."
——*Mark Leslie*

"To go out in a gondola at night is to reconstruct in one's imagination the true Venice, the Venice of the past alive with romance, elopements, abductions, revenged passions, intrigues, adulteries, denouncements, unaccountable deaths, gambling, lute-playing and singing."
— *Peggy Guggenheim*

Max

The Orient Express from Paris to Venice. That's the plan. Until my brother plants his big feet into everything.

"Can you change your booking?" Ian peers at me through my small screen. I'm walking down the Rue de Rivoli, trying not to walk into the masses of tourists moving as a small herd from window to window on one of the busiest shopping streets in Paris. Cress wants a small enamel plaque that says "Chats Lunatiques." I'm meeting her at Eglise Saint-Eustache for the memorial service being held for the victims of the terrorist attack two nights ago at the Victor Hugo House in the Place des Vosges.

"Why should we do that, Ian?" The testiness in my voice makes no discernable impression. I add a ferocious scowl.

All that does is make his long-suffering drawl even

longer and more suffering. "Since our house in Clerkenwell was blown up, the insurance adjusters need to see both of us. And a detective has more questions."

"Why would the police think I'd know more now than I did ten days ago?"

"Reflection."

"Fuck reflection. I'm still processing what happened in Paris."

"They are connected," he observes moving on to loftier tones. "You can tell them a lot about Arslan and his plot."

"He's dead," I state in my most repressed, matter-of-fact voice. "They can just stamp case closed on the dossier."

"Look, take the Eurostar tonight and I'll meet you at St. Pancras. You'll be on your way the day after tomorrow. Cress will love the extra travel time."

"Fine, we can come tonight. Right now I'm on my way to a funeral."

Ian in properly silent.

I walk into the massive medieval building where a massive crowd stands in the relatively short nave. I look over where Cress, face spotted with tears, speaks with members of the funeral party. This is the memorial service for the people who died in the terrorist attack. We stayed on extra days in Paris so we could attend, grateful that none of us were victims. My fingers twitch. Yavuz Arslan and his brothers may have paid for kidnapping Cress, but if he was in front of me, I'd have my fingers around his neck.

"Max, are you still there or have you frozen?" Ian's voice seems distant.

"Sorry, I'm not just standing still you know. Hold on while I check the times." I tap keys, the slow internet maddening. Once I know what's what, I continue, "meet us 22:30. And make sure we have a place to stay."

"Righty-o." The jaunty expression rubs my already irritated nerves. "See you soon."

He rings off before I can say more. Grumbling, I sidle over to Cress, who is holding the hands of a small Frenchwoman in a black silk dress and hat with a veil that hangs to her shoulders. Next to them is her husband, gaunt, frail, propped into a wheelchair with a rug over his legs. He was injured in the attack.

Cress smiles. "Max, this is Monsieur and Madame Comfrey. Madame et Monsieur, voilà mon copain, Max Grant. We all nod in recognition, then mouth a couple of anodyne phrases before we take our seats in one of the rear pews fumbling with the order of service and the unfamiliar prayerbooks.

Afterward the prayers, singing, and memorials, we stand to the organ playing Bach's Toccata and Fugue. We turn out of the pew toward the door and my hand goes to the small of her back. I sigh as the tension in my neck and shoulders releases. I steer her out of the church, past the priest and the families, and out into late afternoon April sunshine.

"Did you find my plaque?" Her voice is brighter than I expected after a solemn service on a drizzly afternoon.

"Yeah." I pull the small packet out of a slightly damp pocket and thrust it at her.

She grabs the tiny rectangle and squeals with delight. "Can we put it on the front door?"

"Let's think about that when we get home."

My voice is flat as I remember my conversation with Ian. I'm tired and I'm sick of constantly having to fit in with other people's wishes. Right now being in Chicago seems like heaven.

"What's up?" Her eyes are curious but unworried.

"Ian called. Change of plans." I sigh.

"So what else is new?" She still seems bright rather than worried.

"We need to go to London. We'll do the Orient Express trip from there."

"Why London?" Now she looks concerned.

"Ian and I have to meet with the police and insurance adjusters over the terrorist attack. Not a big deal, but it needs to happen tomorrow. I have us booked on the Eurostar tonight and he'll meet us at St. Pancras. But first, we need to eat. We'll stop by Chez Casimir for some nosh before we catch our train."

Our luggage is in a locker at the Gare de l'Est, a short walk from the Gare du Nord. We can pick it up, then go to dinner.

"You were able to adjust our train reservations." A flat statement, not a question.

"All taken care of. And a pleasant add-on to the trip."

She nods her acquiesce. "Do we have somewhere to stay?"

"That's Ian's task."

I wrap my fingers around her elbow and we head out for our final Parisian meal, wheeled cases clattering behind us. The green awing is welcoming and the diners who can't give up their cigarettes spill out onto the sidewalk tables. Cress agrees that indoors is preferable. It's a homey neighborhood place with round, wooden-topped tables, matching chairs with green upholstered seats, everything slightly worn. The tiles have an eight-pointed star design.

"They look like quilt-squares," Cress says, glancing at the floor as we are shown to our table, close to the traditional zinc bar.

The oysters are plump, fresh, tasting of the Atlantic. The rillettes of duck with juniper and pink peppercorns burst with flavor. Cress follow with a dish of pan-fried wild mushrooms and while I have a Côte de cochon du Perche, which is a fancy name for schnitzel. We finish by sharing a Tarte Tatin and a selection of farm cheeses before strolling over to the Gare du Nord to catch our train.

We arrive in London slightly late. Ian is pacing on the platform. Once we collect our luggage, he walks us over to the St. Pancras Renaissance Hotel. The Gilbert Scott neo-gothic Victorian pile is right at the entrance to the station.

"I'm living in one of the Chambers Suites at the moment and I was able to book one for you. Almost home from home really. I may just stay permanently rather than find new digs."

Looking up the decorated grand staircase, Cress whispers, "This reminds me of the Saint-Chapelle. The renovation must have cost a bomb."

"Incredibly expensive and ten-years work, but definitely worth it. Hard to believe the building was slated for demolition."

"Isn't it a grade-one listed building?" Outrage has Cress quivering.

"It was derelict," Ian says, carelessly. "The government had the option and it was an eyesore." He takes a breath, ready to wax on but Cress is wilting.

When he notices her slumping against me, he relents. "Do you need something to eat before bed?"

"We had a huge meal at Chez Casimir before we left," Cress says.

Ian looks like he has more to say, so I butt in. "Where's our room?"

After check-in, we follow him to the elevator and ascend to a private floor and the Hayward suite, complete with separate living room. Cress grabs a complimentary bottle of water. You'd think she'd just emerged from weeks in the Sahara.

"Ordered you a paper for tomorrow. And breakfast is available in the Chambers Club."

The suite is a feast of walls the rich burgundy of a museum gallery, with contrasting cream wainscoting, thick area rugs with understated designs, and raw silk drapery. The furnishings have a low-slung, modern feel that creates a comfortable space within the grandeur of eighteen-foot ceilings and the meticulously created medieval ambiance of the public rooms.

Cress

The bustle at platform 2, Victoria Station, reflects the general excitement of people going the trip of a lifetime. It may only be two days, but heightened expectations surround the crowd waiting to be escorted onto the first phase of their Orient Express experience. A dress bag hangs over my left arm making my grasp on the handle of my dressing case awkward. Hard plastic cuts into my palm. Our luggage has been whisked off to the baggage compartment and we won't see it again until it's delivered to our Venice hotel.

My new traveling costume was a last minute purchase. While Ian and Max spent hours with police, insurance adjusters, and estate agents, Grant women descended en masse.

I compare my spa experience with the recent one before Brian's birthday party. Although only a few weeks ago, it seems more like a lifetime. This spa is very Victorian, as befits the hotel. We begin with a session called Journey to Harley Street. Over two hours of exfoliation, aromatherapy, and a facial. We also manage a percussive back and shoulder massage before we indulge in lunch and hours of shopping in Bond Street, where I wince at the prices.

Meggy sterns informs me that I will not be allowed on the train unless I am suitably attired—which does not include sweatpants or t-shirts or, god forbid, jeans. These edicts are backed up by her massively pregnant sister Diana and sister-in-law Liz. Prudently prepared with a suitcase, they pack up all my clothes, replaced by more suitable wear.

Now I'm in cream gabardine slacks with a matching long jacket and a silk top with Durer's hare peeking out. I have comfortable low-heeled brown Mary Janes and the thinnest stockings I've ever worn. The dress bag contains a long evening gown in sapphire with silver ballet flats.

Max and I sip Bellinis and munch on scrambled eggs with smoked salmon and caviar while chugging through the Kentish countryside to Folkestone, where we'll transfer onto luxury buses that will take us to the Eurostar for the Channel Tunnel leg of our journey. Once on the other side, we're met by our personal steward, who hands us glasses of sparkling wine, takes my hand luggage, and escorts us to our compartment. We settle in until, sooner than we expect, it's time to change for dinner. We need to leave enough time because I know when Max helps me remove my current garments, he is going to be distracted for at least a little while.

Eventually, I am in my clingy, almost too-sexy backless dress and Max is resplendent in his new tux.

Once he knew he'd need dinner clothes for the trip, he contacted his tailor, who was able to make up a new one as a rush order, based on the fittings for the one severely damaged in the Paris attack. He'd had it delivered directly to Victoria and was sublimely confident that it would fit perfectly, which it does. I smooth down his shirt front, tuck a tissue or two into his cummerbund, and pull lightly at his lapels, earning a lingering kiss. Long, thin fingers caress my spine, the combination sending waves of pleasure through me. Neither of us wants to break the moment, but, scheduled for the last dinner sitting, Max's phone alarm signals that it's time to go.

Our steward escorts us to the bar car, where we have the specialty of the house, a Guilty Twelve cocktail, created to celebrate Agatha Christie's novel. The barman, as expected, refuses to divulge the twelve secret ingredients and the flavor is so complex I don't even try to guess. Then we try the other special cocktail, Chaos, made with Monkey 47 Schwarzwald Dry Gin, Chartreuse, and a few drops of Boker's Bitters, a distillation of dried orange peel, green cardamom pods, catechu, quassia bark, star anise, cloves, and angelica root. Only three ingredients, but the bitters alone give it an incredibly intense flavor profile. I'm almost tempted into second but as the train bumps along the track, I worry that I might lose my balance.

In their tiny kitchen, the dinner chef and his team create a gourmet's dream meal. The restaurant car, lined with Lalique glass panels, is the perfect setting.

Lobster with caviar, roast beef with truffles, cheese, and dessert—I'm stuffed to the gills. We adjourn to the bar car to listen to live piano for a few hours and chat with fellow travelers before dragging ourselves to bed. Max doesn't miss an opportunity to tell all and sundry about my writing and, unusually prepared, I promise to hand out bookmarks at lunch to anyone who's interested.

Morning arrives with stunning Swiss mountain scenery and breakfast in our compartment. Pastry, fruit, coffee, and tea keep us lingering in our room although the urge to move around finally wins out and we get up, dressed, and off to the bar car, where we find some of our friends from the night before. Word has spread and I have a continual line of people asking for bookmarks and telling me how much they like the chance to meet a real author. Two people have read at least one of my books so I pull out a couple of book-plates and sign them to stick in their copies when they get home.

We finish with more scenery, lunch, tea in our compartment, and a stroll to shop in the boutique. Max buys me a silver-foiled, laser cut popup card of the train as a memento and I pick out an enameled tie pin for him. And then we pull into track 9 at Santa Lucia station and move from the magic of the train to the enchantment of Venice.

I imagine myself as a glamorous 1920s socialite as I step out of the wagon-lit, new dressing case in hand. The Orient Express to Venice is an experience every romantic should have once in their life. A special fund to enable people to taste the pleasures of the past in the present would be a brilliant idea. Maybe I could interest the company and some other historical fiction writers to get together and create a yearly reader contest.

A large hand curls around one shoulder. "We should move out of the way, *la mia stellina*," Max whispers, his warm breath making my neck tingle. "The porter is here to collect the luggage."

A water taxi is laid on to take us to our hotel, all part of the service.

Max

I originally thought we could stay at the Danieli, with all its associations with famous authors, but the chance for Cress to stay in a newly renovated fifteenth-century hotel is too good to pass up.

When the water taxi arrives at our stop, I hear her take a deep breath when she sees the big square building with its Venetian gothic windows. "Is that...?"

"Somerset Maugham said, 'There are few things in life more pleasant than to sit on the terrace of the Gritti when the sun about to set bathes in lovely colour the Salute, which almost faces you.' Don't you want to see for yourself?"

"I suppose." The caution in her tone surprises me.

"I thought you deserved some luxury."

She snorts with amusement. This isn't the first luxury hotel we've stayed at on this trip,

As we walk into the splendid room, Cress' eyes widen at the large flower arrangement sitting on the coffee table. Then she turns and tries to push past me. "Easy, Cress." I grab her around the waist. "They're silk flowers. No need to panic." I rock her gently, nuzzling her neck.

Then I think of a joke to lighten the mood. "A truck loaded with Vicks vapor rub overturned on the highway." She stands still, expressionless. I reposition her so I can stare at her luminous hazel eyes and, with a grin, give her the punchline. "Amazingly, there was no congestion for eight hours."

Cress' lips turn up slightly. Is she trying to suppress a laugh. The reaction's fleeting, but some of my exhaustion rolls away.

We have the Punta Della Dogana Patron Suite, with sumptuous decor, rare art work, and amazing views of the Grand Canal. "Is this what our life has come to?" she asks. "One luxury hotel after another?"

"Isn't that what life is supposed to be?"

"I think I'm ready to go back to normal, whatever that is," she says. "Even if your house isn't my original normal, it's more like home than this."

"I've scheduled in an in-room couples massage for tomorrow. That should perk us both up before your paper."

"My paper," she groans. "Maybe I should have

canceled after all rather than be at the end of the conference."

"Too late now," I tell her with an airy wave.

She falls onto the bed with all the lack of grace I so love about her.

"Hey, let's relax in the bath," I suggest. "You'll love the dark green marble bathroom and the extra deep tub. Then we'll have a nice late-night dinner at the Club del Doge restaurant. Daniele Turco and his staff turn out amazing meals. "

"How do you know about the bathroom? Have you stayed here before?" She gives me side eye. "Not sure whether I can eat dinner. I'm stuffed after all that food on the train."

"When I was thinking about booking this place originally, I read a lot about the renovations. That's why I chose this suite."

"You're getting as bad as me," she moans.

I give a little snicker. "Just get undressed and I'll run the bath. And don't worry about dinner. You'll have worked up an appetite by the time our reservation rolls around.

Cress

Where is the damn outfit I packed for this book panel? I only had three hours before showtime. The couples massage relaxed me yesterday but the effect hasn't carried over and now I'm vibrating like a lute string. The only thing hanging in the closet is the dress bag with the evening gown. I'm swathed in the oversize hotel robe, feet shoved into complimentary slippers. Walking in any backless footwear is a problem and I have to shuffle, constantly pushing my feet forward so I don't walk out of them.

The careful packing of the new clothes was messed up by rummaging to find things during our train travel. When I dump out my suitcase, my clothes look like they were balled up in a dryer for three days. My simple black suit with a pencil skirt and a cream cashmere turtleneck looks like a pile of rags. "Max," I shout, "how do I save this situation?"

He comes in from the bathroom, wiping shaving cream off his neck, shirt sleeves rolled up to his biceps. I point to the rat's nest on the bed.

"What the hell happened, Cress?" He sounds bemused.

"Beats me. Guess with all the excitement, everything was just stuffed in willy-nilly. Can these clothes be saved?"

He strides over to the house phone. "This is Max Grant in the Punta della Dogana Suite. Do you have an emergency laundry service?" He waits, examining his nails. A squawk at the other end makes him smile. "Excellent." He hangs up the phone and throws the towel into the bathroom.

"Would you like some coffee?' he asks, sorting clothing into piles. Holding up my turtleneck, he asks, "Is this part of the outfit?"

"Yes, that, the black skirt, and the matching jacket. And coffee would be lovely."

A knock at the door interrupts my train of thought. Max lays the outfit over his arm and lets in someone from housekeeping. They have a chat in Italian and he hands over the clothes, then pulls a bag out of the closet and shoves in the rest of my stuff. Everything except what's in my lingerie bag. Then he points at his watch and the man bobs his head, grabs the clothes, and walks off.

As I see my clothes disappear from view, my teeth start to chatter and I can't stop shaking.

"Cress!" The alarm in Max's voice causes me to shake harder. He grabs me by the shoulders. "Cress." With one hand under my chin, he forces my eyes up to his. "Your clothes will be back in plenty of time." He gently pushes me onto a chaise longue. Then he calls for room service.

Several cornetti con crema and too many macchiatos later, I have an hour to spare when my suit reappears. Max tells me that everything else will be in the room by the time we return. He's wearing the business suit that he brought for his London meetings but I'm not sure I want him to come to the talk. The threat of rain means he's got both our raincoats over his arm. As I place my "Caterina Cornaro" Murano glass bead necklace over my head, I say, "Max, maybe you can sit in a nearby cafe. Have a spritz. Read Dante."

He puffs out a breath of indignation and picks up his dual language version of *Inferno*. "You don't want me to come?"

"Would you be very hurt?"

"Wounded but I'll live."

"Sorry, I'm just really nervous."

With a crocodile grin, he starts a joke. "There were two guys in a lunatic asylum and one night they decide they don't like living there any more. They climb onto the roof, and just across a narrow gap they see the rooftops of the town, stretching away in the moonlight. The first guy jumps right across with no problem. But his friend's afraid of falling. The first guy says 'I have my flashlight with me! I'll shine it across the gap between the buildings. You can walk along the beam and join me!' The second guy shakes his head. 'What do you think I am? Crazy? You'd turn it off when I was half way across!'" He laughs. I feel a rumble in my chest but I suppress it with a tight smile.

A chill wind makes the walk to the venue slightly unpleasant but at least it's still dry. Max hands me my coat and presses a kiss into my cheek. "I'll be at that bar on the corner, drowning my sorrows in spritz. Break a leg."

I watch him until he disappears through the door, then I turn and enter the building behind me. The Ateneo di San Basso, an eleventh century church right by La Fenice opera house, is now a place for conferences and concerts. Beautifully decorated, it underwent reconstruction from fires in 1105 and 1661, the theft of its decoration under Napoleon in 1806, and its use by a marble and sculpture center and as offices until it was reconstructed in the 1950s.

The audience for the panel on Researching Historical Fiction is full and the pre-talk chatter lively. When we're introduced, I feel my insides starting to liquify, but I manage to control my muscles so no one sees the anxiety pouring out of me. I look over at the other two panelists. Their names are familiar but I don't know either one. Michael Madsen writes American Civil War novels and Philip Excelsior writes about the Ming Dynasty. Philip leans over, hand outstretched. "Congratulations on your award nomination. So sorry that the dinner ended the way it did."

After trying not to fidget through their presentations, I take a deep breath and plunge in, speaking too fast at the start, but eventually getting into my proper pacing. Now I'm close to twenty minutes and need to wind up. "In the end, imagination is the companion of research," I say. "No matter how much I know about my historical characters, only when I manage to get inside their heads can I create a convincing portrait. While the real Ivan the Terrible may never be knowable, I hope my readers can get a glimpse from my interpretation of the man and his motivations. Always leave space for inspiration, no matter how closely you want to stick to the facts."

"Thank you for a most interesting presentation, Dr. Taylor," the moderator intones.

I flush as the audience applauds, my stomach in knots. "I believe all of our speakers are willing to take questions," the moderator announces. After a few questions about working with sources in languages you don't know and getting permission to do research in foreign archives, a well-dressed man in a designer suit stands up.

"Dr. Taylor, how do you feel about recent accusations that you have plagiarized other authors, primarily historians, in writing your novels?"

My mouth dries and I feel the blood drain from my face. The events of last December come down like ton of bricks. Tina's well-publicized attack and current stay in a mental hospital should have put paid to the allegations. And yet, social media makes everything, consequential or not, live on and on.

Above the buzz of speculation, the moderator says,

"These questions should pertain to the topic at hand, doing research for historical novels ..."

The interlocutor breaks in, "it is relevant if she uses her 'research' to steal from other authors."

The hell with this. I've just been through a terrorist attack and kidnapping while at an awards dinner, where this disputed book was nominated for an award.

Several authors try to shout down the questioner. His stolid posture, arms folded, scowling, signals his immovability.

I come out from behind the panel table, fold my arms, and glare at the questioner. "Excuse me. Perhaps you haven't followed the events since that accusation was made. My accuser, who never offered proof of her assertions, set fire to my condominium and then shot me outside the Palmer House in Chicago. She has been undergoing psychiatric evaluation since her arrest last December."

He tries to interrupt, but I'm on a roll. "My book was nominated for the Dumas-Hugo Award in Historical Fiction, and after the accusations, the committee thoroughly vetted it and declared that there was no evidence of plagiarism. I am tired of these false accusations surfacing over and over.

Applause breaks out in the audience.

And then the truly unthinkable happens. The man holds up my book, takes out his lighter, and sets it on fire. He waves it above his head like a brand before dropping it to the floor. Immediately panic sets in as a mad scramble ensues to stamp out the flames or search out the fire extinguisher.

Emotional overload hits and I check for a pathway out of the room. I grab my briefcase and walk out, the continued cries ringing in my ears. I feel angry and as if I've been physically assaulted. I pass by the cafe where I know Max is drinking spritz, but I'm not ready to talk about this. I need to process what's happened, so I go on past the building and off to one place where I know I can find a quiet refuge. When the marble facade of the fifteenth-century church, Santa Maria dei Miracoli, comes into view, my breathing slows and a feeling of peace steals over. Passing through the portal of Pietro Lombardo's creation, I contemplate the fifty-two wooden panels of the coffered ceiling and wish I could stay forever.

Max

Third spritz while I wait for Cress. The bar is only a few steps from the venue and she should have been here at least half an hour ago, even if she dawdled, chatting with colleagues. I turn my mobile over; still no messages.

This particular bar is a gathering point for operatives from a variety of agencies so I know it well. A former MI6 colleague, Zachary Lemon, has turned up and we've taken the opportunity to catch up. He lives nearby with his Venetian wife and, even though retired, this bar turns out to be one of his hangouts. Zach is short and stocky, his blond hair long on top, tapering to short back and sides. A navy roll neck sweater, brown corduroy trousers, and a heavy unbuttoned pea coat make him look like a docker on holiday.

Sipping a spritz bitter, Zach says, "Still no word from your fiancée?"

"She must be talking to other conference attendees. Watch my drink. I'll check out the Ateneo and bring her back."

"Don't forget we have a reservation at Ai Cugnai at eight." He waves me off, already immersed in checking his messages.

The Ateneo is empty except for a couple of workers cleaning up after the program. Ashes cover a portion of the floor, along with paper fragments. When I look closer, the charred cover of Cress' book on Caterina Cornaro warns me that something serious has happened. I grab the sleeve of one of sweepers. "Scusa, è finita la conferenza?"

The older of the two rubs the silver scruff on his chin. "Sì finito un'ora fa."

Sweat drips down my spine. An hour ago. Where the hell is she?

I pull out my phone and send a text. She hasn't answered the others, but maybe...

Leather-soled shoes tap along the terrazzo floor. A short, thin man with tortoiseshell glasses and thinning black hair stops in front of me.

"May I help you?" His British accent makes it likely that he was involved with the conference.

"My name is Max Grant and my fiancée was giving a paper here earlier, but she didn't turn up at our meeting place after."

His face creases. "Dr. Cressida Taylor?"

I nod. He must know her.

"Marshall Mongomery, the convener of this session." We shake.

Then the story spills out. "She made a wonderful statement, then left in the confusion," he finishes. "I'm sure she'll turn up. Please give her my apologies on behalf of the organizers. I'll be in touch soon. I'd like to take you both out for dinner. We had no idea that one of the attendees was a disgruntled loser from the Historical Novel Awards protesting because he didn't make the short list."

"Thanks for your help," I tell him. "We'd love to but tonight we have plans with some friends but we'll be at the Gritti for a few days so you can leave a message there."

I trail back to the bar, where Zach still nurses his drink and munches on crisps.

"No luck?"

I shake my head no but don't volunteer the story. "I'm going to call her best friend and see if she has a favorite spot in Venice."

"Absentminded professor?" he grins, taking a final swallow and pushing out of his chair. "Off to Coop for some shopping, then home to the wife. Good to see you, Max."

"You too, Zach." My farewell is perfunctory and I dial Micki's number.

"Micki, this is Max. You in Vancouver?"

"We got here yesterday." She sounds fed up. "Something wrong?"

"I've been trying to find Cress. She didn't show up for our rendezvous. Where might she be in Venice?"

She doesn't ask what happened. "If the Frari is open, she might be there, at the Bellini altarpiece or Monteverdi's memorial. If not, she might be at the Miracoli. Those are two of her favorite spots."

"What's the Miracoli?"

"It's probably the most beautiful small church in Venice. It was renovated some years ago through the Save Venice Foundation. Cress adores the coffered ceiling."

"Thanks," I hang up, Google the Frari. It has been closed for about half an hour. Then I locate the whereabouts of the Miracoli church, and turn my steps toward Castello. It's not much over a minute from Campo San Fantin to Campiello Miracoli but I'm out of breath after I pelt down the small streets, dodging pedestrians.

I walk to the small kiosk and pay my admission to the almost empty sanctuary. Cress, partly hidden in the shadows, stares at the ceiling. Careful not to crowd her, I stand next to the pew she occupies, and gaze at the curve of her neck. Without moving, she moistens her lips. I clear my throat and she twists to look at me.

"Look up, Max," she says. "This church has the most beautiful fifteenth-century ceiling. I wish I was allowed to just lie on the floor and look up at the miniatures for a couple of hours. We'll have to come back so you can really spend some time studying the paintings. It's my favorite church in Venice."

"I know. Micki told me."

"Is that how you found me?"

I nod.

"I was so angry when that guy brought up all Tina's lies. But when he set fire to the book, and the crowd went crazy, I just had to leave."

I choke. "He did what?"

"Pulled out a lighter and set the book on fire. I ended up here. Kind of looking for sanctuary."

Sliding in to the pew, I grab her shoulders, turning her to face me. The glazed-over devastation in her eyes brings back memories of last December, when the accusations emerged. My heart mourns the loss of bright enjoyment and the sparks of enthusiasm that had attracted me from the first time I'd seen her on a long-ago Oxford afternoon.

"When you didn't show up, and didn't answer my texts, I checked the Ateneo. Then I called Micki. She didn't seem best pleased to hear from me, though."

"JL's mother wasn't as welcoming as they hoped. Nothing to do with you." She sniffs. "I'm sure we'll get the whole story eventually." She leans against me. "I forgot to turn my phone back on. I turned it off for the panel. Sorry." She pulls it out of her pocket and flips it back on.

I make a sad face of commiseration, then pull her in for a hug that is part consolation, part comfort, and a lot of desire. "Let's get a drink and something to eat. You'll feel better after a spritz and some cicchetti. And," I pause with a slightly mischievous grin, "a few good jokes to go on with."

Bacaro Risorto is a tiny ciccheterria at the corner of Campo San Provolo. There aren't many places to sit, but I manage to grab a chair at the outside counter where I get Cress settled. A couple of spritz bitter with Prosecco and a plate of assorted cicchetti—meatballs, arancini, pizzette, and bruschetta with different salt cod preparations—should keep us fueled until dinner.

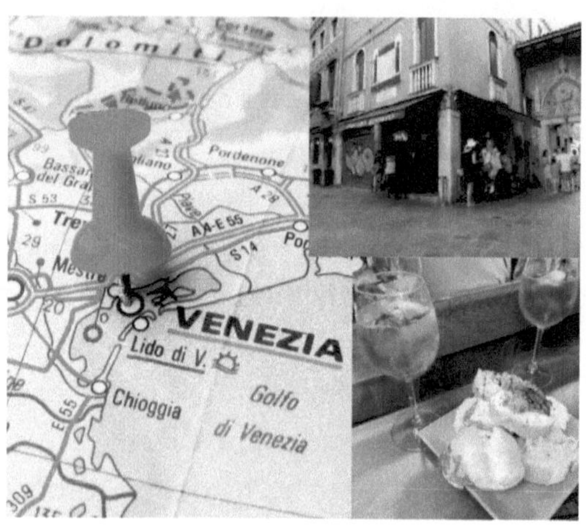

"Our reservation isn't for another hour and a half, so we have plenty of time to relax, enjoy our drinks, and just nibble." Leaning down, my lips brush against her temple. A man taps me on the shoulder. "Need a chair? We're just going." He sounds like he's visiting from the deep southern U.S. "Thanks." I grab the chair and sit across from Cress just as a waiter comes over with our selection."

"Cin cin," I say, tapping my glass against hers.

"Salute," she responds, taking a big gulp.

I tell her about my drinks with Zach, how his wife and son stopped by before going to a children's playground near the Giardini, and make her laugh describing the sight of four-year-old Paolo being dragged out of the bar by their miniature pointer, Porcini, while yelling Smettila!

"By the way, we're having dinner with them at Ai Cugnai tonight."

"Oh." The flat syllable isn't a good sign.

"Do you want me to put them off until tomorrow or something?"

"Don't think I'm really up to being with your friends tonight. Maybe just a room service dinner?"

Instead of a meal in our room, I convince her to go to the restaurant of an old friend, sure we can find a quiet corner. We walk through San Marco into Cannaregio, through the sotoportego, down the stairs and into Campo Santi Apostoli where we have a quiet dinner at Trattoria da Bepi. Bepi has a rustic decor with wood paneling, storage barrels, and wood-beamed ceilings. I'd met the eponymous Bepi through a mutual friend and had become a regular during my stint in Venice. I came for the fish and stayed for the jokes.

I let Bepi arrange the meal, which starts with a bottle of Prosecco, proceeds with several delicious courses including razor clams, fegato alla venezia with polenta, and a seafood risotto and ends with tastes of various dolce and shot glasses of limoncello and grappa along with espresso. By the end, Cress is smiling and my heart unclenches.

Cress

Venice is pretty crime free, but pickpockets are a problem. As we bid goodbye to Bepi, a couple of kids jostle past me and I feel a slight tug. When I look down, my bag has disappeared, neatly cut from my shoulder.

"Max," I shout. "My bag". The kids start to run and Max takes off after them. Fortunately I'm wearing practical shoes, so I'm not too far behind.

When they scatter, I keep my eyes on the one who has my bag dangling from his fingers. Turning right into a dark, narrow salizada, he makes a quick turn into an even darker and narrower calle. Giving chase, my arms practically scrape the damp building walls, as we zig and zag, turning sharply into another, even narrower calle. Fortunately the calli are empty of strollers since there is barely room to get through in some places. Then the calle unexpectedly widens and lights glare out from a hotel entrance.

"Faster, Cress," Max shouts from a few yards in front. I can hear footsteps receding as Max and the thief jockey for position in the suddenly wider space. Anger gives me a new burst of adrenaline as the calle narrows again just past the hotel. I scan ahead through the darkness, hoping I haven't missed a turnoff.

Suddenly a steep staircase looms. Shit, a bridge. Scrambling up, I slide over the smooth plateau at the top, and almost fall down the other side, before making a razor thin turn into a campo, which seems empty. While looking for an exit, I hear footsteps behind me and realize I'm being outmaneuvered. Max runs past. "Turn around, Cress," he yells.

The noises seem deafening with runners footsteps, heavy breathing, and shouts bouncing off the bricks. Loudest of all is my heartbeat. I'm on the edge of collapse. Almost blind in the dim light of the campiello, I'm not sure where to go next. The entrance to a sotoportego echoes so I take a couple of breaths and run off again. The next turn, however, takes me to a canal. Should I turn back? Seeing steps down to a motorboat moored to the side of the canal, I put a hand on the slimy wall and carefully descend the slippery stairs.

And then I notice a profound silence. The footsteps, shouts, and heavy breathing have disappeared. All I hear is the sound of water slapping against the sides of the canal and susurration of the boat moving. I creep back up the steps and slowly retrace the path and reapproach the opening to the sotoportego. A figure looms out of the darkness and I scream.

"Cress." A familiar rumbling baritone is freighted with relief.

"Max?"

Arms outstretched, my bag dangles from long thin fingers. "He dropped this and went out a different way."

"Thank god."

"Let's move off." He finds another opening and we

stroll down the calle casually, two lovers out for a stroll. But the experience has shaken me. This trip to Venice has darkened my feelings. No longer inhabiting a magical place, I feel menace everywhere.

Back at the Gritti, all I want to do is go to bed and pull the covers over my head. Dimly aware that Max had been trying to initiate conversation, I've withdrawn somewhere he can't reach, seemingly trapped into inescapable memories. He kneels on the Persian rug, taking my cold hands in his big warm ones while I stare out the window as if he's invisible, his touch evanescent.

He brushes my cheek with his fingers. "Wake up, Sleeping Beauty. Talk to me." Then, pulling my stiff body gently into his arms, Max begins running his fingers through my hair. *"La mia stellina,"* he whispers, *"mon petit chou, mein ganz besonderes Kätzchen,* please talk to me."

"I'm tired," I say, and snap my mouth shut. Stop being a bitch, I chide myself as I stand on tiptoe and kiss his cheek in apology.

"Let's get you to bed."

<hr>

Max

I wake Cress up with gentle kisses. "How are you feeling?"

"Fine." Her voice is heavy, drugged with the dregs

of sleep. She notices the room service cart. "Is there coffee?"

I pour her a cup and add a dash of cream. She sighs with pleasure while I butter some toast and slather on marmalade just the way she likes it. "Thanks for getting my bag back," she says through a mouthful of tartina marmellata. "I'll have to look for a new one, but at least they didn't make off with my wallet."

"Did you have anything important in it?"

She smiles. "Nope, everything important is either in the safe or my money belt. The wallet itself is nice and I had a couple of euro coins, and they could have gotten a tube of Chapstick, but that's about it. I just feel violated."

"Well, now that it's over, I'm looking forward to taking you to some of my favorite spots. And, something else..." I pause.

She narrows her eyes and purses her lips. In her experience, surprises are rarely good. "Ok. What is it?"

"I made arrangements for us to stay a few extra days, then take the Orient Express back to London and fly home from there."

Cress' head bobbles as she takes this in. "When did you make arrangements?"

"I've, uh, I've been up for a bit," I stammer. "Had some work calls to answer."

The surprise on her face is adorable. "And you made arrangements for staying longer as part of these 'work' calls?"

Reaching across the breakfast table, I grab her hands and squeeze. "Hey, this is supposed to be a good thing. Besides, I got a message from Clay, and I have to meet with the bankers in London again before we go back. He'll send the company plane for us, so that's a nice perq. Jarvis is happy to spend more time with the cats and we can take a bit of time to look for a flat or small house. But if you don't want to go with me, you can fly back from here."

"Back to the fairy tale," she whispers.

"You bet. No way our memories of Venice are going to be nutcases and pickpockets."

Her beaming face makes everything right. "How much longer will we be in Venice before we go back?"

I get off the couch, stretch, then sit back down, crowding her against the arm until she squeals in protest. Feeding her cut strawberries, I say, "We're booked on the train next Wednesday. We get in on Thursday and stay at the Milestone Hotel. Friday I meet with the bankers and the estate agent can take us round to likely places on Saturday and Sunday. Your choice about how long we stay after that."

I wipe my hands on a napkin and kiss strawberry juice off the corner of her mouth, "Now, is there anything special you want to do in Venice?"

Cress

Monday morning sees us at the Gallerie dell'Accademia. Most museums don't open until nine or ten, but my favorite Venetian museum opens at 8:15. Instead of breakfast at the Gritti, we go to Torrefazione Marchi where I quickly down several café macchiatos. Then we stop at Suso Gelatoteca for panettone stuffed with gelato, breakfast of champions. Well fortified, we stroll through Campo Santo Stefano, through Campo Vitale, and over the wooden bridge to the Accademia. After visiting my favorite paintings by Bellini, Carpaccio, Veronese, and Lorenzo Lotto, we wander down toward the Peggy Guggenheim Museum, stopping at Pasticceria Toletta for some tea and pastry.

By the time we finish our snack, my favorite jewelry shop is open. It's in a campiello just around the corner from the Guggenheim and the Murano glass pieces are exquisite. The small, crowded, but inviting space dazzles with color from counter surfaces, display cases, a table in the center of the room, and necklaces displayed on the walls. A desk sits near the back.

"*Bongiorno,*" I call out.

A woman came out, smiled, and said *"Bongiorno, signora."*

"Is Leslie here by any chance?"

"You're in luck, she just stopped by."

"Could you tell her Cress Taylor is here?"

The woman nods and goes behind the curtain to the back of the shop. out. Leslie comes out with a big smile and hugs me with kisses on both cheeks. " Good to see you, Cress. It's been a while."

"Probably two years. When I was doing the research on Caterina Cornaro."

"I saw that the book was out and you'd been nominated for an award."

I grimace. "A mixed blessing. But I'm here to look at jewelry." A tap on my shoulder reminds me of my manners. I pull him around, even though she can hardly miss the giant standing behind me. "Leslie, this Max Grant. He's my ..."

I pause and Max says smoothly, "I'm her fiancée." He holds my out hand to display the heirloom ring to its best advantage.

"Very nice," Leslie says.

Originally from the US, Leslie Genninger came to Venice to learn how to create Murano glass. She produces some of the most interesting Murano glass jewelry around, employing master artisans on Murano to create beads to her specifications. I'm fascinated with the non-jewelry pieces she has on display now—-insects, sea creatures, birds. When I look around Max and Leslie stand to one side, chatting. I wonder what they're cooking up.

Lunch at Trattoria ai Cugnai, surrounded by lunching gondoliers and other locals, makes me almost feel Venetian. Hearty portions of spaghetti alla vongole and caprese salad presupposes a nap but instead we stand in line at Santa Maria Gloriosa dei Frari. "I stayed in an apartment near here one summer in Campo San

Tomà," I tell Max, trying not to yawn. That second glass of red wine might have been one glass too far.

"The Frari was remodeled in the fourteenth century and both Titian and Monteverdi are buried there." Noticing that the names didn't seem to register, I explain, "Monteverdi was a famous composer at the beginning of the Baroque era. He's credited as one of the creators of opera and wrote the 1610 Vespers as an audition piece to become the music master for Saint Mark's. It's one of my favorite musical compositions. I'll play it for you some time."

Max nods but doesn't say anything.

"And Titian," I continue. I never seem to be able to restrain my annoying pedantic side, Max puts his palm over my mouth."I know who Titian was, the most important painter of the Venetian school in the sixteenth century."

"Art more than music, then."

"Titian is very popular in England," he says drily. "We had him in school." And then he mumbles something I don't catch.

"What did you say? I couldn't hear you."

"Just a little brag. Grant House boasts a painting by his nephew, Marco."

My eyes widen.

"I take it Mum didn't show it off." He sighs. "Well, we tend to prefer the Canalettos and Guardis anyway."

We pass from the bright spring sunshine into the darker confines of the Frari. I'm excited. No matter how often I've visited, I never get tired of this place.

"Let's go in and look at the art and the tombs. I really want you to see the Bellini altarpiece. To me it's the treasure of the place."

"Sure."

After paying our respects to the tombs of Monteverdi and Titian, we gaze with awe at the Bellini altarpiece, check out Donatello's "Figure of St. John the Baptist and Titian' "Assumption of the Virgin." Max is eloquent, explaining some of the fine points of Titian's masterpiece. Then I reluctantly point out the monument for Canova.

"Not one of my favorites. The original design was intended as a tomb for Titian. When Canova died, his students created it for him, but only his heart is buried here."

After such a full day, we agree to go back to the Gritti for a long nap before our evening activities.

Max

For our last day, we decide on the breakfast buffet while watching the sunrise over the Grand Canal from the Gritti Terrace. Having greeted the sun, we go back to the suite. Hang the "Do Not Disturb" sign on the door handle, and spend the rest of the morning in bed. When we finally emerge, early afternoon shadows are already beginning to color the city.

We drop into Ballarin for espresso macchiato, then continue toward the ghetto to tour the Jewish museum, which was created out of three of the historic synagogues. Leaving all our stuff at the counter, we spend an hour looking at the exhibits before connecting the guide from Context Travel who we'd booked earlier to take us on a two-hour walking tour.

"Do you have other plans?" our guide asks as we finish.

"A couple of things," I tell her. "We're going on a gondola ride and then a cicchetti tour."

Cress hits me in the arm. "You didn't mention either of those."

"Do you hate the idea?"

"No, I just wasn't expecting them."

"Fun." The guide enthuses. "A gondola at sunset is a marvelous experience."

"I booked a special private tour, twice as long as the usual."

"Perfect. And who can resist cicchetti? Make sure your guide takes you to Al Timon, Do Spade, Bacarando, and All'Arco." She grins and smacks her lips. "Oh, and Alla Vedova for meatballs and very cheap wine. When do you leave Venice?"

"We're on the Orient Express to London tomorrow," Cress says. "Then a few days in London before we go back to Chicago."

Back at the Academia Bridge, we meet our gondolier for a private one-hour ride that will coincide with sunset. We enjoy a violinist and champagne while we float through the canals, our gondolier guide pointing out sights along the way. Cress leans against me as we pretend to be in our own timeless bubble. An air of silence envelopes us, cushioning us from the busy traffic of tourist Venice, the sounds of the violin and the splash of water blending with the voice of our consigliere. We pull up at the gondola stop to applause as onlookers gawk at our passionate embrace.

Cress

A man dressed in the uniform of the Venice-Simplon Orient Express has just taken our bags from the lobby of the Gritti out to the water taxi waiting for our arrival.

Back to platform 9 and the return trip on the Orient Express to London. Originally, Max insisted that we just take a vaporetto. Line 1 is the most popular, traveling from the Piazzelle Roma to Lido and is frequently jammed with locals running errands and tourists, being tourists. I didn't really think that would work.

Then we find out that our trip back on the Orient Express included transfers from the hotel, so here we are, still in luxury's caress.

"Are you ready to finish our travels?" Max asks, slipping his arm around me. "Venice to London to Chicago? Or do you want more adventure?"

"Are you proposing another add on?" The idea is tempting but, no.

"We could get off in Paris and take the special trip

from Paris to Istanbul. Pretend you're Agatha Christie and I'm Max Mallowan." He's looking off into the distance, enjoying a last view of the Grand Canal.

I snort at the idea. "I'm older than you, but not that much older."

"I don't feel five years is much of an age difference," he says. "I wasn't even thinking about that."

"Not sure he was always faithful, either."

Holding his hands up, palms out, Max protests. "I will always be faithful. Maybe this was a bad comparison." He rubs his jaw. "In the end though, I take it your answer is no."

"Could we do it another year?" I try to sound excited but I'm burned out. I'd loved my one trip to Istanbul and I'm sure I'll love it again, especially with Max, just not now.

"Whatever you wish, *la mia stellina*. Let's think about where we want to live when we're visiting London."

The taxi pulls in and the VSOE representative sees us into the station and guides us to the platform, where we check in and a porter handles our bags. The trip back will be the exact reverse of the trip from London—lunch, tea, dinner, breakfast, brunch, and tea again after we transfer from the Eurostar to the final train in Folkestone, before our final arrival at Victoria Station, where we'll transfer to the Milestone Hotel.

Now, settled in our compartment, where the steward has handed us glasses of Prosecco, I turn to

Max and gaze deeply into those cloudy gray eyes. "I thought the book burning and the bag grab has ruined Venice's magic for me."

"We recovered and the magic returned." He clinks his flute against mine.

"Venice," I breathe into the rarefied air as I take a last look before we pull out. "Gelato, gondolas, romance. What more could we ask for?"

A Hotel in Istanbul

At the Crossroads is book two in the Global Security Unlimited series.

Max Grant is a former MI6 operative with a new life in Chicago, a promising relationship with author Cress Taylor, and a past that's about to catch up with him. Ten years ago, Max was caught in an ambush in an Istanbul alley, where most of his team died, and his testimony put a terrorist mastermind in prison. Now, the terrorist has escaped, and he's coming after Max. As Max is inexorably drawn toward confrontation, he must race to stop the mastermind before he eliminates them both. If you like travel and pulse-pounding suspense, combined with a continuing romance, you'll love At the Crossroads.

Initially, I planned on having the book end in Istanbul, but in the end, my editor convinced me to wind it up in Paris instead. Everything from this scene until the end of the book all disappeared from the published version of the novel.

I hope you enjoy revisiting Max and Cress as they spend time in one of my favorite cities.

Sharon Michalove, January 2025

Paris-Istanbul, May 2015

Max

Once we clear airport security, I go to the departure lounge at Charles de Gaulle to wait for our flight to Istanbul to board. Yavuz and I had gotten separated at check-in and so far, he hadn't appeared.

I stare out the window at the rain that started just as we left the Victor Hugo museum. Dampness creeps up through my limbs as I question whether I made the right decision, taking off for a confrontation that will certainly mean the end of Faez, or me, or perhaps both of us.

For the hundredth, no maybe thousandth time, I pick up my phone. I have a text from Metin telling me the NSA and CIA still can't find out where Yavuz was in the last, blank year and a half, which is definitely bad news. As he is still my conduit to Faez, I will have to see this through.

My fingers itch to text Cress. Find out if she's safe. Tell her I'm all right. Let her know I am on my way to Istanbul. But I can't. I don't have a burner phone or the time to buy one. If she stays in Paris, at least she won't be in danger when I face Faez.

Remembering the chaos at the museum dinner, my heart sinks. I should have stayed and protected Cress. I could have made that choice but it wasn't an option. I had to entrust her safety to JL. We discussed the possibility before the dinner. The plan was, if an attack occurred, he would stay with Cress and Micki and I would follow any trail I could that would lead me to Faez.

My last glimpse of Cress was seeing her duck under the table. And I turned away, knowing this was as close as we were going to come to seeing a fire-eater in Paris. I followed Yavuz down the corridor and out into the Place des Vosges and my date with fate.

My mobile is easily traceable. I send a coded message to MI6, telling them where I'm going, what flight I'm on, and asking them to pass it on to Allan. Then I message Metin and Clay to tell them where I'm going, turn off the phone, take out the battery and walk into the men's room. Fortunately it's empty, so there are no witnesses when I stamp on the mobile and crush it. I brush up all of the pieces, dump them in the loo and flush until everything disappears. A wall of isolation surrounds me as I cut my last tie.

The last boarding call sounds over the tannoy as Yavuz runs into the lounge. "Damn security," he grumbles before heading off down the gangway. I wonder if he's been calling Faez in Istanbul. If I will be ambushed at the airport. Nothing I can do now except try to get a little rest.

We aren't sitting together. Yavuz is short enough at five-seven to travel comfortably in economy while I am in business class for the extra leg room. He can't afford to sit there and I'm not feeling generous.

As soon as Yavuz and I reunite at Istanbul International Airport, I retrieve one of the many passports I always carry and stand in the visa line to pay for the paper stamp. So far I haven't seen any signs of an attack. Yavuz leans nonchalantly against a convenient wall, pulls out his mobile, checks his messages, then makes a call.

"Hello, brother," he says. "Are the arrangements set?"

Brother? I thought his brother was still in London. Then I remember he has another younger brother.

"What the..." His face darkens and his body stiffens as he moves out of earshot. Whatever is happening must not be good. After some inaudible exchanges, he pushes the phone into a pocket and strides over to where I am still in a long line.

"Sorry, Max."

"Emre?" I query.

"No. My closest friend, but like a brother. He is trying to set up a meet for you."

"I take it the news isn't good."

He shrugs. "This isn't merely a matter of snapping your fingers. It will take some time."

"And in the meantime, he may show up and try to kill me."

"A risk, for sure."

Yavuz looks down at himself. He's still wearing the dress clothes he got for the dinner. "Can't wait for you. I have to go home and change, then straighten a few things out. Meeting another contact. Where will I find you?"

Should I tell him or not? Can't make any of this work if I keep my whereabouts secret. Besides, I don't want him to know I don't trust him. "I made a reservation at the Pera Palace Hotel."

Yavuz's mouth twists. "You've come up in the world, Max. No more ratty hotels or sponging off my sister. Now you stay in one of the most lavish hotels in the city." The bitterness he expresses reinforces my misgivings.

I shrug. "Not an MI6 operative anymore. May as well be comfortable while you are making the contact."

Yavuz sighs. "Sorry. Tired. Stressed. I will come by as soon as I know something. Not sure how long the negotiations will take." He pauses. "Faez will probably set a trap. Agree to meet, and then…" He throws his arms up, as if emulating an explosion.

"We'll need to be smarter than he is."

His expression is dubious. "Like 2003?"

I run my fingers over my scalp. "No. We had no warning. This time maybe we can gain the upper hand." I don't say I thought someone on our team sold us out. Now I wonder if the traitor was Yavuz. Unlikely since his sister was one of victims. But you never know. The line inches forward.

"I'll be off then."

"I may be out finding more suitable clothes."

He gives me a curt nod and races off to find a taxi.

Visa safely pasted into my passport, I take the hour-long drive to the hotel in fierce Istanbul traffic. At the Pera Palace, I ask for the Agatha Christie room in case Allan got my message, and can't stop Cress from coming with him.

Wrung out, I have to drag myself away from the desk and toward the exit. If I go to the room, I will probably fall onto the bed and sleep, so I pocket the key and walk five minutes to Istiklal Caddesi to browse the men's wear shops. Then I wander the streets for a while, reacquainting myself with a city I haven't visited since the disaster of 2003. Fortunately, this is an area I don't associate with Zehra, which makes the whole exercise more bearable.

Two hours later, I'm back at the hotel with a pair of jeans, a few golf shirts, pants and socks, and some toiletries. I changed at the shop from my suit and brogues to a second pair of jeans, a T-shirt, and some work boots. I topped it with a navy peacoat.

Throwing the coat over the back of one of the numerous chairs crowding the space, I put my few purchases into the bureau and flip on the TV. International news broadcasts have the whole Paris attack on a loop. The dead include two dinner attendees—the President of the society, and Cress' agent, who was sitting with him—and all the gunmen. Paris police took no chances.

I take a deep breath, my muscles relaxing. No mention of Cress, JL, or Micki. Allan and Inspector Poulliot must have gotten them to safety. I cross my fingers. Maybe Cress will go on to the conference in Venice. Otherwise, JL needs to take her back to Chicago. Switching off the box, I appreciate the silence —for a minute.

Then, not able to concentrate, I pace. Where the fuck is Yavuz? I expected to hear from him by now. Maybe he hasn't been able to make contact. Worse, everything could have backfired. Maybe he's dead.

I eat lahmacun, a Turkish flat-bread pizza,

followed by some roasted chestnuts, but it only satisfies me briefly before my stomach rumbles again. I bring back döner, beer, and a bagful of bagel-like simit. Sinking onto the couch, I open a bottle and nibble on one of the ubiquitous sesame-crusted circles.

After a second simit, I recommence pacing, thankful the room is huge. I check another news broadcast. No reports of dead men turning up in alleyways. I unwrap the döner, pick at a little of the still warm, greasy meat, then my stomach decides to rebel. I re-wrap the whole thing and toss it into the trash. The smell of grease and roasted lamb pervades the room, so I retrieve the slimy package from the bin to dispose of elsewhere.

Easier said than done. After a fruitless search for a service room where I can toss the offending article, I take it out of the hotel and eventually find a rare municipal bin. Then I trudge back to the hotel and ask if there are any messages. There aren't any, so I trail up to my room. The ridiculously elegant space feels cold and empty without Cress.

I sit alone in an oh-so-British chintz armchair, regret flooding me while I think about my impulsive action. When Yavuz suggested taking off for Istanbul to confront Faez, I thought it was a brilliant idea. Whether Yavuz was on my side or not, he could lead me to my goal. Now, waiting for something to happen, I realize how foolish I've been.

Yavuz. Had I trusted him because of my guilt over

Zehra? Was I wrong in suspecting him now? A prickling sensation has me rubbing the nape of my neck.

The sudden shock when the hotel telephone rings propels me across the room, hands shaking as I pick up the receiver. I fumble, trying to push the communication button.

"Yes?" My voice grates from hours and hours of not speaking.

"Mr. Grant?" The voice is deferential.

"Yes." Impatience floods through me and I clench the handset. Skip the niceties and put the call through.

"We have a group of people in the lobby asking for you."

Not Yavuz, then. I visualize a clutch of Turkish security officers, or perhaps gunmen. Either way, this doesn't sound good.

I stall. "Did they say who they are?"

After a pause, the desk clerk comes back on the line. "There are two men and two women. One British, two Americans, and a Frenchman."

My heart lifts, then sinks. Frustration overwhelms me and I snap, "Didn't you ask their names?"

"Sorry, sir. I'll ask now." A mumbling noise alerts me he has put his hand over the mouthpiece.

Finally, after what seems like hours, he says, "The British gentlemen informed me his name is Allan Mason."

Of course it is. Thank God they got out, and he received the message about my whereabouts. But why is my troupe of raggle-taggle gypsies with him?

"Send them up," I tell him. Then I sink back, exhausted, onto the bed and listen for the nearby elevator.

Cress

Our taxi pulls up to the seven-story Pera Palace Hotel, in the heart of Beyoğlu. On my bucket list as a destination, I never expected my introduction to be like this, chasing Max across Europe after being shot at in Paris. Anger at how he left me behind wars with relief that he's still alive.

Pain runs through me like hot lead. I know he thinks his job is to protect me, but I'm not an assignment. All he really needs to do is to love me.

As soon as I see him in the doorway of the Agatha Christie Room, my knees buckle with relief. He catches me as I topple. The twist of his lips turns to a radiant smile as he pulls me in, frowning over my head at the rest of the crew.

"Shove off." He tries to shut the door.

Allan wedges his foot into the door frame. "Not a chance, mate."

Max jerks back. Allan has probably never called him "mate" before in their lives.

A deep rumble of laughter shakes his chest. It feels like a minor earthquake as he pulls me backwards to let in the horde. JL is the last to enter. He turns, looks down the hallway, then closes the door with a decisive snick, turns the lock and fastens the mechanism that only allows the door to open an inch.

We go through the long hallway, Max never taking his arm from around my waist. Everywhere, pictures and knickknacks surround us, including antique furniture and shelves of Christie's books. A vintage Underwood typewriter catches my eye, and I try to pull away and examine it, but Max's grip is like an iron hoop around me.

"You can check it out it later," he whispers. "It's for atmosphere. Christie never used it."

"Shatter all my illusions, why don't you?" The corners of my mouth turn up in a grin belies my words. I elbow Max lightly in the ribs. "Did you pick the Pera Palace because Ian Fleming stayed here?" Max has a James Bond obsession. He even tried to buy a 1930 Blower Bentley, Bond's first car, but with only fifty-five of them made, he hasn't been able to fulfill that wish.

"Not really. When MI6 sent me to Istanbul, I stayed in seedy hotels, and then…" He swallows convulsively, rolls his shoulders, and continues. "And then I lived with Zehra." He's still holding on to me and I rub his back.

"Let's sit down." JL gestures to the various pieces of furniture. Max heads to a large, red velvet armchair and sits down with me in his lap. Allan grimaces. JL and Micki cozy up on the long red velvet couch facing the chair. Ever the odd man out, Allan grabs a desk chair and angles it, to face us. A faded chintz armchair, angled toward the windows, looks forlorn.

A entirely unwarranted sense of peace comes over me. Even though I know we aren't safe, Max's presence envelopes me with a sense of security. I think about my anger when he disappeared. His innate desire for secrecy and his overprotectiveness have caused most of our clashes. Every time I'm convinced we are finally partners, he proves we aren't. And yet, thinking about the guilt he has carried all these years over Zehra's death, I can't blame him. I don't want him to carry the burden of losing anyone else.

With his lips pressed to the nape of my neck, he says, "Do you forgive me for coming here without you?"

I take a few breaths, then answer. "Yes. I didn't want to, but I understand." I wrap my fingers around his. "Do you forgive me for following?"

"No," he breathes against me. "Do I wish you were somewhere safe? Of course. But I've been aching ever since I left you in Paris and hoping you would be here." He glares around the room. "I wanted to wind up the whole Faez thing before you arrived."

"And with that segue," Allan says, "it's time to make a plan."

AEGEAN PERSUASION

When Damson Fitzwilliam pranced into the small sitting room at Castlebrooke House, her employer, Lady Agatha Carstairs, laid down her teacup next to *The Guardian*, open to an article on Brexit. The housekeeper waved a square, Imperial blue envelope like a small flag at a parade.

"This is for you, Agatha. Looks like some sort of invitation. Perhaps you'll be having tea with the Queen."

"Or it's a very posh appeal for a donation," Agatha responded, catching sight of her name in large gold calligraphy as Damson pushed it at her. After forty-five years together, there was no formality between them, Agatha reflected, inwardly amused at her housekeeper's capers. Firmly grasping the envelope, she said, "Would you bring me the letter opener, please?"

An inveterate mystery reader, Agatha fancied herself a real-life Miss Marple. Bringing her detecting sense to bear on the mysterious item, she gave it a sharp once over before picking up the Venetian glass-handled opener her parents had brought back from their Italian honeymoon.

The envelope was made of heavy cotton rag paper, surprisingly soft to the touch. A commemorative postage stamp affixed to the corner depicted the seventeenth-century sailing ship Sovereign of the Seas. Elaborate calligraphy in gold ink spelled out her name and address. When she turned it over, the flap was sealed with gold wax impressed with a ship under full sail. Underneath was an engraved word, *Persuasion*. She carefully prised it open, making sure to preserve the seal.

The thick cardstock of the enclosure fit tightly against the gold tissue lining the envelope. Agatha eased it out gently, making sure not to damage the edges of the card or tear the fragile lining. A small white card in a plain envelope fell out. She laid it aside and examined the invitation, admiring gold, beveled edges before touching the engraved words in raised gold ink.

The rustling paper rousing her rescue greyhounds, Wickham and Willoughby, who were lying at her feet. They lifted their heads in unison at the sound, then subsided with soft snuffles.

She laid the missive back on the tea table, leaned over to fondle each dog's velvety gray ears, then picked up the delicate porcelain vessel. Cold, scummy. Her lips twisted in disgust as she put the cup down and reached for the silver bell to summon Damson just as the housekeeper bustled back into the room with a fresh cup.

"Have you read it yet?"

"Don't rush me," Agatha said. When Damson smirked at her, she murmured, "No one is indispensable."

"You would never fire me," Damson said confidently. She patted her short, silvery hair. The two women had a brief glare off, a common occurrence after so many years in close proximity. Agatha sipped her refreshed tea.

"Fahin," Damson said, a reminder of her Yorkshire accent still discernible, even after a lifetime in Hampshire. "I'll read it for you."

With a voice as majestic as Lady Bracknell in *The Importance of Being Earnest*, Agatha said, "I am perfectly able to read it myself. Just fetch my glasses." She threw a razor-edged glare at the other woman before adding, "Please."

Once her glasses were settled on her nose, Agatha slowly read out the ornate engraved script.

Congratulations!

Please accept this personal invitation to experience the luxury yacht, Persuasion, on her maiden voyage to the Aegean and Ionian Seas. An exclusive opportunity awaits you as one of eight passengers to explore the delights of the Greek Islands. Our resplendent suites provide unparalleled comfort. The voyage will also offer world-class cuisine, a full-featured spa, and an olympic-sized swimming pool.

Our itinerary will take us from Athens to Cyprus. We will visit the legendary site of Odysseus' palace in Ithaca and the lair of the Minotaur on Crete. Whether you choose from our carefully curated tours or want to explore on your own, our experienced staff is ready to make your dreams a reality.

Upon your acceptance, you will receive a detailed itinerary, flight information, and the dates of the voyage. Please return the enclosed card at your earliest convenience.

"I don't understand. Why would I be invited on this cruise?" Agatha shook her head and handed the card up to Damson. "Rather mysterious, don't you think?"

The small response card had her name printed with accept printed below. The envelope bore another stamp in the Royal Navy series, the Mary Rose, and the printed address of a post office box in London.

Damson was turning over the invitation. "I can tell you why you were invited."

"You had something to do with this?"

"When I was at the hairdresser a few months ago, I filled out an application for a cruise giveaway."

"Why aren't you and Cap the recipients?"

A broad smile spread over Damson's face. "If you don't know the answer to that, you don't understand my husband after all these years. Cap would never leave Chesney Hardcastle and his precious garage to go on a Greek vacation, or any vacation really. But ever since I came to work for you, I've known how you regretted calling off your wedding to Victor. And missing your honeymoon. So I thought..."

Agatha felt her jaw drop. She wiped a film of tears from her eyes. "I-I don't know what to say."

Damson folded her arms. "Say you'll go."

"There are no dates. I would be going into this blindly."

"What difference do dates make? Not like you have other obligations."

"The estate..."

"Bother the estate. That was the excuse before. Philip can take care of the estate while you're away."

Agatha flushed. The past rose up and she was twenty-three again, confronting her parents.

Her father's voice bounced off the furniture in the small sitting room while he glared like a bull ready to charge a toreador. "Seriously, Agatha, how can you imagine we would let you marry Victor Macdonald?"

Forcing herself to straighten her spine and not look away, she protested, "You like him. You've always pointed out what a thoughtful, decent man he is."

"He is," her mother said. "But he's no longer a suitable husband."

Agatha, cheeks fiery red, stuck out her chin. "Why? Have you heard something against him?"

"No, Agatha, we've not heard anything to his discredit." Was there a hint of sympathy in her mother's drooping eyelids and compressed lips?

With a ragged cry, Agatha fought back. "Then nothing has changed. Victor's still the same man you welcomed when he proposed months ago. We're to be married in a few weeks." Her father's stony expression told her that the entreaty had not softened his attitude. A sob tore from her throat. "I love him. That's all that matters."

Lord Carstairs' posture softened slightly as he took

her hand. "Love doesn't come into it, my dear," he said gruffly. "Now that your brother is no longer with us…" He choked, but quickly regained his composure. "Nothing is the same. You are the heir, Agatha. That changes everything. Your responsibility, your loyalty, is to preserve the family and the estate. Victor doesn't have the status, or the money, to be an appropriate consort for the heir to Castlebrooke Park."

His last words echoed in her ears as the past faded away. She brought her attention back to Damson, who stood, legs slightly apart, arms folded across her chest. An electric shock ran through Agatha as she realized her loyal housekeeper was helping her follow her dream.

Silence stretched while Agatha collected herself. "I've decided to accept. At twenty-three, I gave up everything for family obligations. But I can safely leave the estate in my nephew's hands and rectify one of the few regrets of my life." A small smile tickled her lips. "I've been offered a second chance. At my age, this might be my last opportunity."

Then she retrieved the walking stick leaning against the chair, hoisted herself up, called to the dogs, and almost waltzed out of the room.

Agatha loved October, and not just because her birthday fell in the middle of the month. The crisp days, smells of bonfires, blazing leaves coloring the landscape and crackling underfoot. But this year would be different. The cruise would fill the calendar and she could use it as an opportunity to celebrate her seventieth birthday. She particularly wanted to explore Ithaca, where Victor had planned they'd spend most of their honeymoon. Would she feel elated or bereft?

At the airport in Athens, Agatha felt a shiver of excitement that reminded her of a time when the romance of travel fired a vivid imagination. When her parents were killed in a car accident a mere two years after she rejected Victor, Agatha dedicated her life to the preservation of Castlebrooke Park. She'd never married, closing off her heart to dreams of romantic love.

Leaning on her stick, she exited the arrivals hall, a porter trailing behind, pushing a trolley heaped with luggage. Drivers waved cards with travelers' names scrawled across their surfaces and called out for their passengers. Her gaze roved the crowded space as she tried to find one with her name. A liveried driver in blue and gold caught her eye as he held up a card neatly printed with her name. She moved stiffly in his direction, handbag looped over her wrist, still trying to recover from hours of sitting. Even though Agatha enjoyed the luxury of a first-class seat, she felt creaky. Old bones, she thought resignedly.

The liveried man tucked the card under his arm and moved forward, hand outstretched. "Lady Agatha Carstairs?" She was surprised by his Scottish burr, but she nodded. "Right this way, milady." He waved the card toward the exit. Holding the door, he focused on the porter, and said, "It's the Rolls."

Strong sun shone down as they emerged from the modern terminal complex gleaming bright white. Agatha blinked and scrabbled in her bag for sunglasses, almost sagging with relief when she slid them onto her snub nose. No hat was needed for the short walk to the Roller, but she glanced back to make sure the old-fashioned hat box, containing her wide-brimmed straw sunhat, remained securely loaded onto the luggage cart.

The miniature procession moved briskly toward the dark blue car sporting *Persuasion* in gold calligraphy on the passenger door. When they reached the curb, he clicked a button and the boot popped open so the porter could stow the cases. Agatha stared at the Phantom convertible resembling a classic motorboat, with elegant lines and a teak roof deck lid. She ran her fingers over the wooden slats, disappointed that the convertible top was up. Tasteful or OTT? Agatha's opinion wavered back and forth between admiration and amusement as she slid onto the buttery seat, leaned back, and blew out a breath as the seatbelt buckle clicked home. "Thank you so much," she said to her escort, watching him settle into the driving seat and secure his own restraint. "Would it be possible to have the top retracted?"

"Sorry, Lady Agatha, but I'm afraid not." He didn't elaborate. She swallowed her disappointment and settled back to enjoy the drive as the chauffeur smoothly pulled into the snaking line of vehicles.

Considering the short distance from Athens, the heavy traffic between the capital and the port in Piraeus meant the journey took close to an hour. Agatha suppressed a groan when the arthritis in her hips and knees caused little stabs as the car started and stopped on the overcrowded roads. Her relief at finally reaching the cruise terminal left her limp, gratefully grabbing the driver's arm as he helped her out of the car. The hubbub made her ears ache while her eyes were assaulted by bright colors swirling around her as passengers crowded near the boarding areas. She sniffed the air, redolent of salt, motor oil, gasoline.

A crew member waited to deal with her luggage while a short, bearded man strode over and took her hand, bowing low. His white captain's uniform, adorned with gold braided epaulets at the shoulders. A badge with a sailing ship and *Persuasion* in gold thread was sewn onto the pocket, gleamed in the bright midday light.

"I am Captain Makris. It is my honor to escort you to the *Persuasion* and welcome you to our maiden voyage."

"Thank you so much, captain." Agatha's dry throat made her voice sound scratchy. She swallowed. "I've dreamed of cruising the Aegean for many years and the invitation to join you for this journey has brought me great joy."

As they strolled up the gangplank, Makris said,

"The other passengers are already onboard. We will set sail soon."

A tall, thin uniformed woman with light blue eyes, sharp cheekbones, and very pale skin approached, her white-blond hair pulled back into a severe bun. "This is your steward, Kirsten. She will show you to your cabin. When you are ready, she will escort you to the lounge to meet your fellow travelers."

Agatha studied Kirsten, noticing the steward keenly appraised her as well. Finally, in a slight Scandinavian accent, the woman said, "Pleased to meet you, Lady Agatha. Your luggage has already been transferred to your cabin and, as your personal steward, I will be happy to fulfill any of your wishes during the voyage. We have full service and I am also your concierge, so I can arrange spa services on the ship and make arrangements at the various ports we will visit, if there are particular sites you want to see or restaurants you wish to sample. I can also help with any shopping needs you have. While you are at lunch, I will unpack your bags."

"So kind," Agatha murmured. They had reached her cabin and, as the door swung open, the air whooshed out of Agatha's lungs. The suite was enormous, with a lounge that led to closed French doors on one side and what looked like a small kitchen and dining area behind the lounge.

"Your bedroom," Kirsten said, indicating the closed doors. "There is a bath attached, of course, with both a tub and a separate shower. As you can see, you have a veranda as well. Perfect for enjoying an Aegean sunset or entertaining a lover."

She dropped her voice to a confiding whisper. "Even the King of Norway hasn't a yacht like this."

Agatha checked herself in the mirror hanging over the credenza to the right of the door reflecting the opulent space spread out behind her, ran a hand through her short gray hair, and adjusted the black contrasting collar of her white polka-dot blouse. "Astounding," she agreed. Turning to the steward, she straightened her shoulders and smiled. "Ready.."

After the elegance of her suite, Agatha was sure nothing else could surprise her, but she was wrong. Entering the yacht's lounge, her eye caught on the row of Venetian glass chandeliers swaying gently with the movement of the ship. The long rectangular lounge was flanked on both sides by enormous windows. The view left her speechless and unable to take in anything else. She stood frozen, open mouthed. Kirsten led her to one of the overstuffed sofas and pointed to the bar, champagne flutes resting on the mahogany top. "Please take a seat, Lady Agatha. I'll fetch you champagne."

Agatha sank into the soft cushions. Kirsten returned with a glass and slipped the stem into her hand. "Thank you so much," she said as Kirsten moved away. Following her retreat, Agatha noticed a knot of stewards gathered in one of the corners.

She scanned the other guests. Six people of differing ages and genders gazed back. A lover of puzzles and mysteries, Agatha tried to guess their backgrounds, certain that they had pegged her as an ordinary, elderly English woman, perhaps a little dim. Outside her small circle, she knew that people underestimated her and the assumed dithering personality she often displayed in the company of strangers made her feel safe, almost invisible.

Captain Makris arrived just as Agatha realized that there were only seven passengers. Someone was missing. With the ship under sail, no one would be joining unless they were picking up the last passenger on one of the islands. She was determined to solve the conundrum.

A gong reverberated. As the room stilled, Makris threw his arms wide. "Welcome to the *Persuasion*. Most of you have already met but, I would like to introduce Lady Agatha Carstairs to her fellow travelers. Perhaps each of you will say a bit about yourselves so we can all be comfortable acquaintances. Would you begin, Major Jeffries?"

Jeffries stood. He was tall, gaunt, and stood as if at attention, hands clasped behind his back. Khaki cargo shorts and a golf shirt with an insignia on the chest added to the impression of a stereotypical military man. "Pleased to meet you."

Agatha blinked. Jeffries voice was unexpectedly a high tenor rather than the rumbly bass she had anticipated. She wondered if he would have risen higher in the ranks if he could have produced a more suitable timbre.

Shifting from foot to foot, Jeffries said, "I'm retired from the army and live in Colchester." Then he abruptly sat down. Agatha fiddled with the butterfly on the gold chain she always wore, and wondered if he hid a dark secret.

Captain Makris flashed a sympathetic smile before focusing on the honey-blond waves and the red bandage dress that accentuated the curves of the Marilyn Monroe lookalike sprawled on a light-blue velvet settee. "Mrs. Kingsway, would you go next, please?"

"Certainly." Her voice was low and husky as she gave the captain a come-hither look. She licked her carmine-colored lips. "Lady Agatha, a pleasure to meet you. I'm a widow and all my children are grown and scattered around the globe. I live in a small house in Hampstead, near the Keats House. Cruising is a passion of mine so I was over the moon to be invited on this journey."

With a nod, the captain acknowledged her introduction and moved on to a couple who defined the adage that married couples grew to look alike as they aged. On the other hand, Agatha thought, maybe they were twins traveling together. Regarding them with interest, she realized that they seemed even older than she was. Except when she visited old Mrs. Smithers, who was ninety-eight, she was accustomed to being the oldest person in the room. An unsettled feeling stole over her, as if she had somehow lost status.

"Harry Fredericks." The small, gray-haired man who popped up had the deep voice she expected from the major. He wore a loud Hawaiian shirt, black shorts, and boating shoes. "This is my twin, Francine."

"Fran," the woman piped up. Her clothing was identical to her brother. "We live in Milton Keynes and this is our first trip abroad." She smiled shyly. "It's a fairytale dream for us."

"I'm a retired accounts manager, and Fran was a librarian." Harry gave a self-satisfied smirk as he returned to his seat next to his twin.

Agatha's eye was caught by an older woman sitting with a teenage boy who leaned forward, his forehead resting on closed fists. She wore a twin set and plaid skirt, while the young man was in jeans and a T-shirt emblazoned with a picture of Freddie Mercury. Captain Makris said, "Mrs. Zachary and her son, Theo." Mrs. Zachary's lips curved into a chilly smile while Theo raised his head, threw Agatha a hostile glance, then looked away.

In a toneless mumble, the thin, silver-haired woman said, "Nice to meet you, Lady Agatha." She cleared her throat, then said at a normal volume, "Theo and I live in Mayfair, but I also have a country house in Devon." She gave no clue as to her marital status but Agatha noticed she did not wear a ring.

Pushing up onto her short legs and leaning slightly on her stick, Agatha said, "I am Agatha Carstairs and I live at Castlebrooke Park in Hampshire. You needn't use my title. Too tiresome." She looked around, smiling. "This is my first trip abroad and I am looking forward to seeing all the sights." She plumped back into her seat. "Very nice to meet all of you." She turned toward the captain. "I was told there would be eight passengers. Was someone unable to join us?"

Makris shrugged. "The other passenger is our owner. At the moment, unfortunately unavailable, but I hope you will be able to meet sometime during the cruise." He looked over at the doorway, where a man in a white uniform hovered. "And now, I believe, luncheon is ready in the dining room. I will lead the way." He took Agatha's arm and led the little convoy out of the lounge and deeper into the ship.

Sunlight poured into Agatha's stateroom. After several days of cruising, she found that the sea air and unaccustomed exercise made her sleep exceptionally well. When a brisk knock sounded against the cabin door, she sat up and straightened her nightgown as Kirsten walked through with a morning cup of tea.

"Grattis på födelsedagen, Lady Agatha," she said with a broad smile. Guessing at the meaning, Agatha said, "Thank you. How did you know today is my birthday?"

"It was asked for on the forms when you agreed to the voyage." She handed Agatha the tea. "The captain has arranged for some special treats today in honor of your birthday."

"Aren't we in Ithaca today?"

"Certainly. You have the morning to wander around Vathy, the capital. Then lunch at a very nice taverna. In the afternoon I have arranged for you to have a private tour of the island so you can visit Odysseus' palace, the Monastery of Panagia Kathariotissa, and the Byzantine frescoes and mosaics in the medieval church of Anogi. Then you will join your fellow cruisers for a celebratory birthday dinner at one of the best restaurants in Ithaca."

Kirsten's words made Agatha's stomach gurgle. She took a last swallow and handed the empty teacup back to the steward. "Will I have time for breakfast before we leave for the island?"

"You have at least one hour before disembarkation."

Hopping out of bed, Agatha waved her thanks to Kirsten and rushed to take a shower. She regretted her lie-in, leaving no time for a leisurely bath.

After five days of cruising, Agatha felt in equal parts delighted, drained, and disgruntled. The identity of the mysterious owner remained unrevealed. She had probed the other passengers, but no one had any ideas. Even the crew professed cluelessness about their employer. Perhaps the puzzle would finally be solved at her birthday dinner.

The breakfast buffet was a feast of English classics from kippers to kedgeree complemented by Greek specialties. Agatha splurged on bacon, thick slices of toast, a boiled egg, cheese pie with nuts and honey, and fruit with thick yogurt. With a lot of walking on the docket, she wanted a fortifying start to the day. She nibbled on bacon while scrolling through her messages, all birthday wishes from friends and family. A small pang of regret struck her at being away from loved ones. Philip had included a reassuring update on the estate.

When Mrs. Zachary stopped by her table holding a mug of coffee, Theo was nowhere in evidence, which was, frankly, a relief. The young man continued to be sullen and uncommunicative, two traits Agatha found tiresome.

"I understand it's your birthday. May I join you?" Mrs. Zachary asked, her voice low.

Agatha gestured to the empty chair across from her. "Your son sleeping in?"

"He's already had breakfast and is up on deck. He seems to prefer the company of the crew. Of course, some of them are much closer to his age than us old folks."

"Well," Agatha said, "perhaps he will appreciate the voyage in retrospect."

With a nod, Mrs. Zachary sipped her coffee, but gave no indication that she wanted to say anything. Agatha wondered why she had come over. Finally, she asked, "Do you have any idea why the travel company might have chosen this group of passengers for the *Persuasion's* maiden voyage? I was entered into a contest. Was that the way you were chosen too?"

For a moment, Agatha thought Mrs. Zachary looked like a deer caught in headlights. But the expression was so fleeting, she thought she must have imagined it. Certainly, the smooth explanation, "I subscribe to an email travel newsletter about cruising. I thought the company might have picked us at random from the subscriber list," seemed natural enough.

The responses she'd had from the other passengers had been similar. She was fascinated that her fellow passengers were dedicated to hours of searching for travel opportunities. So many other pastimes occupied her days that the idea of spending time in front of a computer had never crossed her mind.

"*We travel not to escape life but for life not to escape us*," Mrs. Zachary said. "I write that Thomas Jefferson quote in the front of my journal every year, but I never have the courage to follow it."

"Until now."

"Yes, I..."

A voice came over the public address system. "The tender will leave for Vathy in half an hour. All passengers should assemble on deck in twenty minutes for today's excursion. Thank you."

Whatever Mrs. Zachary had been about to say was lost in the moment.

Agatha took a last bite of marmalade-laden toast, leaned over for her stick, and maneuvered her way between the chair and the table. "Nice talking with you," she said. Mrs. Zachary gave a little wave and sipped her coffee. But Agatha felt her eyes burning into her back as she out of the room.

Spending the morning in Vathy had been surprisingly enjoyable. She wandered around with Major Jeffries, discovering that the reason he had come on the cruise was to relive his vacations in Greece when he had been stationed in Gibraltar. A friend had somehow arranged the invitation. It came at an opportune moment as he had just been diagnosed with terminal cancer. Still well enough to travel, this was a bit of a last hurrah for him, he told Agatha sadly. She patted his arm and they walked companionably around the town, visiting the Church of St. George, the Archaeological Museum, strolling past Venetian-inspired houses, most rebuilt after the 1953 earthquake, and stopping for elevenses at a small cafe, where they enjoyed kourabiedes with small cups of syrupy Greek coffee.

The seven regrouped for lunch at Kohily, a small restaurant overlooking the bay. After a nice meal of meze including grilled octopus, taramasalata, grape leaves stuffed with lamb and rice, sliced tomatoes and cucumbers, glistening grilled peppers in oil, chunky eggplant, and olives. Cheeses included several made with sheep and goat milk, some hard and some soft. Skewers of grilled chicken, pork, and shrimp sent up a delicious aroma. Heaped platters of fruits and nuts rested alongside colorful woven baskets of crusty bread and pita. Servers passed platters of spanakopita and fried halloumi.

After all the savories had been consumed, each diner was presented with a beautifully decorated plate with small portions of baklava, galaktoboureko, and portokalopita, a Greek specialty redolent of orange. While the staff wished Agatha, *Chronia Polla*, the captain, explained that it was a popular Greek expression meaning they hoped she would enjoy many years.

Kirsten magically appeared at the end of the meal and escorted Agatha to meet her tour guide, Nikos. Dressed in fashionable jeans and a pristine white shirt, he lounged against a red Land Rover, looking at his phone. Sunbeams glinted off his black hair.

"Nikos," Kirsten said sharply. When he raised his eyes from the screen, she continued tartly. "This is Lady Agatha Carstairs. She will be touring with you this afternoon. You remember the itinerary?"

"Of course," he countered, his Greek accent overlaid with British intonations that marked where he had learned English. Pointing to the car, he said, "And I have it printed out as well."

"You will end at Dona Lefki. The reservation is for eight p.m. Do not be late."

"Don't treat me like a child. All the timings are worked out and, barring a road blockage, everything will be like clockwork." He made a shooing motion. "Go back to the boat, Kirsten. I will see you this evening at the restaurant."

Frowning, Kirsten turned away toward the harbor, but Agatha heard her mutter, "Just because you're his son doesn't mean you can speak to me like that."

Another puzzle. Perhaps Nikos was Captain Makris' son? This trip was proving full of questions with no answers.

Nikos took Agatha's arm and helped her into the back of the vehicle. "We will start at the church so you can see the frescos, then go on to the monastery, and finish at Odysseus' Palace. You know the story? Penelope waited there for her husband to return, besieged by suitors, telling them she would choose one when her weaving was finished. Every day, for the last three of the twenty years, she wove cloth by day and unraveled it at night."

At least, Agatha mused, Penelope's Odysseus finally came home. When Victor left, it had been forever.

Nikos cleared his throat. "After that, a nice ride in the country will be refreshing before your special dinner." He gave Agatha a wink, climbed into the Land Rover, and they drove off toward adventure.

On the way to Anogi, Nikos explained the history of the village and the church they would be visiting. "Anogi was the capital of Ithaca during the sixteenth and seventeenth centuries. But the church dates back to the twelfth century, when all of Greece was Byzantium."

Agatha looked out at the landscape. "What mountain is that?"

"Mount Niritos. It is the highest mountain in Ithaca and Anogi is on the eastern slopes. Practically no one lives in the village now, but we will be able to get the keys from the caretaker so you can see not only the mosaics but the frescoes and the icons. It is one of the largest and most important churches in the Balkans. The bell tower is Venetian."

"Is there anything else to see in the village?" Agatha was looking forward to viewing the art in the church, but she hoped there was more to see.

"We will rest in the cafe and the owner can tell you stories about the history of the town."

"Perfect," Agatha said. "And then?"

"Then we will go to the monastery. We can drive but it is only 2.5 kilometers away if you would like to walk. Unless," he turned his head slightly and glanced at her stick.

"I can certainly walk that distance, even if it is uphill." Agatha couldn't help her indignant tone. She hated people assuming that because she needed to use a cane, that she was incapacitated. She wasn't in a wheelchair yet.

When the Rover juddered to a stop, Agatha jolted awake. Her head felt heavy and her eyelashes stuck to her lower lids. The world was a blur. Nikos helped her out of the car. She was stiff and a bit wobbly, so he took her arm and they walked to the cafe on the central square. Once he had her settled at a table, he went to find the owner, who was in the kitchen supervising dinner preparations. He came out taking off his apron and shook hands with his guest. "Would you like a coffee or some tea?"

"What sort of tea?" Agatha asked.

"Chamomile. It is very popular here."

Even though she would have preferred a nice Darjeeling or Assam, Agatha didn't fancy another coffee. "That sounds wonderful. Thank you."

When he returned a few minutes later with her tea, the owner sat at the table and regaled Agatha and Nikos with stories about Anogi and the island. After an hour of conversation, he reached into a pocket and handed Nikos the keys to the church. "I hope you enjoy your visit," he said, waving away the offer of payment.

After an in-depth look at the church, Agatha turned to Nikos. "You are a marvelous guide, Nikos. Where did you learn all this?"

Not meeting her eye, he said, "At university. I studied art, architecture, and archaeology in Bath."

"And now you're a driver? How did that come about?"

"I am equivalent to a Blue Badge guide in England. So my job is to take visitors on tours but I also drive on the side. At some times of the year, the demand for tours is not so high and I need income. Driving is a way of making extra money."

"What about your family?"

Nikos stiffened. "I prefer to make my own way. My family is very generous, and we are close, but I want to show that I can be independent."

Agatha fiddled with her straw bonnet, untying and retying the ribbon under her chin. "Shall we walk to the monastery? Or will you want to have the car available for the drive to Odysseus' Palace?"

"The climb up is steep and I think driving will be more practical. The monastery is one of my favorite places to take tourists. There is a famous icon and spectacular views."

The short ride to the monastery was uphill and Agatha was secretly relieved not to have walked. When they arrived, Nikos said, "There are renovations going on here, but don't worry, we will be able to see the icon of the Nativity of the Theotokos. It is much older than the monastery itself and a real treasure. Why don't we go in and see it, then we can enjoy the views?"

When they walked into the church, a man in a white shirt, gray trousers, and burgundy suspenders stood in front of the icon. Click, click, click. Agatha's stick tapped against the floor as they came closer, and he turned to face them. He was about six foot, rangy, with a wind-burned complexion, and a shock of white hair. Agatha thought he was probably a few years older than she was. His eyes crinkled as he smiled, holding out his hand. "Happy birthday, my dear Agatha," he said, his voice a rich baritone with a strong Scottish accent.

Her brow furrowed. Who was this man?

"Thank you, Nikos," the stranger said, clapping the younger man on the shoulder. "I will escort Lady Agatha to see the view after we have appreciated the craftsmanship of the icon. I hope you don't mind waiting with the car?"

"Not at all. Enjoy yourselves." Nikos turned quickly and left the church.

"You don't recognize me?" He sounded resigned. "I suppose expecting that after all these years was a bit optimistic."

Agatha studied him carefully, straining her neck slightly because he was so tall. After a few passes, the years fell away as she realized who stood before her. As recognition dawned, the man facing her grinned, deepening the grooves around his eyes. Finally she blurted, "Victor? Is it really you?"

"It is indeed. Welcome to Ithaca. A little late, but better than never."

Coincidence? Serendipity? "Bu-bu-but..."

Wagging a finger at her, Victor Macdonald said, "I'm disappointed. I thought you would have solved the mystery by now."

"The-the-the mystery?" She frowned. "The only mystery for me is how I ended up on this Aegean cruise."

"And?" When she saw the glint of amusement in his eyes, the last piece clicked into place.

"It was you?"

"The *Persuasion* is my yacht. I built it for you." He

took her hand. Agatha felt heat rise from her toes to the top of her head. "I see you still wear the necklace."

He reached out a finger to touch the filigree butterfly. "We missed our honeymoon. And I thought, perhaps Ithaca could still be ours."

Agatha removed her sunglasses and wiped her eyes. "I've never left Britain," she said.

"And now you have your chance. And perhaps we have a chance, another chance at life."

Victor leaned forward, put his hands on her shoulders, and touched her lips in a gentle kiss. "I've kept an eye on you all these years and I know you never married."

"When my parents persuaded me to give you up for Castlebrooke, I knew there would never be anyone else." She sniffed but didn't move away. "Did you marry?"

"You never checked? I'm not exactly anonymous."

"I wondered but I didn't want to know. Once I'd lost you, I built a wall to keep thoughts of you out. Buried myself at Castlebrooke where it was unlikely I'd ever hear any news of you."

The light in his blue eyes dimmed. Agatha thought she saw moisture collect at the corners. "And you were successful in forgetting me, I take it."

"You were often in my thoughts, but I never wanted to know what your life was like. That would have caused more regret than I could handle."

By this time they had walked out of the church with barely a glance at the icon. He led her to a wall where they could look over the Ionian Sea, blue water glimmering in the late afternoon glow.

"I've done very well for myself," Victor said.

"You must have if you can afford that yacht. Why did you say you'd built it for me?"

"Because I did. I did marry, twice. I have two children and one grandson. My first wife was a lovely woman, but she always knew that she was second best. She wasn't you."

"Wasn't?"

"She died a long time ago. Cancer. She had a long, painful decline."

"And you remarried?"

"Yes, some years later. My second wife was Greek. We were married about ten years, then divorced. When she went back to her family, she took our son with her. She died last year." His face drooped, reminding Agatha of a bloodhound. She wanted to put her arms around him but forced herself to stand still.

"After the divorce, I looked you up and found you were still unmarried and living at Castlebrooke. I decided to persuade you, after all these years, to take a chance with me."

"Did your wives know about me?"

"My first wife did. We married about a year after you broke off our engagement. She read the society news and knew she was my rebound. Our engagement hadn't been a secret. And I'm sure she suspected that I never got over you. But I was a good husband, so she had nothing to complain of."

"But you married again…"

"After I dealt with everything to do with my wife's death and getting my daughter settled, I was at loose ends. When I met Agata…"

"Agata? She had my name?"

"Yes. I…" He swallowed. "Unfortunately, that was the only thing you had in common. Once we cut ties, I knew that I shouldn't have given up all those years ago. Now I had a chance to make things right. I made a plan. Once I'd settled on the yacht, it needed to be designed to my specifications. The build took four years. And I bought a house on Ithaca. Set everything in motion. Visited Chesney Hardcastle and enlisted your housekeeper in my scheme. Not to mention getting my children on board with the idea."

Damson had colluded with Victor? Agatha set the thought aside for the moment. "Are your children ok with this?"

"My daughter is still a bit wary. I believe you've met her, and my grandson."

"Have I?

"Mrs. Zachary, Clarissa, is my daughter and Theo is my grandson."

"And your son?"

"Nikos. He was fine with the idea from the beginning."

"And the other passengers? Are they involved?"

"Major Jeffries is my cousin. I'm glad I could do something for him. He's been dealt a rotten hand." He began pacing. "Carol Kingsway is his nurse. And Harry is my business partner."

"Really?" Agatha could hardly credit that. "Is Fran really his sister?"

"Yes. She is our information specialist." He paused and ran his fingers through his hair. It stood up in spikes and she could hardly keep from laughing.

"But right now is about us. I'm taking my shot. After all, romance isn't only for the young."

"Why *Persuasion*?"

"When you called off the wedding, I felt like Captain Wentworth in the Jane Austen novel, rejected by Anne Elliot."

Agatha's jaw went slack with surprise.

"All this is my Wentworth moment."

Ah, Agatha thought, the famous letter. She quoted, "*I must speak to you by such means as are within my reach. You pierce my soul. I am half agony, half hope. Tell me that I am not too late, that such precious feelings are gone forever. I offer myself to you with a heart even more your own than when you broke it...*" Her voice fragmented as tears flowed down her cheeks.

Victor took out a handkerchief and blotted away the moisture. They gazed into each other's eyes for a long moment, then the mood was broken by a car horn. Victor looked at his watch. "That's Nikos, reminding me that we need to leave if we are going to visit Odysseus' palace before our dinner reservation at Dona Lefki. And we can plan our future life."

"Nikos reminded me about Penelope's weaving while she waited for her husband's return. Will I be able to see the loom?" Agatha asked. "After all, I waited forty-seven years for you."

Victor's delighted laughter rang out, reflected by the seawall. "Of course you had to find a flaw in all my careful preparation. I should have had a reproduction made to commemorate our visit."

Hand in hand, they left the monastery to commune with another pair of timeless lovers.

SYLVIE AND ALICE

Author's Note

"Sylvie Green" was originally part of an anthology project that was done by the Off Campus Writers Workshop in collaboration with high school teacher Jay Rehak, who came up with the original idea for a collection of short fiction all stemming from the same framing story—celebrating a writer who is receiving a lifetime writing award as she celebrates her 100th birthday.

A Reason to Be Here: Tales from the Writer's Convention was published in 2019 and "Sylvie Green" was my first published piece of fiction. At the time, I had decided to use the name Deborah Kahn so my work as a historian would be separate from any short stories or novels I might publish.

In the end, having a pseudonym was too much work and I decided that my readers wouldn't mind that I had published nonfiction earlier in my career.

Now, having published four novels and some short stories, I'm glad that you can find me as Sharon Michalove.

The story as it stands now is as much about Alice as it is about Sylvie so I've retitled it to reflect that. My writing has developed over time and I revised extensively. The original 1800 words has expanded to just over 8K and the whole thing is now in first person, reflecting the voices of both Sylvie and Alice.

I hope you enjoy reading about the encounter between two writers, one at the beginning and one at the end of their careers with a budding romance too.

High expectations are the key to everything.—Sam Walton

Sylvie

"Where's damn the book?"

Belle opens one yellow eye, stretches, turns around on the chair, and starts to wash her ears. She doesn't know and, more important, she doesn't care.

Loud honking sounds from the street below. Wondering who's making all the noise, I see Mike, my colleague at Granville College, in the purple Porsche Boxter convertible that he calls Viola, after his favorite Shakespeare heroine. He'd bought the sporty car instead of investing in a house or condo.

And would probably rent forever if he didn't win the lottery.

I rush from the living room to the bedroom to the study muttering expletives under my breath. Belle, her black fur electric from the continuous outdoor cacophony, stays two leaps away. Even though I'm sure that looking in the kitchen will be fruitless, a glance shows me the battered hardcover sitting next to the mug of now-cold coffee on the counter. With effort, I cram it into an overstuffed brief bag, breaking one of my just-polished nails. A shake of the little purse slung around my neck assures me that my keys are clipped to the fob. I practically tumble headfirst down the stairs, in my rush out the door.

Mike frowns, tapping his fingers on the window frame. The building door slams and the black wrought-iron gate clangs, adding to the strident blare from his horn.

"What the fuck took you so long?" His voice reverberates around the neighborhood. I look around, hoping neighbors aren't hanging out of the windows, gawking.

Breath puffing out in gasps, I slide into the plush gray leather interior, and sink into the roomy bucket seat.

"Couldn't find the book." Can't catch my breath. Damn asthma. I dump everything from my bag into the footwell, scrabbling for my inhaler.

His mouth flaps like a hooked fish. "You did find it?"

I take a few inhales while my foot taps the blue and yellow cover. I slide my phone into my sweater pocket; shovel the rest of the bag's contents willy-nilly back into the butter-soft burgundy cowhide. "It was in the kitchen. With my cold coffee and uneaten toast." My voice rasps. I swallow a few times.

Mike's face twists into a simulacrum of resignation. "Fine, we'll go through a drive-through and get you something."

Beneath the growl, I hear underlying fondness. Good to be with a friend who knows your ways. Then, with his schoolteacher voice, he quizzes me. "You have *your* book too?"

My hand wriggles into the case and caresses the no-longer-crisp paper cover of my new novel. Presenting Alice Bainbridge with a less than pristine copy will be so embarrassing. I grind my teeth slightly before putting a hand on his arm.

"I need to go back and get a clean copy. I can feel the cover of this one is bent."

The heat of his glare should burn me to a cinder. "Forget that. We're late and already have one extra stop. Put the damn seatbelt on."

"Fine." I sniff. "She'll never read it, anyway."

I'll bury it in the heap of sacrificial offerings. Every author will give her a copy of their book.

"Hey, be optimistic. I am." Mike's wry smile acknowledges that his military thriller might not be to the genteel author's taste.

"Let's face it, at her age, she probably doesn't read

a book a day anymore. I expect mine will be lost in the pile and find its way to a second-hand bookstore after she dies."

I spy a tube of lip balm rolling around and unbuckle the seat belt so I can reach down to grab it.

Success. I wave the renegade in the air.

"Put your seatbelt back on." He frowns.

I click it closed, making a face at him.

"Nah, she'll live to the end of her TBR pile."

I double over with laughter, the seatbelt cutting into me. "Owwww." My howl sounds like a TV cartoon character.

Mike rolls his eyes, then tears away from the curb, almost hitting a dog racing across the street. Breaks screech. My forehead bumps against the curved top of the dash as Mike lowers the window and yells, "Stay out of the street, you mangy cur." Then he heads north.

With just two fingers on the steering wheel, his turn into the drive thru has us swaying from one side to the other. His brakes squeal as we approach the order window. Then we wait until my sandwich is heated before heading out, Starbuck's Pike Peak in the cup holder and a sausage, egg, and cheese sandwich clutched in my hand.

Two newly published authors on their way to a writers conference.

Remembering that I'll be dead soon is the most important tool I've ever encountered to help me make the big choices in life. Because almost everything - all external expectations, all pride, all fear of embarrassment or failure - these things just fall away in the face of death, leaving only what is truly important.— Steve Jobs

Alice

Colorful corpses, three outfits lie inert, uncommunicative, on the bed. I ask them to plead their cases. Silence. I used to talk to my characters. Now I talk to my clothes. Unlike the former, the latter have no opinion.

I know any of them will be fine. I don't resemble a withered old crone and the advantage of reaching the magic age of one hundred means no one expects me to look like a fashion model. I expel a noisy breath, just because I can, leave them there and opt for the beige sweater and oatmeal colored slacks I usually wear. Not as dressy as the suit or the caftan, but definitely comfortable.

After small tussle to get the outfit on, I maneuver my chair, Zippy, through the wide doorway, zooming toward the kitchen. I've thought about moving to a senior center in the hopes of wide corridors for wheelchair races.

My grandnephew, Eddie, sits drinking coffee. I swallow to keep from drooling. It's easily been twenty years since I was forbidden coffee, and chocolate, and cola. The acid, caffeine, and my propensity for too much cream and even more sugar means a ban, not a suggestion. At the thought of an icy cola with a glug of cream, my eyes mist with desire.

Eddie glances up from his scrutiny of the Chicago *Tribune*. "There's a whole article about you in here. Excited?" His bright blue eyes twinkle behind thick glasses as he brandishes it in my direction, the page neatly folded to show an old photo of me.

With a fond smile, I wheel toward the table. I'd never expected him to move in with me after his divorce. His son and daughter grown and gone, he was looking for someone to fuss over. Now that I need a constant companion, the arrangement suits us both.

Once settled in my usual parking spot at the table, I reach for the tea cup, one of the family collection. It had been given to me by an aunt when I graduated from bottles, and I'd loved my Beatrice Mallet children's cup with two children fishing, ever since. I always quoted the rhyme painted on it before drinking.

"Fishermen two, Bobbie and Sue, Fishes for tea, Straight from the sea."

Eddie had just filled it and the stringent herbal scent of the tea casts a soothing atmosphere over the room.

"I'm gratified that the society wants to honor my career, although I don't imagine I'll rank among the greats for posterity. But I don't really want to make a speech."

Curiosity makes his eyes glitter. "What do you want to do?"

My mind swirls like a mini tornado with ideas and strictures. Easier to know what I don't want so I study the yellow-and-blue flowered wallpaper as if the design will transmute into a coherent list.

"I don't want to tell stories. I've done that all my life. Now I want to hear other people's stories."

"Don't you get that from reading?" Eddie's puzzled expression surprises me.

"I want to have people tell me stories. Their stories. Not made up ones."

"So that's what you'll ask for?"

Fiddling with my spoon, I manage to drop it under

the table. Eddie folds his long body and reaches for it. Grabbing it, he expertly throws it into the sink and pumps a fist. "Still have the eye."

I want to laugh but the ordeal of being lauded as a treasure gnaws at me. "I'll thank everyone, then ask them to tell me stories."

"You're in for a long day. All those people. Hours and hours of stories."

"I have all the time there is. And you can do crowd control."

Sipping green tea from the delicate porcelain, decorated with colorful song birds inside and out, a rush of memories displaces my unease. The kitchen chair, squirmy on the seat covered in red vinyl that makes my behind stick in the heat. Legs swinging, heels tinging against the metal legs. My parents drink thick black coffee while I have warm milk with a drop of the pungent brew to make me feel grown up.

Our birthday tradition included one present at breakfast, along with the first cake. My sixth birthday. Mouth full of chocolate, I unwrapped the gift. A black composition book, page after page of white ruled pages, and a pack of yellow pencils, just for me.

"You love to tell stories," Dad said as he sharpened a pencil with a tiny penknife that hung from his waistcoat watch fob. "You should try writing them down. Then you can read them to Phil."

"He's too young," I protested. My baby brother wasn't all that interesting and I didn't think he'd make a good audience.

"No one is ever too young or too old for stories," Dad chided.

I still believe that.

I am not a people person. It's not that I am shy, but I am more comfortable in an atmosphere of one-on-one. I hate crowds and parties. - Bethany Joy Lenz

Sylvie

The event is at the Norris Center at Northwestern University. The Evanston campus is beautiful in the crisp autumn air. After ten minutes, Mike pulls into the nearby South Campus Parking Garage and we start the hike into the building.

The roar coming from the Louis Room rolls out the open doorways. This is an invitational event, but when I peek in, two hundred people are crushed together, and tempers are already rising. I turn around and bump into Mike's chest.

He growls. "Get going, Sylvie."

Tears gather in my eyes. "Can't," I whisper.

Strong fingers grab my shoulders. "You can." His snarl makes me jump.

When I push past him, back out to the foyer of the building, he follows behind. His feet crack against the floor as he rushes after me.

Blindly, I keep a hand on a corridor wall. The tears are falling now and my sight is blurred. Moisture drips down my cheeks and falls off my chin, spotting my blouse. My nose runs. As soon as I'm in the open space, I slide to the floor and drop my face to my hands.

A hand touches my shoulder. "The fucking hell, Sylvie. You're a mess."

When I look up into Mike's grim face, he shoves a bunch of tissues at me. "Tell me what's going on." His hand waves around wildly.

Tissues crumpled in my fist, my whole body shakes. No words come out. The panic that engulfs me can't be explained. I'm here to meet my idol, and somehow I can't go through it. A sense of desolation washes through me and I just want to slink away, tail between my legs.

"Wipe your face, Sylvie and I'll get you to the bathroom so you can wash up and compose yourself."

The compassion in his voice makes everything worse. I don't want his pity and I don't deserve his sympathy.

'Just get me an Uber, Mike. I'm not staying."

His laugh is humorless. "Yes you are. This is your chance to meet the writer you never stop talking about, and I'm not letting you run away. I thought you were braver than this."

"I'm not brave," I wail.

"Pretend you are. When you get home, later, you can collapse. Give in to hysterics. But right now, pull up your big girl panties and get back into the game."

Hand held out, he grasps mine, pulls me up, gives

me a hug. Then he checks his shirt front to make sure I haven't stained it. It's a little wet but nothing that will show.

"Good thing I'm not wearing any makeup."

"You never wear makeup. Lucky you have such good skin. But now you look snotty and disgusting. Let's get you cleaned up before you meet Alice."

Success comes to those who dedicate everything to their passion in life. To be successful, it is also very important to be humble and never let fame or money travel to your head.—A. R. Rahman

Alice

Good thing Eddie got us here early. Except for the organizers the generous space is empty. I survey the room. A table near a stage. A huge cake takes up most of the top. Alongside are stacks of plates and rows of forks wrapped in napkins.

Some kind of trophy sits at one end. Kind of like an Oscar, only bigger. Instead of a naked man, a slender woman, posed like a dancer, arms upraised, stands delicately balanced on tiptoe. Words are inscribed on the base but I'm too far away to read them.

Eddie asks where I should be placed. Like a flower decoration or something. Not sure I like that.

An hour later the place is jammed. Can't believe

all these people turned out to see me. Maybe my idea of listening to stories is naive. Two hundred people, two hundred stories. We might be here until midnight, or tomorrow. My bones ache and my ears buzz.

"You okay, Aunt Alice?" Eddie's face creases.

I touch his hand. "A bit overwhelmed, but fine. Wondering whether I've bitten off more than I can chew."

"We'll give people a time limit for their stories. No more than five minutes. I'll be the timekeeper and make sure you get breaks too." He drops a kiss on my cheek.

I love how he sees this as a collaboration. A joint venture rather than an imposition. "You're so good to me, Eddie. Your parents brought you up well."

He smiles. "Dad was so sorry he couldn't be here. And Grandpa..."

"I know. Funerals suck." Vaughan's best friend just died and the funeral is today. Philip, my earliest audience, hasn't "been" for a long time. He lives in a memory-care facility in Florida. My sister-in-law died years ago. Vaughan would like to move his father up here, but at ninety-six, he's too frail.

A whiny crackle from the microphone alerts the crowd that we're ready to start and Eddie pushes my chair up the ramp to the stage.

The tech taps the mike a couple of times and mutters. "Testing. Testing." Such a cliché.

Clearing her throat, Millicent Franks, one of my

mentees and a fine short-story writer, calls the crowd to order.

"Thank you all for coming today to honor one of the greatest writers of her, and perhaps any other, generation. I won't rehearse all of Alice Bainbridge's accomplishments. You know them or you wouldn't be standing here now."

She goes on for ten more minutes. I tap my fingers on the arms of my chair and try not to look bored. Eddie checks his watch, then clears his throat loudly.

Millicent subsides. "Without more ado, let's welcome Alice."

Vigorous applause ensues.

They present me with the award. Heavy, gold-plated bronze. The words on the base are from the Czech author, Milan Kundera. "The characters in my novels are my own unrealised possibilities."

When Millicent plops in my lap, I practically tip over. Eddie saves me, picking up the award and putting it back on the table.

"The cake will be available for everyone while they wait to speak to Alice," Millicent bellows into the noisy crowd. "But first, Alice will say a few words."

I know the crowd expects a speech, capped by one of my stories. Some new tale that will show that I still have it, whatever it is. Instead I say, "Thank you for the warm reception. And the beautiful award."

I cough. "Being old has its privileges, I suppose. Once you've outlived most of your peers, you win by being the last one standing."

There are titters from the crowd, as if they aren't sure whether I'm being funny or serious. I'm silent.

"Tell us a story, Alice," Jason Carson calls out. He's a thriller writer. Tales of violence and sex. Jason's popular Mannheim novels are a lucrative film franchise these days.

"I've been telling stories all my life. I wrote the first in pencil sitting at my parents' kitchen table."

Eddie hands me a water bottle and I take a sip. The crowd is silent, waiting for more words of remembrance. The awe I see is so misplaced.

Everyone here is a writer. We've suffered the same slings and arrows. Rejections. Bad reviews. Books not selling. The well of ideas running dry. Writer's block.

"Now I'm tired. And I have no more stories that I want to tell."

The crowd gasps, shifts, groans.

"No, Alice, not true," someone calls out.

"It's your turn to shine. Tell me your stories. I want to know about all of you, your journey, why you're here, why you want to meet me."

Chattering turns to a dull roar.

Eddie grabs the mike, the crowd quietening as he begins.

"There will be some ground rules. There are a lot of you. If you want to tell Aunt Alice a story, make it a short one, five minutes max. And she will need breaks throughout the day."

He thrusts out his chest and I stifle a laugh. "I'm the gatekeeper."

An elderly man in an old-fashioned but well-cut navy suit calls out, "We could be here for days, Alice."

"Then let the young ones tell their stories, Horace. I already know yours."

The crowd titters and Horace guffaws. "I'll take you for a nice dinner at the end, Alice."

"Hear that Eddie? We'll be dining out. You know all best places."

Know how to ask favors. There is nothing more difficult for some people, nor for others, easier.— Baltasar Gracian, 1601-1658, Spanish writer

Sylvie

As the line forms in front of Alice's wheelchair, anxiety floods back into my chest. My breath rasps as I struggle for air.

I reach into my pocket for my inhaler, but come up empty. I panic. Taking a second dose from my inhaler is the only remedy. This would be the third today, but I'm desperate.

When I can 't find it, I wonder. Did I give it to Mike?

He's in line, getting coffee. I don't have the breath to call out. Instead I squeeze my eyes shut and concentrate on getting air into my lungs. Ragged sounds make the people around me stare. After a few minutes, I'm stable again.

A woman stands at my shoulder. "Is this yours?" She hold my inhaler loosely between two fingers.

"Where did you find it?"

"Must have fallen out of your pocket and rolled away. Hit my foot." She drops it into my open palm.

"Thank you."

"Got to get my place in line." She turns away with a smile.

"Wait. You can get in front of me."

She looks at the horde behind and shakes her head. "Nice of you but the blood-thirsty Madame Defarges would just cart us both off to the guillotine."

The jostling of writers keeps me shifting. A slow trickle leaves the line, getting cake, irritable at the long wait. What did they expect?

Everyone in the room wants to get close to Alice. Touch her hand. Tell their stories. Receive words of wisdom and encouragement.

But all these stories will be the same. Won't she get bored? Maybe she'll throw up her hands after the first hour and roll away. It's her party and she can leave if she wants to.

A guy a little ahead of me complains. "Five minutes! Can hardly get started before time's up."

"Just think of it as flash fiction," his companion tells him. "A sound bite."

My heavy bag rests at my feet, Alice's book on top. The crowd shuffles slowly forward. At a shove from behind, I whirl, glare. The guy smirks, palm still raised, then points his chin. "Move up," he hisses.

A noticeable gap has opened up that I need to close. I rush to move forward before two people can cut in front of me, tripping over the bag, now an obstacle. They grimace as I get up and brush off my knees. This day has turned into a nightmare.

Mike comes up and hands me a cup of coffee. "Careful. It's hot," he warns.

I make space for him, take a sip, and burn my tongue. "Shit."

"Told you to be careful." Mike blows on his own cup.

Once the dual stings, knees and tongue, subside, my mind goes back to woolgathering, but I keep one eye peeled.

My first novel goes on sale next week, and I've been deliriously excited to meet my "mentor." I've visualized gently taking the bird-like hand of the frail centenarian and staring intently into her light-colored blue eyes. And I would explain how Alice and her writings had changed my life.

How trite. I'm a writer, dammit. Why is it so hard to think of something to say?

Discouragement creeps in, like fog on little cat feet. Nothing is what I expected. First, that boring presentation. Even Alice looked impatient to have it over.

Now she's besieged by hordes of writers, all wanting to meet her, fawn over her, and maybe tell her a story. The centenarian already looks tired. By the time I get to the head of the line, Alice might have expired from fatigue. Bleah.

Thirsty, I chug cooled coffee.

I think of the box of author copies sitting on my dining table.

I kick my bag, then bend down, checking that the signed copy and that precious book, the one by Alice, are still there.

The not-quite-empty cup tips and spills into the bag. I shriek, drop the cup, and dump everything everywhere to keep the liquid from soaking the books. The tall guy standing behind me sighs and drops to his knees.

"Calm down. Let me help."

Mike runs off, then back with napkins, lots of napkins.

Frantic, I try to blot the paper while the tall guy retrieves my wayward belongings. Mike scrabbles to pick up rolling pens. I put the two coffee-speckled books on top of the higgledy-piggledy mess swimming in the bottom.

Standing up, I feel a tap on my arm. Apprehension turns to shock when I glance around and see Alice's grandnephew, Eddie.

"You seem a little flustered. Need some help?" He hands me a runaway pen.

Eddie is tall and balding and only vaguely resembles Alice. He strikes me as a comfortable sort in his plaid sport coat and open-collared shirt. Not so forbidding close up as he appeared on stage.

He smells vaguely of vanilla. I've read that men like

the smell of vanilla. To me the scent is slightly cloying and old-fashioned, but the aroma was faint.

"I've got it." I push my hair behind my ears, and fiddle with the clip. Frown at the reddish strands caught in the clasp. Why is he standing here? Shouldn't he be the guard dog, standing by his aunt?

When I look toward the table, Alice isn't there.

"She's taking a break," Eddie says. "So I thought I'd stroll around a little and noticed your little mishap. That you were flustered. Thought maybe I could be of assistance."

My mouth drops open.

"Watch out for flies," Mike says.

Eddie peers at the line of writers ahead of me. "Are you hoping to tell Alice a story?"

I swipe my suddenly teary eyes. "I do have a story to tell, but I'm not sure it's worth Alice's precious time."

"Is the story important to you?"

"Yes." I'm surprised at the vehemence that rings in my ears.

"It's the story of how I became a writer." Then, suddenly less sure, I add, "but I'm sure everyone here has that story. Alice will be tired of that tale long before I have the opportunity to speak to her."

I sound flat and whiny at the same time. Come on, Sylvie, my inner voice scolds. You're better than this.

My helpers pat my shoulders. "You got this," my former critic tells me.

I look up and see crinkles around his eyes, his compelling sapphire blue eyes.

"Maybe you and your friend will have a drink with me after this ordeal."

Mike looks at him with interest and sticks out his hand. "Sounds great. I'm Mike Warren. I write military thrillers."

I'm silent, so Mike gestures to me. "This klutz is Sylvie Green. And you are?"

"Frederick Zane. But you can call me Rick. And I'm sure."

He checks his watch and surveys the line. "By the time we get through, the sun will be over the yardarm."

We're all speaking in clichés.

Eddie smiles and takes my hand. In a kind voice he says, "I think my great-aunt would like to meet you. What's your name?"

"Sylvie Green," I mutter.

"What do you write, Sylvie?"

I straighten, willing myself into sounding confident. "My first book comes out this week." I notice Rick listening intently.

"What's it about?" Is Eddie interested or just being polite? I go for the former, even though I'm convinced it's the latter.

"The book a historical mystery about a murder in the Arctic during the nineteenth-century Franklin expedition. All fictitious of course. The theme is uncontrollable desire and the willingness to do anything and give up everything to appease that appetite." I'm bouncing on my toes as I recite my carefully rehearsed book blurb.

Eddie nods and looks again at the queue, still shuffling slowly.

"Alice's interested in polar exploration, and young writers."

"Reading her book on polar exploration sparked my interest in the first place."

"She'll love to hear that."

Turning toward Mike and Rick he says, "I hope you gentlemen don't mind if Sylvie jumps the line?"

Mike grins and pushes me. "Go, dork."

Rick nods his agreement.

Taking my elbow, Eddie urges me forward. Alice is back in her place, being guarded by two minions until Eddie can return.

When we reach her, he says, "Aunt Alice, I think you'll want to hear the story that this newly published author, Sylvie Green, has to tell."

It's impossible to explain creativity. It's like asking a bird, 'How do you fly?' You just do.—Eric Jerome Dickey

Alice

"Take fifteen," Eddie whispers in my ear. "I'll get you another bottle of water."

"I'll float away."

"Nah. You don't want to get dehydrated and this place is too warm. I'll see if I can get the temperature lowered a bit."

The long line of writers doesn't seem to have diminished, even though after two hours I've listened to twenty-four stories. Eddie is a brilliant timekeeper but we're at max speed with no reprieve in sight.

I wheel myself off to the restroom, mostly to get away from the crowd. Nice that the accessible bathroom is a single and empty. I splash water on my face. Eyes closed, I enjoy the solitude and the quiet until pounding on the door reminds me that my time is up.

Now back at the table, I worry that I will wear out before we ever get to the end. I examine the young woman and motion her over to the table. My hand looks like a frail, arthritic claw and I wince at this sign of my ridiculous old age as we shake hands.

"My hearing isn't great these days. What did Eddie say your name is?"

"Sylvie Green." She wets her lips. After a pause she plunges straight in, "My mom got sick when I was in high school."

I give a minute nod of encouragement.

"She didn't die or anything," Sylvie hastens to add. "Anyway, uh, my life changed."

"Of course it did."

"Oh, God, this is so boring." She covers her eyes with spread hands, then peeks through. "I don't know why I thought you would be interested." Her mumble barely reaches me.

I give her my hand to hold. "Just relax, dear. Let your story unfold however you like."

Nodding, Sylvie continues hesitantly. "Everything changed that year. I didn't have to take care of Mom, but my sisters were younger and I was expected to watch them, and I did some of the cooking and other housework."

Sylvie had put two books on the table and now she fiddles with a pen, clicking the point up and down.

"With all that going on at home, I didn't have time for much else. No time for friends, clubs, movies, dates. My life was a desert." She falls silent.

I'm sure five minutes have passed but Eddie doesn't interrupt. Mutter is coming from the line but I don't point out that her time is up.

Instead, I prompt. "Go on dear. The natives are restless."

Sylvie shakes herself out of her torpor. "Reading was my only outlet. I mostly read fantasy novels, although I couldn't let my dad see them. He thought they were unhealthy."

I laugh as Sylvie continues. "I read them late at night, in my room . . ." She hesitates again. "When Mom's pills worked, life seemed almost normal. When she didn't take her medication . . ." Her voice is thick and she breaks off.

She rushes on as the crowd makes restless noises. "Then, in junior year, your novel, *The Queens*, was assigned in our English class."

She relaxes at my smile. "Your writing, like my mom's pills, brought order out of disorder, cleared my mind, gave me focus." She reaches out to the table for a ragged hardcover edition of *The Queens*. Pushing it into my hands, she says, "Could you sign it? Please."

"Always one of my favorites," I tell her. I take the book and the pen Sylvie has clutched in her hand, and scrawl a few words and my signature, gravely handing both back to Sylvie, who can hardly stay still.

"Oh, thank you," she gushes. "This means so much to me. Wow."

Best wishes on your writing career.
I'm sure you will succeed brilliantly.
Alice Bainbridge

She looks at the inscription. Words pour out like a waterfall. "I'd never read anything like it. I was blown away. We studied it for a month and I probably read it six times. History came alive. I studied old maps, and read biographies. I hunted down every book of yours that I could find. I've read everything."

Eddie's voice interrupts. "That's very nice to hear, but..." He gives a pointed look toward the queue.

"Give her a little more time." Still, I can feel the resentment building up around us. "Be quiet," I call out to the crowd. "This is my event and I make the rules. If I choose to give someone more time, that's my choice"

A strident voice rises above the noise. "Does that mean you're extending our grace period?"

I give the speaker an icy glare. "No."

Then I turn back to Sylvie. "Go on dear."

She puts the book back on the table next to her bag. Her eyes are shadowed. She's afraid.

I wave a dismissive hand. "Don't worry about them."

After a gulp from the water bottle Eddie hands

her, she picks the book back up and grasps it with both hands, like a talisman.

"I could feel the gaits of the horses when characters were out for a ride. My heart broke when David Riccio was murdered, and I shook when the casket letters were discovered."

Her eyes have taken on a faraway look, as if she can see into the story.

"Transporting myself to other places, other times made me feel free. You pushed me in new directions with every novel you wrote. You opened new worlds, gave me new friends, peopled my internal universe."

She gives me an inquiring look and I nod for her to continue.

Freeing one hand from its death grip on the book, Sylvie grabs my hand again. "I started having conversations with my imagined version of you."

More grumbling came from the crowd and Eddie's commanding voice, warned the impatient horde.

Speaking more quickly, Sylvie continued. "Your book on arctic exploration refocused my interests. You whispered in my ear that I should apply for the Arctic Circle program enabling me to write my first novel, the book I just published, *Cold Death in the North.*"

In a confiding whisper, she finished. "I'm hoping it will sell well enough that I can give up teaching and write full time. I'm writing my second novel, the first in a series about murders at the court of Francis I." Despite the soft tone, her glee is palpable.

I sit still, mulling over her words.

She looks stricken when I don't respond. She finally squeaks. "I'm so sorry for taking up your time. Just another gushing effusion. Not really a story. Totally wasting your time. I'll go now." She shoves my book into her bulging bag.

I reach out a restraining hand. "You remind me of another young writer. I'd love a signed copy of your book." Her smile lights up the room.

[I]f you want the rainbow, you gotta put up with the rain!—Dolly Parton

Sylvie

My legs wobble as I walk away from Alice. Seeing Mike and Rick in line, I go over.

"OMG, OMG, OMG. I can't believe it. She actually asked for a signed copy of the book. And she listened to all that drivel and never laughed at me."

"Twenty minutes," Mike crows. "You killed it."

The brief feeling of elation turns to shame. When I glance over at Rick, I expect a scowl. But he grins. "Well done. You must be a natural storyteller to captivate Alice that way."

"I made the crowd angry."

He lifts an eyebrow. "She could have stopped you any time. But she didn't. Don't beat yourself up."

The line snakes forward. "I'm going to find a place

to sit down. I need to process all this. Come find me when you're done."

Mike shakes his head. "We may not get there. Only half an hour left before they turf us out."

Again, shame washes over me. I had enough time for four people and they might not get any.

'I'm sorry. Got carried away. And now you two may never get a chance."

Eddie stands up on the stage and taps on the microphone. "I realize that not all of you will be able have Aunt Alice sign your books. For those of you who don't get the opportunity, there are signed bookplates available along with a URL for a website where you can record your story."

A rumble of voices starts up and Eddie holds up a hand. "In addition, there's a table available if you have one of your own books to give Alice. We both want to thank you all for being here today."

Mike says, "I think we should avail ourselves of the signatures and the website."

"Wise man. We aren't going to make it to the front in the next half hour." Rick pulled a book out of his backpack. "And I want to leave my book, just in case..."

A breath-taking photo of Lake Michigan catches my eye. My indrawn breath is noisy and Rick beams.

"I'm a photographer. This is my latest photo essay, a love story about the lake."

The book is plucked out of his hands. Mike starts turning pages. "Cool."

I try to grab the book out of his hands, but he holds it over his head. "Wait your turn."

Rick pulls it away and hands it to me.

Mike just laughs. "Where are we going for this drink? I have my car, so Sylvie and I can just meet you."

"Didn't drive," Rick says. "I live close by, so I just walked over."

"Think I'll just Uber home," I tell them. "I have some new ideas for my book." I'm on fire and itching to get back to my computer. Alice is even more inspiring in person than in my imagination.

"Oh no you don't," Rick says. "Writing can wait until tomorrow. Tonight we're going to celebrate your brilliant achievement. And we'll do it in style. An upscale bar crawl. And you're going to tell me your story and all about your book. And what you think about mine."

Mike's face falls. FOMO setting in.

Rick notices. "Yours too, Mike. As fellow authors, we all need to brag a bit."

"We want to hear your story too," I tell him. "You don't get to be the mystery man."

"My story is very boring but I'll tell you while you fall asleep over drinks." Rick produces an ostentatious and totally fake yawn.

My friend and colleague squints at him. "Driving may be a bad idea if we're doing a lot of drinking. We can drive to my place and drop off Viola. Then we'll Uber around."

"Mike's car," I tell him when I see confusion cloud his face.

"Viola? You named your car after a Shakespeare heroine?" Rick looks admiring.

Puffing out his chest, Mike says, ""It's a purple Boxter. Best car in the world. Special color just for me."

Rick snorts, his eyebrows up at his hairline.

Mike chuckles. "Just because I teach literature doesn't mean I name things after literary characters. Unlike Sylvie, here, who named her cat after Dido Elizabeth Belle."

Rick looks straight into my eyes. "Do you have a particular watering hole? He pauses. "And has anyone told you those greenish-gray eyes are amazing?"

Instead of thanking him, I say, "A man usually praises a woman's eyes when she's not attractive and he's looking for something nice to say."

Mike guffaws while Rick appraises me from head to toe. "Fishing for compliments?"

"Just stating a fact."

Mike butts in. "You know you're nice-looking Sylvie. And her favorite place is The Violet Hour in Wicker Park."

"Let's save that one for the end of the evening. Definitely a place to wind down." Rick puts my arm through his. "We'll start in Logan Square, at Scofflaw."

Mike strides toward the doors to the center, but Rick stops me, hand on my arm.

Then he leans down and whispers in my ear. "You

are beautiful, Sylvie. And I plan to get to know you better—much better."

Heat rises, up through my gut and into my face. The tips of my ears burn. "I'd like that," I tell him.

Despite his earlier protest, Mike turns at the door, sees us standing there, and raises his voice. He can't resist a literary reference. "Lead on Athos. One for all and all for one." Heads turn as, arm in arm, we parade through the doors and out to the street.

***

For what is it to die but to stand naked in the wind and to melt into the sun? And when the earth shall claim your limbs, then shall you truly dance.——
Kahlil Gibran, artist and poet.

Eddie

At the end of the day, Aunt Alice is exhausted. But happy. She got her wish and heard stories all day. Happy stories, sad stories, and above all Sylvie Green's story. The young woman, she tells me, reminds her of herself as a young writer.

We take a raincheck on dinner.

"I'm too tired to eat," she tells Horace. "Why don't we make it for tomorrow, when we're all fresh. And we can tell each other stories."

"Deal," he says and walks us out to my car.

Alice wheels herself into the parking lot while I pull a cart full of books, her award wedged tightly in to keep it steady. Halloween will be here soon, the time will change, and darkness will come early. But now, leaves, orange, red, and brown, swirl around us in the golden late afternoon sun. I let Alice enjoy the air while Horace and I stow the books.

"Did you hear some good stories today?" Horace's face is alight with avid curiosity.

"A few," she says, her voice feeble with tiredness. "I'll tell you a few tomorrow when we get together."

"If people take you up on recording, can I listen in?"

"Looking for ideas?" I ask him. After all, he's a writer, and I'm used to the thought processes of authors.

"Of course," he admits. "I'll call in the morning and we can set a time and place."

"It will be a public site, so anyone who wants to will have access."

"Perfect. I'm looking forward to that." Then he marches off to the car and driver nearby.

"Bye Horace," we call to his retreating back.

I settle Aunt Alice in the front passenger seat, fold up her portable wheelchair, and slide it into the trunk.

When we get home, she moves to sit in her special chair. I haul up the books and other items, then make tea.

"Where do you want your new cup?" I ask her.

Her lips twist. Not sure if it's a smile or a grimace.

"Put it on the porch. I'll think about what to do

with some other time. For now, out of sight, out of mind.

I hand her the tea.

Taking the mug, she asks, "Could you find Sylvie Green's book? I liked that young woman and I'm curious about her writing."

Rooting around, I find it near the blue-covered book near the bottom of the heap. The cover shows an Arctic landscape, a ship frozen in the ice, and lost men. I hand it to her.

"Let me know when you want to go to bed. Going to spend a little time working in my office."

She nods as I switch on the table lamp. She already opened the book, which is propped on her reading pillow. The mug is securely on the table, refreshed with more tea. Next to it is her ever-present notebook and a fountain pen presented to her when she received a P.E.N. award some years ago.

Aunt Alice doesn't summon me and I get absorbed. By the time I'm tired enough to sleep, the clock shows three a.m. The light in the living room reminds me that Aunt Alice needs to be helped to bed.

She seems to be sleeping, Sylvie's book is on the table, the notebook on her lap with the pen poised on top. I glance down. Her spidery handwriting covers a page. I slip the notebook carefully away so I don't disturb her.

I take it back to my office and begin to read.

Review of Cold Death in the North by Sylvie Green

Reviewed by Alice Bainbridge

Set in the nineteenth-century Arctic, Cold Death in the North is a clever mystery by debut author Sylvie Green, who draws on her own background in polar exploration to construct a murder mystery that she places on the Franklin Expedition in 1848.

Franklin was searching for the Northwest Passage, as so many had done before him. He commanded two ships, the Terror and the Erebus and Green designs a plot that has several of the crew dying in mysterious circumstances on the Terror after the ship is trapped in the ice.

The ingenious twists and red herrings are allied with a fiendish motive, insightful exposition of character, and a liberal sprinkling of historical fact. The oppressiveness of the setting enhances the suspense.

The solution is as powerful as it is

unexpected and this reader came away with the conviction that a new star has risen on the literary horizon.

I bring up a blank email and address it to the book review editor of the New York Times. They are alway interested in Aunt Alice's reviews. Once it is typed and proofread, I send it off with a covering note. With a smile, I think of the astonishment Sylvie will feel when the review is published.

An hour has slipped by and I really need to put Alice to bed. Back in the living room, she hasn't moved. I can let her sleep here so I grab a throw to cover her. My hand brushes hers. A cold hand. Colder than it should be. I put two fingers against her neck, feeling for a pulse. Nothing.

I glance into the corner, where Zippy, her faithful steed, sits waiting for races that will never come. The house is silent except for the ticking of the mantel clock.

Then I gaze at her peaceful face and I know, somewhere, she's dancing.

GRACE AND FAVOR

Grace Cromwell and her husband, Chris, have dreamed for years of a real English Christmas and finally it looks like their fantasy will come true. But when Chris dies unexpectedly, Amanda goes alone to a historic fifteenth-century English inn. There she meets Mark Sinclair, the owner. He's charming and single, but harbors an inner sadness. Perhaps Christmas will bring surprising gifts to both of them.

Epigraphs

"The earth has grown old with its burden of care, but at Christmas it always is young, the heart of the jewel burns lustrous and fair, and its soul full of music breaks the air, when the song of angels is sung."
Phillips Brooks

"The best of all gifts around any Christmas tree: the presence of a happy family all wrapped up in each other."
Burton Hills

Christmas is most truly Christmas when we celebrate it by giving the light of love to those who need it most.
Ruth Carter Stapleton

Three Days Before Christmas

Nothing beats waking up in a huge four-poster bed in a charming old English inn, I tell myself. Some owner painted rebuilt in 1420 on the outside wall.

The tap on the door means morning tea has arrived. I look out the window at the small walled garden, rosebushes partially buried in fresh snow, peach-colored blooms still clinging to the stems. Must be a microclimate.

By late December, common wisdom would say that the plants should be bare but instead show signs of vigorous growth.

This could be an Agatha Christie country house

mystery. I luxuriate in the chance to have someone bring me tea and toast in bed to tide me over until breakfast in the dining room.

Chris laughed when I told him early morning tea was the deciding factor.

"I'm opting out," he'd said.

When we met, I couldn't resist asking whether he was related to the famous historical Cromwells. Sheepishly, he admitted he was a distant descendant of Oliver Cromwell, the general and head of the Commonwealth after the overthrow of King Charles I. He was an even more distant one of Thomas Cromwell, Henry VIII's notorious minister.

Despite his English background, he hated tea and loved to sleep in. But he slept like the dead, so I knew no one would disturb him.

Dead. Tears gather at the corners of my eyes. Dashing them away with the back of my hand, I force a smile for the woman in the black dress topped by a neat white collar, a lacy apron around her waist. Straight out of the nineteen twenties.

She sets the tray on a small walnut table, removes the teapot, cup, plate, toast rack, and condiments. Rich bronze liquid flows into a cup covered with peach roses, much like the ones out my casement window.

"Darjeeling, second flush," she informs me.

Is it somehow better? People usually prefer the first of everything, like the first pressing of olive oil. These questions used to excite me, but now I can't muster any enthusiasm.

"Is peach the theme for this room?" I indicate the dark peach duvet cover and lighter peach linens and the peach and butterfly design used for the bed hangings and curtains.

Her laugh tinkles like she'd plinked a fingernail against the china cup. "They named all the rooms for royalty. This is the Queen Eleanor of Castile bedroom. There's a little card with history about it in the chest of drawers."

My hand strokes the bedding, but it is no replacement for Chris. A small sniffle escapes. "Allergies," I mumble.

"Milk? Sugar?"

"Plain is fine." I hesitate. "Is there lemon?"

"Sorry, no. I'll mark it on your sheet so you'll have it tomorrow."

She hands me the cup, then slides the silver serving dish under her arm. "Nice little start to the day. Breakfast at nine in the small dining room."

"Does it have a name too?"

"The Prince's Hall."

I mumble my thanks, then stare out at the still-dark sky.

She closes the door. I hear her footsteps patter down the wooden hall floor.

Nestling into the silky pillows heaped against the headboard, I warm my hands around the teacup and inhale the fruity aroma. I heard somewhere that tea experts often compare Darjeeling tea to champagne.It tastes of citrus and flowers and doesn't have the malty, roasted flavor of my usual Harney & Sons English Breakfast Tea.

Once I finish the tea and manage to eat two triangles of wholemeal toast thickly spread with butter and marmalade, I fall back to sleep, hugging a pillow to myself as if it's Chris.

The banging of a gong alerts me that breakfast is now available. I quickly shower, dress in something Christmassy, and cross my fingers that I can find my way back downstairs.

After several dead ends, I stumble on the twisting, uneven corridors that are my route to the stairs. Clinging on to the barley-twist rail, I reach the bottom of the twisting staircase, and the sound of an angry voice stops me in my tracks.

The owner of the Swan Inn, Mark Sinclair, stands behind the reception desk, holding a telephone handset up to his ear. His fingers grip it so tightly that they are white at the tips. With his face twisted into a snarl, I instinctively back up three steps, reluctant to move into the entrance hall.

After a long, frustrating trip down from London on the train, I barely looked at him last night. I'd had the fleeting impression of a tall, good-looking man, but that was all. Too exhausted for curiosity, I'd just scrawled my name in the book and followed the porter up the stairs to my room.

His deep baritone sounds hides the frustration. "I'm truly sorry but, as it says in the brochure, there are no refunds after December 15."

There is a pause, and I hear his pen tapping against the marble-topped counter. "I'm sorry you feel that way, but there's nothing I can do for you."

Another period of silence. "Merry Christmas to you too." His voice has a sour note to it now.

The receiver bangs down on the phone, and I hesitantly edge forward.

He looks up from paperwork fanned all over the counter. The tall man has thick chestnut hair, a slim oval face, and high cheekbones wears a classic Fair Isle pullover with colors that reflect the brown, blue, and green hues in his large hazel eyes. A frown mars his full lips, his cheeks are flushed, and a shadow hints at sadness much deeper than his current anger.

His long thin frame is the polar opposite of my medium-height, sandy-haired, stocky husband, whose round, cheerful face reflected a sunny disposition. A pain strikes my breastbone as I picture him, dead from a thoracic aortic rupture. Nine months later, watching his collapse haunts me, waking and sleeping.

"Sounds like your day isn't starting well."

With a shrug, he says, "Late cancellation and wants a refund."

"A medical emergency?" I suggest.

"No, they bloody well decided that they want to go on a Christmas Caribbean cruise."

I feel my eyes widen.

"Hope you had a good sleep," Sinclair says in a voice that suggests the north of England. "The wind was a bit noisy."

"After the flight and the track disruption at Ashford, I was exhausted when I got in. Just fell into bed and didn't wake until the tea arrived."

Paperwork disregarded, he gazes at me for a long moment and butterflies beat their wings in my gut. "You look quite festive."

My hands reflexively brush against the playful kitty Christmas sweater, last year's present from Chris. My last present from Chris. The remembered texture of the red, gold, and green flocked wrapping paper makes my fingers tingle.

Chris insisted I wait until we had opened all the other gifts, even though the large rectangular box had pride of place under the tree. Then, ceremoniously, he bowed and proffered the box. It was light, surprising from the size of it.

Slow and deliberate, I freed the box from the wrapping. A ridiculous amount of tape held it in place. As I avoided ripping the paper, Chris fidgeted. Every groan elicited a wicked grin. I loved making him suffer.

Finally, paper gone, the white box appeared. I slipped off the top and laid it carefully on top of the neatly folded paper. I put the ribbon into the box top, then pushed open the holiday tissue paper. Inside was a beautiful holiday sweater with adorable cats appliqued onto the knitted body of the garment.

On top was a large white mailing envelope postmarked Rye, UK. Inside, I found a pamphlet about the hotel, Sign of the Swan, one about Rye at Christmas, and the confirmation of our reservation for the following Christmas. Chris booked one of the historic rooms furnished with a four-poster bed. And now, here I was, wearing the sweater, fighting the despair that threatened to overwhelm me.

Mark clears his throat. "Breakfast is through there." He gestures openhanded to the left of the counter. "Have anything. The package is all-inclusive. So eat up. It's going to be a nice day to see the town all decked out in holiday cheer."

"Thanks." I turn left and try not to wobble as I fight to get my suddenly rubbery legs to work.

When I move away, he mumbles, with sharp jabs at the telephone dial. Who'd run a hotel? Not me.

The dining room has wooden beams and white plaster walls. The tables and chairs are in the same walnut as the bedroom furniture. A stone fireplace houses a merry blaze. Christmas wreaths and garlands are everywhere, fortunately without the twinkling fairy lights so often a feature of restaurants during the season.

Set into the fireplace stonework is a relief of an eponymous swan and a tabby cat, partially screened by the tree, cuddles a stuffed reindeer toy.

A young woman, probably no more than sixteen, approaches me. "Mrs. Cromwell?"

I nod and she leads me to a small table for two near the windows, where I can admire the medieval houses and concentrate on the bustling crowd wandering down the narrow street. Everywhere, decorations are in evidence. Wish some of the spirit of the season would imbue me with joy.

Breaking into my thoughts, the girl asks, "Coffee or tea?"

"Coffee, with cream." My response is automatic. Then I remember other experiences with coffee in England and I look at her anxiously.

"It's not Nescafe, is it?"

"No instant stuff here. My dad would never allow it. He buys the beans special, grinds them himself. We brew the coffee in a cafetière. Funny, too, 'cause dad never drinks it—only tea for him." She gives a giggle and moves off, presumably to bring the coffee.

The staff set the tables with gleaming silver, pristine white tablecloths and napkins, crystal water glasses. A charger decorated with a holly design has a long tube wrapped in red, silver, and gold foil. Resting in the middle of the table on a tartan runner is a small white porcelain bowl etched with a relief of gold stylized trees. In the center of the bowl, a pinecone sits, surrounded by fir branches and red berries. The arranger dusted the ensemble to look snow covered.

Under the mysterious tube is the menu. I study it, trying to decide what to eat when a shadow stretches across the table. I raise my head to see Mark Sinclair hovering. His face displays a professional smile. Nothing to get me excited. But something sends a zing through me.

"Wondered if you needed some help with the menu. American guests are uncommon this time of year, so breakfast foods might be different from what you're used to.

My gut reaction is to say, "I can figure things out." But his eyes have a hopeful gleam and suddenly I don't want to come over as a defensive foreigner.

Thanks so much. I studied in London ages ago, and there are some things here that are new to me."

Sinclair hooks a chair with his foot and pulls it over next to mine. I can feel the heat from his arm against my sleeve, causing delicious shivers.

Shaken, I move away as I ask, "Fried bread?"

"We put some oil in a pan, heat it up, and fry triangles of stale bread in it. It can be any bread but we alway use white, baked here. You have it in place of regular toast. Golden and crunchy. Spread it with marmalade and add a slice of back bacon. Lovely."

My lips quirk. "Sounds greasy."

"Not if it's cooked correctly. Makes a lovely change. Any other mysteries?"

"I know about black pudding, but what is white pudding?"

"The easiest explanation is that it's black pudding without the blood, but that's too simple. In our case, we use cooked oatmeal and barley mixed with onions, mace, white pepper, and parsley, all held together with beef suet. Then it's packed into a casing. Once it's cold, we slice it into thick rounds and fry it."

The front desk bell pings.

He moves the chair back and gets up. "I'll leave you to decide. Eirlys will be over to take your order."

"What a lovely name. How is it spelled?"

"E-I-R-L-Y-S. It means snowdrop in Welsh."

I jot the name down in the small notebook I always carry. "You're Welsh?"

"No, but my ex-wife was."

Ex-wife. Why does that idea cause a pang? I

wonder how long ago they divorced. And is his daughter just visiting for the holidays?

Instead of pursuing those questions, I say, "How do you pronounce it, again?"

"Ire-liss. At the moment, she hates it, but I think it's just her age."

His laugh is deep and musical and makes my bones reverberate at the sound.

And then, like the Cheshire Cat, he vanishes. The memory of the smile warms me to the toes.

When Eirlys returns with more coffee and a glass of freshly squeezed orange-pomegranate juice, I order the full English breakfast without the baked beans and decide to try the white pudding.

"Aren't baked beans American? From Boston?"

"We don't eat them for breakfast."

She sighs. "We eat them any time. I'm sure when I get to university my diet will be beans on toast, with an occasional runny egg on top."

Involuntarily, my nose wrinkles, and she laughs. "I'll just pop your order into the kitchen." She turns to leave, then has another thought.

"If my dad returns, make sure he has tea and pulls a cracker with you."

She taps on the beautifully wrapped tube. "He only has me, but I have a boyfriend to pull crackers with. Since you're on your own..." Biting her lip, she glances at me from under long, dark lashes. "Well, why not?"

Food for thought until my hearty breakfast arrives.

After breakfast, I stop by the desk, where Mark is handing over one of the ornate old-fashioned room keys to a couple in their late sixties or perhaps early seventies. "Same room as always."

"Such a pleasure to be here for Christmas, dear Mark." The slender, silver-haired woman's voice sounds like a flute. She pats his cheek with a gloved hand. "How many years have we been coming here, Brian?"

Her husband, who stands like he's on a parade ground, hands behind his back, furrows his brow. "Must be thirty-five years at least. Before your time, of course, Mark."

"My uncle Charles owned the place then."

"I remember when you and Angharad first arrived." The woman smiles, then bites her lip. "Sorry, Mark, I didn't mean to..."

He reddens slightly, then waves a dismissive hand.

"Why not go in and have a cup of tea. Eirlys is in the dining room. She'll be thrilled to see you. Your bags will be in your room when you're finished. I know you can find your way."

A few more pleasantries and they move toward the breakfast room.

Mark spies me loitering. "May I help you, Mrs. Cromwell?"

I pretend to be surprised, but I don't think he's fooled. "Oh, uh, I could use some recommendations on what to see this morning."

"Plenty to do in Rye." He taps his pen on the open guest register, gazing at the ceiling for inspiration. The shrill ring of the phone interrupts and he picks up the receiver. I motion leaving, but he holds up a hand to stop me.

"What can I do for you, Mr. Kilpatrick?"

A squawk comes through, as if a gaggle of geese is on the line.

Mark squeezes his eyes shut, running his free hand through his hair.

"How many can you provide?"

I hear his foot tapping as he listens to the response.

"That's only half what I need. Any suggestions?"

Lips pursed, he scribbles on a piece of paper.

"Christ. Guinea hen. That's so much more work. Do you have ducklings at least?"

He straightens up. "Perfect. We'll do that then. Delivery in the morning?"

He says goodbye and hangs up with a couple of deep breaths.

"Sorry, supply issues. Nothing to worry about. It's more or less sorted."

He squints at the writing on the pad. "What were we talking about?"

"What I should do today in Rye."

"Right. If you like nature, you could go out to the Rye Harbour Nature Reserve. Lovely area. Or there's the Castle Museum and Ypres Tower. A walk around town is pleasant and the unusual weather means that some of the gardens still have some color. Lots of late medieval houses. Unfortunately Lamb's House isn't open this time of year."

"The Museum sounds good. I'm something of a history buff."

"We're stuffed with it, being one of the Cinque Ports."

I know all about the Cinque Ports—Sandwich, Romney, Dover, Hythe, and Hastings. Although designated earlier, their influence grew in the eleventh century, when they were first granted important legal and fiscal privileges, as well as valuable commercial benefits and social status, in return for providing ships and men to meet the naval and transportation require-ments of the English Crown.

In the fourteenth century, the Corporation added Rye and Winchelsea. Today, Dover is a working port, but some of them, like Rye, are no longer on the coast as harbors silted up over time, pushing the towns inland.

"There's a nice circular walk between here and Winchelsea. I have a guide you can take. You'll find out all about our importance as a port but also how in bad times the people survived as smugglers." Then he declaims,

> If you wake at midnight, and hear a
>   horse's feet,
> Don't go drawing back the blind, or
>   looking in the street.
> Them that ask no questions isn't told
>   a lie.
> Watch the wall, my darling, while the
>   Gentlemen go by!
> *"A Smuggler's Song," Rudyard Kipling*

"How could the town survive just on smuggling?"

"It was big business. The Hawksworth Gang's headquarters were at the Mermaid Inn. Six hundred men. You can imagine the amount of merchandize that passed through Rye."

Rummaging under the counter, he pulls out "Shifting Sands," by the Royal Geographical Society.

I open the thin green brochure and am immediately hooked by the introduction.

A harbour two miles inland. A town that fell into the

sea. Sheep that like to live by the coast. Smugglers sneaking across tidal marshes. Pilotless planes appearing from across the water. A coastal walk where you only glimpse the sea from afar.

"Normally I'd tell you to check out St. Mary's, but I'd suggest that you wait for that until and go to the Christmas Eve service instead. Lovely singing by the choir. I'll also have a tour of the hotel tomorrow, showing off the secret doorways and hidey holes. Later, we'll have storytelling in the bar."

Walking over to the staircase, I hear Mark's voice call after me. "There's a lot of nice shops too, if you fancy a few bits and bobs to remember your trip."

"Thanks," I call back. "Plenty to choose from." Then I slowly sashay up the steep steps, feeling his eyes burning a path up my spine.

***

Rye is every bit as charming as its promotions promise. The two-hour walk between Rye and Winchelsea will give me an introduction to both towns, so I opt for that. The weather is blustery, but sunny.

Some parts are challenging, but I persevere, wishing I had an arm to cling to on the upward traverses. The town council has decorated to the hilt, and in the town center, sweet-voiced choirs take turns serenading passersby, while handbell players are farther off, ringing carols.

Vendors hawk roasted chestnuts and I pick up a brown paper sack, burning my fingers on hot from the coal morsels as I continue on through the streets, gawking at the festive store windows.

My hotel welcome package said that there would be a gift exchange on Christmas morning after break-fast, so I plan to stop back in a few shops and find things that would be welcome for anyone, have them wrapped, and return to The Swan for lunch.

I struggle through fields between Rye and Winchelsea, but the walk is worth it. Sheep are all over, especially the unusual chocolate-colored sheep near Camber Castle. When I get to Winchelsea, I stop in a corner shop and ask about them.

"Ryeland Sheep," the man at the counter. "Rare, they are. All registered. If you like the wool, there's a shop in Hastings that carries jumpers and such."

Hastings. Not likely. If Chris was here, we could rent a car and go. With an internal slap, I stop the pity party. If I decide I want something, I'll check out the internet when I get home.

I'm dragging and ready to eat when I get back. A quick wash and I go down to the Prince's Hall. The setup is much the same and Eirlys tells me I will have the same table each day for breakfast and lunch.

I'm not used to so much exercise, but it certainly sharpens my appetite. After the huge breakfast, I didn't think I'd want to eat again.

As I go back to "my" table, the room fills with chattering groups, couples and families mostly, although a few larger groups are friends who meet every year here to celebrate the holiday together. One quartet of particularly raucous women sits just over from me.

The woman I saw this morning comes over from a table of six.

"Forgive me for the intrusion, but I noticed that you're all by yourself. Our little group," she gestures toward her table, "has space, and we'd love to have you join us, at least for this meal. If we mesh, then we can make it work for the rest of the break."

Her smile is all flashing white teeth. "Would you like me to speak to Mark?"

My heart warms, and I am momentarily speechless. Perhaps this trip isn't a mistake after all.

From the consternation on her face, I know she's afraid to have overstepped.

Mark comes rushing into the dining room. "Francine, nice of you to welcome our new guest. This is Mrs. Grace Cromwell, visiting from America. And Grace, this is Mrs. Francine Fanshawe. She and her husband have been coming here since 1988."

"Thank you, Mark. I admit I was remiss in not introducing myself, Mrs. Cromwell."

"That's all right," I assure her.

Mrs. Fanshawe turns a gimlet eye on Mark Sinclair. "We noticed Mrs. Cromwell sitting all alone and invited her to join our merry crew for lunch."

"Do you want to move, Grace?"

"I'd be happy to try it out."

Francine Fanshawe takes my arm and we thread through the tables. Mark follows with a chair, but stops to have a word with Eirlys. She nods and scurries off.

I see a busboy clear a place for me and Mark sets down my seat, making sure there is enough space for me to slide in.

"Eirlys will bring a table setting and menu. Bon appétit, everyone."

My table companions are delightful. Colonel Fanshawe instructs me in the fine art of bird photography and offers to take me to Rye Harbour Nature Reserve early the next morning.

"Up with the lark," he says jovially.

"The crack of dawn, more like," Francine says with a theatrical shudder.

The Zacharys, who are from the Isle of Man, are founts of information on late medieval shipping and trade. Ian and Mary Louise Grant, also first-year participants, are more my age. He's Scottish. she's American.

"We were just finding out why Ian and Mary Louise are at the Swan rather than spending the holiday with family," Francine says.

I can tell she is going to be a nosy parker who will try to ferret out every secret.

"My family is visiting my younger brother and his wife in Chicago this year. I don't have enough leave for that, so we decided on a Christmas break instead. I must be back in Casablanca just after the first of the year."

"Casablanca. How romantic." Eileen Zachary's eyes mist over.

Her husband puts his palm against hers. "Of all the gin joints in all the towns in all the world, she walks into mine." His Bogart impression isn't too bad.

Ian warbles, "I left my heart in Casablanca..."

"Do you go with him, Mrs. Grant?" Eileen Zachary's features contort as if she has contracted a severe case of FOMO.

Mary Louise, who looks like she's aching to say "Ms." smiles sweetly. "Yes. I write travel articles and have a contract for a series on Morocco while Ian is at the consulate."

"So birds without a permanent nest," the colonel remarks.

"We have a small flat in London and spend time up in the Highlands with Ian's family when we get the chance." Mary Louise smiles with genuine warmth.

"Where in the States are you from?" Ian asks.

"Phoenix, Arizona."

"I'm from Vermont," Mary Louise says, "by way of Iowa. My mom still lives there."

"Won't she miss not seeing you for the holiday?" I feel funny asking, but it just slips out.

"She'll be in Chicago with my in-laws. This way Ian and I can celebrate our first anniversary as if it's a romantic getaway."

Francine turns her gaze to me, ready to pounce.

"And what brings you here, all alone, for Christmas?" Francine feigns innocence, while her husband casts an admonitory look.

"My husband and I planned this trip last year, but he died nine months ago. We'd already paid for everything and it seemed a shame to cancel, so here I am."

The expressions of condolence from people I had just met are kind but jarring. I stare at the lunch menu, trying to master my emotions.

"We've all decided on the steak and ale pie," Mr. Zachary says. "The kitchen turns out wonderful meat pies."

Stomach gurgling suddenly, I read the description. It does sound good, but so does the plate of bangers and mash.

"What do you think of the bangers and mash?"

"It's excellent," Ian says. "The dish is my sister-in-law Cress' favorite. She makes us chase down possible pubs and restaurants every time they visit. I know she'd eat it with you if she wasn't in Chicago."

Mary Louise pokes him in the ribs.

"I'll change my order and have it, too. With a half pint of best bitter," she tells Eirlys, who has just come to take the orders.

"Do you want beer too?" Eirlys asks me.

I don't like beer. "Is there something you'd suggest that would go with it?"

Eirlys runs off, then returns like a flash. "Dad says a Pinot Noir or Cabernet. If you want one of those, I'll have him serve it."

Mark comes over with the Cabernet, opens it and says, "It needs to breathe a bit. I'll be back with glasses in about twenty minutes. How many of you are drinking wine?"

Mr. Zachary and Mary Louise are the only ones drinking beer, so Mark opens a second bottle. When the plates arrive, he carries over six glasses, pours a bit into one, swirls it, tastes, and says, "This will be excellent." Then he puts the glass at the one empty spot at the table and pours out wine for the rest of us.

Meanwhile, a chair has materialized. Eirlys serves him a plate of Shepherd's Pie and a side salad. "Hope you don't mind if I join you."

No one demurs, and Mark pours the last of the second bottle into his glass. "Wine's on the house. Beer too."

Drinks are the only extra so this is extremely generous, especially since I imagine these are not bottles of two-buck Chuck.

Everything is what my eight-year-old niece would call scrummy. I taste the steak and ale pie and resolve to have some before I leave Rye. The highlight, though, is the sticky toffee pudding that ends the meal.

Stuffed, and still tired from my walk, I resolve to take a nap.

"Do have dinner with us tonight," Francine calls out as I trundle out the door.

Mark is standing at reception, looking toward the Prince's Hall. His eyes light up when I walk through.

"Did you enjoy lunch?"

"It was lovely. Great food, good company."

"Do you want to share a table with them tonight?"

"They did ask me."

"We do groups of eight for the evening meals. Much more festive. I'll have you seated with them. You can decide after if you want to continue the arrangement."

I nod and continue toward the staircase.

He clears his throat just as I reach the bottom step. "Do you have plans for later?" Mark asks.

I turn. "Probably just a nap. That walk to Winchelsea took a lot out of me."

"There is a Christmas concert at St. Leonard's this evening and I wondered if you like to go."

I clamp my jaw to keep it from dropping. Dumbfounded, I see the light slowly dying in his eyes.

He stutters into speech, to apologize.

"Yes." My hurried gasp stops him. "I'd love to go."

"Great. It's only half an hour away. If we leave about four thirty, we'll have time to stroll around Hastings for a bit before we need to be at Christ's Church in St. Leonard's. We'll miss dinner here, but I know a great place in near the church for a bite before we come back."

While we're waiting for the Christmas Gala concert to start, Mark fills in some history. "The building looks medieval, but dates from 1875 and replaces the first church, built 1860. The impetus for its creation was the Oxford movement, which makes it very high church, but still Anglican."

I'd heard the term before, but I'm not sure what it means. "High church? Like Catholic?"

"Not exactly. They are Church of England but see it as being part of a wider catholic community. They've gone back to a lot of the ceremonial trappings of the service, for example. Very pastoral and evangelical, although not in the same way as evangelicals are in the United States."

The church has a wide middle aisle that Mark says is the nave, with two side aisles. Instead of pews, they set out chairs. The stained glass—painted, I find out—is lovely.

The concert surprises me with its quality even though Mark had assured me they are professional grade. Their coup is getting composer John Rutter to conduct. He brings out all the color and excitement of the pieces with the Hastings Philharmonic Orchestra and their Songbirds chorus.

Tchaikovsky's "Nutcracker" sparkles. "Sleigh Ride" makes us feel as if we are dashing through the snow. And the carols bring nostalgic warmth to the echoing space. The voices soar up to the high ceiling and resound off the stone arches and floor.

By the time the choir is singing "Silent Night," emotion wells up in my chest and my breath keeps catching. One of Chris' favorites, which he would sing in German. A slight tickle starts in my palm. Then I realize Mark is gently cradling my hand, stroking it with his thumb. The sensation comforts me and I don't pull away.

After, we dawdle walking out of the building

before walking over to the Bella Vista Restaurant, which overlooks the English Channel. In front of the blue awning is a space that accommodates outdoor dining in warmer weather. The interior is decorated with contemporary art interspersed with mirrors, white tablecloths offset by small crystal vases. Each holds one stunning bloom.

Neither of us are ravenous, so we agree to share several dishes, starting with an appetizer plate of hummus, grilled zucchini, grilled aubergines, grapefruit, pumpkin seed crackers, figs, nuts, cherry tomatoes, pesto stracciatella cheese, honey & pistachio ricotta, brie, and homemade crostini.

"What made you choose Christmas in Rye? It's not a typical venue for a single woman to choose this time of year." Mark's eyes gleam inquisitively.

For a moment, my thoughts scramble. Then I give him the same story I told to the lunch group early.

"Sorry," he mutters, eyes firmly on his water glass.

"And your wife? Ex-wife?" I can be nosy too.

"Ex. She ran away with a lover when Eirlys was two."

"And you never heard from her again?"

"Dead, actually. She and the man, Iuan, crashed the car on their way to Brecon, in the Beacon Hills, where Iuan lived. It was terrible weather. So no divorce, no reconciliation, and Eirlys never really knew her mum."

He takes a small sip of the wine I'm drinking. "Sorry. Should have asked."

"Don't apologize. You needed it."

"Let's talk about something happier than death," he says. "Tell me about your little corner of the States."

We chat about Arizona, his early life in Yorkshire, and how clever Eirlys is.

"She's aiming for Oxford, Cambridge, York, or Edinburgh."

"What does she plan to study?"

"A joint degree in computer science and maths."

For a main course, we share the Argentine ribeye steak with fries and salad. The chimichurri is so flavorful that we dip the hot crisp strips of potato in the sauce so we don't waste a drop.

The desserts sound yummy, but we decide on coffee and liqueur instead, although Mark just takes a few sips from my small glass.

"Don't want to get breathalyzed. I can have a nightcap when we get back."

After dinner, as we walk back to the car in the frosty evening air, I marvel at the dark blue sky dusted by stars. A few lungfuls When I shiver slightly, Mark puts an arm around me. His face is anxious as he asks, "Is this okay?"

"Yes. I'm feeling the chill."

Back in the car, I luxuriate in the warmth of the heated seat as we make the drive back to The Swan.

Two days before Christmas

Mark and I indulge in a late night drink or two after returning from Hastings and talk for hours about his past and mine.

We slouch on a tweedy couch in front of the lounge fireplace. He kicks off his shoes and stretches his stocking feet toward the fire. I resist the urge to curl against his chest and sit at the other end, watching the moods that wash across his face.

Now it's ungodly early and I've only had a few hours' sleep, but I promised the colonel that I would stalk birds at Rye Harbour Nature Reserve with him. A large thermos and a picnic basket are on the hall table waiting for us.

"Mark's a splendid fellow," the colonel says. "Always one step ahead."

I lift the basket lid and peer inside. "Looks like fruit and sandwiches."

"Probably cheese and tomato. Capital early breakfast and we'll be back to have a second meal in the Prince's Hall."

We're at the Beach Reserve and I'm huddled in a heavy coat Eirlys lent me, drinking hot coffee from a thermos. The colonel has festooned himself with cameras, lenses, and a tripod.

"Perfect time for the ducks. The males have gorgeous plumage this time of year."

My experience with ducks is mostly eating them. White Pekin or Long Island duckling, as it's popularly called. "Are there many kinds of ducks?"

"Oh yes. We'll see Wigeon, Shoveler, Gadwall, Teal, maybe some Pintail." He points to a group with colorful feathers swimming by, lifts the camera, and I hear a whir and rapid clicking.

"Shovelers," he declares, satisfaction oozing out of every pore.

A little later he cries out, "Look, a Marsh Harrier."

"What's that in its claws?"

With a laugh, the colonel explains. "They're called talons. And the Harrier is a bird of prey. It hunts smaller birds."

Horrified, I watch nature red in tooth and claw, while the colonel takes a raft of photos as the bird wings away with its meal dangling in the wicked spikes.

Frozen through, I hop from one foot to the other hoping we're done. By now the sun is up but not really warming anything and the wind is fierce. My cheeks feel chapped and my lips covered with ice crystals. The colonel takes pictures golden plover, lapwings, and linnets before moving on to Castle Water for another hour of torture.

What made me think that winter bird watching would be fun? Grudgingly, I admit to myself that I could be at home, where it's warm, not on the icy fringe of the English Channel.

Teeth chattering, I turn to my companion. "I thought the Gulf Stream was supposed to moderate the temperatures in England. And it's the southeast. Shouldn't that make a difference?"

"Oh my dear, everyone's idea of moderate is different. Compared to Siberia, this is positively balmy. But you come from a warmer clime, so to you, no doubt this is extreme." He pats my arm consolingly.

"Just a few more shots and we can go back to The Swan and warm up with some hot chocolate and a hearty breakfast."

The ride back is ridiculously short and the heater barely has time to start up. The colonel lets me off at the door and takes the car to the car park. I'm a popsicle as I pull open the door and stuff Eirlys' gloves back into the pockets of her jacket.

The sight that greets my eyes shocks the hell out of me.

Mrs. Grayson from room five stands behind the

reception desk. Stands may not be the right word. She's entwined around Mark Sinclair, kissing his face. With his features obscured, I can't tell if he's kissing her back, but he hasn't disentangled himself from her embrace.

A small cry escapes from my chapped lips. Footsteps thunder down the stairs. A man's bright red face glares down from the landing. I bet people can hear his roar halfway down the street.

"What the bloody hell is going on, Sheryl?"

The woman springs back and Mark yelps. She's kneed him in the groin and he falls like a bowling pin.

"Molesting my wife," Grayson's voice has lowered, the tone dangerous. "I'll have you up before a magistrate. By the time I'm done with you..."

As guests and employees rush into the vestibule, his threat lingers in the overheated air.

Mark, huffing and moaning, rises from behind the desk like Lazarus. Pain distorts his features.

Eirlys screams. "Dad. What happened?"

He can't speak and waves the question away as he slowly limps out, skirting Sheryl Grayson, who is immobile. She trains her large blue eyes on her enraged spouse.

Finally, out of her lipstick-smeared red mouth, she snaps, "Shut yer gob, Hugh. No one was molesting anyone. I was just showing appreciation to Mark for making sure we got the same room as last year."

Mark opens his mouth, but the only sound he produces is another low groan. He catches my eye, but

I look away. I don't want to see his treacherous face. Hear more lying words from his lips.

Last night we'd whispered secrets. He'd told me an instant attraction had hit him like a bolt of lightning. We agreed to spend as much time together as we could, see if the attraction held. And now—.

My legs tremble as I instinctively reach for the door handle. When I step outside after opening the heavy door, I hear a whisper on the wind calling my name. Imagination. Wishful thinking.

I run down the steep street, barely keeping myself from falling as the wind pushes me down slippery cobbles. In the distance, I see the welcoming sign of a tearoom. When I reach the safe haven, I collapse at an empty table and order a pot of tea.

To lift my spirits, I spend the day seeing the museum and castle, shopping, and even going to see a film of the Royal Opera House production of "The Nutcracker," at the Rye Kino Cinema. I feel a little better, until I realize that at some point I will have to go back to The Swan.

Having killed the whole day, I go to the sixteenth-century Ship Inn for dinner, but I have little appetite although I sit at the table much too long, enduring sidelong glances from the staff, when they aren't pointedly asking if I want anything else.

Doggedly I play game after game of solitaire until the restaurant closes and I drag my weary body back to The Swan, sure that Mark's overnight caretaker will be the only person up.

But instead of the genial Irishman, Mark stands behind the counter, face pale, doing nothing.

The wind slams the door shut behind me and blood rushes to his face, then as quickly drains away.

"Fergus," he calls out. "Come watch the desk."

The red-haired giant lumbers out from the office. Mark slips out from behind the desk and moves toward me.

I can't move back because I'm already against the door. My eyes slide from side to side, looking for escape. When I try to move, he leans forward and puts his hands on either side of my head, resting the palms against the wood.

His face shows a mixture of fear, panic, and relief. In a roughened voice, he grates painfully. "Grace, we need to talk. I need to explain."

I examine his face, taking inventory. He has a black eye and contusions on his right cheek.

In spite of myself, I choke out a question. "Wha-wha-what happened?"

Rocking back and removing his arms, he touches his cheek with two fingers. "Grayson hit me."

"Did you hit him back?"

He hangs his head, muttering "no. The Hotel Association frowns on hitting guests."

A little frisson of pleasure goes through me that his punishment came so quickly.

"Then what?"

"They checked out. Demanding a refund, of course."

I bite my lip, resolutely staring at the floor.

Mark touches my cheek, then puts a couple of fingers under my chin and lifts my face to look at him. "We need to talk."

"Why?"

"I owe you…"

Anger bubbles up and my voice is harsh. "You don't owe me anything. We barely know each other, and I doubt we'll ever meet again after Christmas."

I twist away and stamp up the stairs, closing my ears to the sound of his plaintive voice calling my name.

But the ghost sound rings in my ears all night.

Christmas Eve

Early morning tea. Today I feel no joy at the prospect. And Eirlys standing outside my door with the tray doesn't improve a mood brought on by too little sleep and too many recriminations about getting involved with anyone and not looking before leaping.

Eirlys' beaming smile as she sets the tray down on the table only exacerbates my foul humor.

"Don't bother to pour it out. I'll do it myself."

Her face falls at my words, and now I have another reason to beat myself up.

"Sorry, sorry. I didn't mean to snap. Just had a terrible night."

"You're not the only one. Dad's like an ill-tempered hyena. Heard him pacing all night and now he just stomps around, slams his fist on the furniture and mutters incomprehensible syllables. Glares too, if anyone tries to speak to him."

"May I have breakfast in my room?"

This isn't a regular offering, but maybe if I tell her I'm ill.

"Sorry. With all the stuff for Christmas Eve and Christmas Day, we're slammed. Everyone will have to eat in the Prince's Hall this morning."

"What if I'm ill?"

She gives me the sort of skeptical look that only teenagers can bestow on adults.

"Enjoy your tea and toast. See you at breakfast." Without a backward glance, she sashays out.

I fall back against the heap of pillows and into a restless doze. When I emerge, I can hear the gong ringing in the distance, the call that breakfast is available. The toast in the rack and the scummy cold tea are unpalatable, so they will suffice. Going out is an option, but with my all-inclusive holiday, I don't need to keep spending money just to display my pique at Mark's behavior.

What should I have expected? Holiday romances are as impermanent as the first snow. I'm not some inexperienced, love-struck teen. And really, what did Mark promise? Nothing. He just said he felt an attraction.

Chris had been the most steadfast man I'd ever known. A once-in-a-lifetime love. Irreplaceable. I'd go home with a painful memory of a flash attachment, something to wrap in tissue paper and sprinkle with rosemary and lavender.

Throwing on a holiday reindeer sweatshirt and

black sweatpants, I stuff my feet into my sneakers and navigate the stairs once again, remembering that today is Christmas Eve, and tonight the magic of Christmas will envelop us.

The last of the steep steps beckons and I try to avoid looking toward the reception desk, but my gaze is drawn inexorably in that direction. One of servers is covering the desk, helping a guest. No Mark.

My lungs let out a breath of relief. My spine softens. A feeling of relief washes through. Then, as I walk through the doorway, I see someone sitting at my table. Mark. He's in a reindeer sweater too. A Santa hat flops over his forehead.

My step falters. Adrenaline rising, my fight-or-flight response kicks in—flight all the way.

Instead of running, I take a deep breath, square my shoulders, and sit down at MY table.

Mark glances at his watch. "'Bout time you got here." The smirk accompanying the comment shows he's not serious.

"Why are you at my table?" Not giving an inch. Not a millimeter.

Hope drains from his eyes, replaced by a desperation combined with fear that reminds me of a rabbit looking up at a hunting owl, talons spread.

Eirlys breaks the tension between us. "You'll both have indigestion if you keep on like this." Her lips compress, arms folded across her chest, foot tapping impatiently.

Mark looks pained. "Just toast and coffee for me, love."

Her expression one of astonishment, she doesn't comment but notes something on her pad.

"And you, Mrs. Cromwell?"

Suddenly, I'm starving. "I'd like the full English, no beans."

Eirlys nods approvingly. "Glad to see you still have an appetite. And coffee with cream?"

"Yes, please."

She marches off toward the kitchen, comes back a few minutes later with a pot of coffee and a pitcher of cream. We haven't spoken in the interval.

I watch the dark, rich liquid flow into the cup. The scent of the coffee, smokey and a bit burned arouses my tastebud and my mouth waters slightly. Mark takes a sip.

"Brewed properly, Dad?"

"Perfect." He winks at her.

Shit, Grace, I chide myself. Say something.

My throat thick with apprehension, I make a stupid remark. "Eirlys said you're very particular about your coffee."

His face serious, he says, "I'm very particular about everything in my life."

Bitter recriminations rise up. "Could have fooled me." Did I say that out loud? I put my hands up to my face. Through my fingers, I see his luminous eyes staring. Then I make it worse. "And you did."

Red patches bloom on his cheeks and I expect to see angry sparks flash from those hazel orbs. Instead, his lids droop and contrition mixed with exasperation gives me a little clue into his thoughts.

"I wish you'd let me explain."

I let my head swivel around the room, looking to see if Eirlys will save us with a well-timed food delivery. But she is nowhere to be seen. The other diners, however, keep ducking their heads, as if trying to look as if they don't notice anything while turning their bat-radar ears in our direction.

A low hiss comes from the back of my throat. "Fine. Tell me what really happened when I saw you in that clinch."

Mark rubs his eyes. "The Graysons having been coming here for a few years now. As you might guess, Mrs. Grayson is something of a flirt, and she has always tried it on when her husband isn't around. I usually manage to evade her innuendo, but this time she didn't dilly-dally. Instead, she threw herself around me."

The revelation stuns me. I visualize the scene, seeing the woman's arms tightly around Mark's body. With the clearness of hindsight, the image shows his arms tightly held to his sides, like she was afraid he'd escape her grasp.

How could I not have noticed? Because I refused to look, like a five-year-old covering my eyes, telling myself that if I ignored events, they didn't happen.

Mark continues, "She must have known that he was on his way downstair and was making a statement. I think she planned he would leave and she would settle in with me. Instead, he dragged her off after a few well-landed blows on my face."

With no clue what to say, I sit silently, twist my napkin.

My silence forces more word from his mouth.

"Look, I'm no Lothario. And I am truly interested in you, even if I have no idea how to make a long-distance relationship work. But I'm willing to try—if you are."

Then, with his thumb, he wipes away tears I didn't know were speckling my cheeks. "Let's pull the crackers," he whispers and I notice the beautifully decorated tubes crackers beside each plate.

I take one end and he pulls the other. A small bang, the cardboard tube gapes open, and a paper hat, snowman charm, and a joke drop out. Picking up the other one, Mark holds the end and I pull, twice, before cracker comes apart.

Taking off his Santa hat, he puts on a crown, then unfolds the second one and settles it on my head. His has a whistle and he blows it, laughs at the weak sound, and puts it down on the table.

Clearing his throat, Mark reads out his joke.

***What do you get if Santa goes
down the chimney when a fire
is lit?***
Crisp Kringle

I groan, then drink some coffee.
"Come on, then. Read yours out."
"Do I have to?"
He folds his arms and gives me a mock glare.

***Why don't you ever see Father
Christmas in hospital?***
Because he has private elf care

Bang, two plates slam down onto the table. Both hold copious portions of the full English breakfast—Mark's with beans, mine with white pudding instead.

"Eat up," Eirlys says, briskly efficient. You'll need your strength to get through the day."

Then she waltzes away, humming, "If Ever I Would Leave You."

How does she even know the music from "Camelot"?

It's Christmas Eve. It's the one night of the year when we all act a little nicer, we smile a little easier, we cheer a little more. For a couple of hours out of the whole year, we are the people that we always hoped we would be. – *Frank Cross*

At dinner, we sit with the Fanshawes, Zacharys, and Grants. They smirk knowingly throughout the meal, as if in on some secret. I had hoped that Mark and I could have a private dinner somewhere, but that wasn't possible. And afterward, everyone was going to the midnight service at the Church.

Tomorrow, we would open our gifts in the lounge, including the guest exchange. My few gifts, wrapped and sitting on the chest of drawers across from the bed, wait for me to put them under the tree. One for Eirlys, one for each of the couples that had befriended me, and one for Mark.

We'll eat Christmas cake in the afternoon and listen to the King's Speech. It would be his first Christmas message. The forecast is for foul weather, so cuddling by the fire sounds like just the way to spend a blustery, snowy day.

Walking back to The Swan after the service, the night is silent, the sky clear, and stars shine brightly down. By morning, a gale will bring a blizzard, but now everything is perfect.

"How long can you stay after the holiday?" Mark's lips touch my ear with every word.

Chris' company is well-managed and I am just the major shareholder. My parents are on a trip through Southeast Asia and won't be back for another two months. No pets, no children, no reason to hurry home.

I turn into him. "At least a month."

"Will you come back?"

"Do you want me to?"

He says nothing, just brings my fingers to his lips and kisses them, one by one.

"Come with me when I leave."

He pulls away slightly.

"Not to stay. To help me decide how best to make the move, sell my house—if you are serious, that is."

"Serious as death. I'll figure out how to make things work here while I'm away."

"Don't you ever take vacations?" I have to wonder what life will be like if I end up in Rye.

"Not really. With Eirlys growing up, I need to make some changes here anyway. You are a good reason to do it now. The best reason."

Our slow walk is an intricate dance of longing, desire, belonging, and peace.

By the time we reach the inn, everyone else has gone inside for a nightcap before bed. Mark takes me in his arms for a passionate before we join the company.

What is Christmas? It is tenderness for the past, courage for the present, hope for the future. – *Agnes M. Pahro*

If you like this story, my short story collection, *Relatives and Relationships,* has stories of love and murder, including how Ian and Mary Louise Grant met at a holiday market in Edinburgh.

CHASING DONATELLO

R aine

Donatello was a pioneer of perspective, and his work anticipated photography and cinema. He is really very modern. Donatello is the best sculptor, perhaps, who ever existed.—Francesco Caglioti

When the last bell sounds, my breath puffs out in a sigh of relief. End of term, grades submitted, and a month in Florence on the horizon. I can almost smell the mingled scents of leather, fish, wild boar, incense, truffles, and a whiff of sewage over the fumes of late afternoon London traffic.

Teaching the glories of Renaissance art to sixth formers, most of whom are only interested in the more salacious aspects, wears you down. The sniggering, whispering behind hands, and passing off of notes create small annoyances that lead to exhaustion.

But I'm out of London now. Relief washes over me as I watch my reflection waver in the mirror-like surface of a stainless steel pillar, one of many in the baggage claim at Amerigo Vespucci airport near Florence. Dark circles under my eyes. Damn hair everywhere. I'm rewinding it into the clip when I hear a snicker.

Graham Spencer-Ross. My art history colleague at Meryton Academy rolls his eyes.

The flight was a nightmare. First, the one daily flight was canceled. We couldn't get a flight to Pisa or even Bologna. Dad, who had been against the trip, hooted like a loon when I finally managed to get home from Heathrow. Then he offered pizza or fish and chips as consolation.

Another trek to the airport. In order to get the flight on track, the airline decided to load less fuel. We ran into trouble and had to divert to Grenoble. A bus was laid on after a two-hour wait for the short drive to Lyon. No direct flights. No available train seats for two days. In the end we flew from Lyon to Paris and, after a four-hour layover, landed in Florence.

I swing round, eyes trained on his quirked lips. Graham, bent at the waist, hands pressed against his stomach, has morphed in a laughing fool. Lift a hand and mimic blowing a poisoned dart into Sir Smugness. Undeniably good looking and superficially charming, the rich playboy isn't my type. Do I have a type? In any case, he's not my flavor of the month.

He blows me a kiss.

I pretend to miss catching it.

He rocks back and forth on the heels of hand-tooled cowboy boots. A look that is incongruous with his Savile Row suit. Squints at the TAG Heuer on his wrist. His eyes dart around the space loud with the chatter of arriving passengers. Does he expect someone?

"Tell me again why you've crashed my plans."

"Why wouldn't I want a month in Italy, looking at art with the best teacher at the school?" He pastes on a winning smile.

"And my father's here, visiting dealers. I thought you might find meeting him interesting." He worries his upper lip with his teeth.

His father is a noted collector. Still... meet his father? Such an unlikely idea. Is he making a move? I'm so bad at interpreting people once they aren't spotty teens any more.

I narrow my eyes and pinch my lips together. He looks past me, as if to speak to someone behind my left shoulder.

"Right now he's chasing Donatello, and, well, I may have told him you were an expert."

Chasing Donatello? Sounded more like a Ninja turtle film than a serious artistic exercise. "You told him what?"

"That you are a renowned expert." Graham draws out every syllable. "Aren't you? You've published about him." Round, wide eyes gaze at me innocently.

"That doesn't make me an expert, especially not a renowned one."

Just then his phone buzzes. With a glance at the screen his mouth sets into impatience; his voice a furious hiss. "Thought you were meeting us at the airport."

The mobile is on speaker and some sort of muffled roaring comes from the other end. Graham's eyebrows lift and his jaw drops.

Out of the corner of my eye I see the luggage conveyor belt halt. No obnoxious yellow molded case. No ostentatious black leather trunk.

I punch Graham's arm. Immediately alert, he glares at me.

I point toward the conveyor. "No bags."

He jerks, slips the device into a jacket pocket, then starts at a run for the baggage claim desk. By the time I catch him up, he's scowling into the face of the clerk, a nonstop flow of Italian spewing out.

He turns to me, then back to the unsmiling face behind the counter. More Italian. After what seems like hours, we fill out forms, take our copies and trail away.

The late hour, the long trip, and no food, makes my stomach growl. I shoulder my small carry-on.

"Let's go." His voice sounds like he swallowed gravel. "I'll flag a taxi."

On the way to the Bernini Palace Hotel, Graham slumps forward, head in his hands.

Alarm bells ring as his façade cracks. I try for a cheerful note. "What's a few mishaps?"

No answer.

"Did you get hold of your dad?"

A minute shake of the head.

"Is your mum with him?"

"Divorced," he blurts. "Since I was ten."

Motherless children. Well, I am. My mother died when I was born. Maybe his mother is still around, but I know he lives with his father—even though he's in his mid-thirties. Even though he has a job and could be independent. Then again, so do I.

I start to ask, then stop. His shuttered face repels questions.

He focuses on the semi clean floor of the cab. "My dad found one of the dealers he went to see dead in his shop. Murdered."

"How does he know it was murder?"

Graham groans. "I don't know. A knife protruding from his chest? A smoking gun? All I know is a man is dead, Dad found him, and he's with the police."

"Do we need to bail him out?"

He moans and I stare as his chest inflates and deflates.

"No. He hasn't been arrested. In any case, there's no bail system in Italy."

He turns a wintry gaze on me.

The cabbie slams on the breaks and we're bumped forward, then back.

"Why did you stop?" My voice shrieks with accusation.

"We're here, Signorina," he says, sounding bored.

Here? Where's here? I scramble out while Graham pays. The name above the door of the palatial building proclaims Hotel Bernini in gold calligraphy.

Raine

Life itself seems to be stirring vigorously in the stone-
Vasari

Hostels or other cheap accommodations fit my purse so I'm not comfortable even walking into the grand space confronting me. Graham's paying, arguing he hired me to be his personal guide, but I can't help wondering what I'll pay in the end.

My mind goes back two months, the day I told Dad I planned to spend a month communing with Donatello.

He snorts. "You'd be better off studying some of the modern Italian masters. A month at the Estorick would be of more value to you. Cheaper too."

Then he turns back to the lump of clay on the armature in his studio. The head of a woman slowly emerges from the amorphous mass.

I shudder inwardly at the thought of the Estorick collection. A listed Georgian building made to house a large collection of twentieth-century Italian art. Eric Estorick, the American collector and art dealer who created it, has a lot to answer for. Too bad he's been dead since 1993.

Despite being the daughter of a well regarded sculptor, I have no taste for contemporary art.

Arms akimbo, I snap like an angry croc. "I don't want to spend the summer in Islington."

Mild astonishment washes across his seamed face. "Why not? You've lived here all your life."

"Precisely my point. I *have* lived here all my life."

"More comfortable than swanning around in the Italian heat. Besides, Florence is overpriced. Ten euros for a gelato. Highway robbery."

"If you're stupid enough to buy it at Il Porcellino." I name one of the outrageously expensive gelateria that prey on unknowing tourists.

He ignores me. "What's wrong with studying Medardo Rosso?" He scrapes clay off his hands.

I wrinkle my nose. "Compared with the elegance of Donatello? I'm not interested. Besides, if I wanted to study Rosso, Marini, or Scalini, I could still do it abroad."

"True enough. Go to Rome. The food's better. And if you need old, have a wander around the forum. Take a day at Ostia."

He walks to the sink to rinse his hands.

Twisting his body, he gives me a sidelong glance. "Or go for the grit. Naples has great museums. And its own atmosphere. No genteel Renaissance there."

"Genteel..."

He stops my protest. "By the by, the Tate Liverpool wants me to be part of a show with Tony Cragg and Rachel Whiteread."

"His stuff looks like things stacked on top of things, or crystal formations. And hers are like discarded bits from construction sites. You do distorted heads. What do you have in common with them?"

"We're all Turner Prize winners?"

Tenuous. "No comment."

A chuckle tells me my words bounce away like water off a tarp.

"New stuff or borrowed?"

"Still to be negotiated. Some of both, I'd imagine. The show will be two years from now." He turned back, studied his partly formed piece, then pinched a bit of clay off, dislocating the notional nose.

Then he rubs his hands and flashes a crooked grin. "How about a curry?"

Graham

Calm purpose and concentrated simplicity - Charles Avery

Bernini Palace Hotel. New to me, but Dad is a regular. Discreet elegance despite the gold decor. I glance at my phone. Room 111.

I take off toward the grand staircase. "Dad gave me his room number," I yell back at Raine, who trails behind. The shout earns me a glare from the receptionist and the few visitors milling around the lobby.

The strap of my leather messenger bag rubs against my neck so I shift it from one shoulder to the other.

When I look back from the bottom of the steps, Raine is hovering around the registration desk.

I come back at a trot. "Come on. What's the problem?"

The stubborn look that comes over her face warns me that I'm in for a bollocking.

"Are we staying here?"

"Of course."

"Then let's check in first."

"No time."

Her lips press into a straight line, hands on hips. "We have time. Your father isn't going anywhere. He's not dying. It's late, I'm tired. I want to get my room key, take a shower, and order room service. We're in a ritzy hotel. Let's take advantage of the amenities. We can see your father in the morning."

Unreal. Maybe glomming on to her trip was a mistake. I could have come on my own. Then I remember why we're here together—Donatello.

The superior smirk on the desk clerk's face as we converge on the counter dissolves when I give him my name. One advantage to being Lord Ravenscroft's son is that people know who I am . Then again, the downside is that people know who I am.

My dad has been my entrée to the world my whole life. I hand over our passports, we sign the forms, and he hands over the keys.

Raine visibly drags. "Is there an elevator?"

"We're on the first floor."

I start up the long, winding staircase. She puffs behind me.

"Come on slow coach."

"Climbing is not my superpower," she manages to get out between sobbing breaths.

Once on the landing I clock that room 111 is to the left and all the other rooms are on the right.

"Going to my room," Raine tells me, still breathing hard.

I take her arm. "We're seeing my dad first."

"You don't need me for that."

Her protest makes me grasp her bicep harder and pull.

Teeth gritted, she growls. "Let me go, berk."

Shame washes over me and I release her arm. "Sorry."

Her eyes shoot flames at me, but she strides toward Dad's door looming at the far end of the corridor. I speed forward to catch her up.

Raine positions herself behind me. I put my ear to the door and hear muffled sounds of water running and classic rock. Can't make out the song.

With a closed fist, I hammer on the thick wood slab.

No response. I bang again, yelling as loud as I can. "Dad, open up."

Twice more I repeat the action before the water stops and the music is switched off. An irritable voice comes from inside.

"Hold your britches."

The door swings in. Dad's head pops out, hair dripping wet. "Oh, it's you."

With a toss of his head, showering me with

droplets, he flings the door wide, now framed wearing only a towel.

Raine gasps.

Dad's eyes sparkle with mischief. "Graham, glad you got here. Who's your friend?"

Raine radiates like a furnace from the climb as she leans around me.

'This is Raine Sheffield, one of my colleagues." I step back , stepping on her foot, so he can see her.

She yelps.

Dad gives her a once over. I call tell he's appraising the disheveled clothes and hair falling over her face. "The Donatello expert. Graham has told me about you." He sounds unimpressed.

"I can imagine." Her tone is dry.

"Your father is Michael Sheffield, yes?"

Standing to the side, my eyes flicker back and forth between them. Her eyes widen in surprise.

"I didn't know you were au courant with contemporary art."

"All art, my dear. Everything interests me." His grandiose arm wave hits me in the chest, but he's oblivious.

Meanwhile, Raine takes in the elegant space. Typical of these historic hotels, the room is filled with antique furniture, tufted silk headboard, and gold-painted woodwork.

"Beautiful space, isn't it?" Dad sounds like he decorated it himself.

"Too much gold, too much everything."

He harrumphs, then moves out of the doorway. "Come in. No reason to stand out there."

With a nudge, I get her to walk forward and follow behind.

As the towel slips from around Dad's waist, I give him a hasty heads-up. "Aren't you cold?"

He retightens it with a laugh. "Have a seat. I'll put on some clothes."

Dad's silver hair sticks up around his scalp in clumps as it dries. Unshaven, eyes red and bleary, a tremor noticeable in his hands, I wonder if he's been drinking.

Closer examination reveals that all the chairs are heaped with clothes, the floor strewn with bits of paper, and a dainty marble-topped mahogany table cluttered with dirty cups, part-filled glasses, and a variety of opened bottles—whisky and wine predominating. A tray rests on the floor near the open bathroom door, piled with crockery and cutlery.

"Just push things off." He picks a shirt and trousers up from one of the piles, roots through another for pants and a Y-front, and ducks into the bathroom.

"How the mighty are fallen," Raine whispers.

She edges in carefully to avoid the detritus, while I move toward the phone on the stand next to the king-sized bed and stab the housekeeping button.

"Just get here as soon as possible." I slam down the receiver. My face feels hot and tight.

I yell at the closed door of the bathroom. "Where's Saunders?"

Dad, in his underwear, buttoning his shirt, doesn't bother to look up. "I didn't bring him. Family matters to attend to."

"Why haven't you allowed the cleaners in? Or room service to take away this trash?"

"Didn't want to be bothered."

"The cleaners will be here in a few minutes and transform this pig sty."

With a glare he slams the bathroom door.

"Dad usually travels with his valet," I say.

Raine's sigh is almost inaudible. She mutter, "starving. Any late-night places nearby?"

"Let's go to Aqua al 2 for something to eat. It's only a two-minute walk and I'm peckish myself after all that time at the police station."

"That would be perfect. We haven't eaten since breakfast," Raine says.

A knock alerts us that the housekeeper is at the door.

"Thank you," I tell her as we walk out.

Raine pokes my arm to draw my attention to a man who peels away from a doorway just as we leave. Is he following us? He walks past, ear glued to his phone. Maybe it's a coincidence.

"Probably from the police," Dad says as if it is an everyday occurrence.

The restaurant, tucked into an ancient building, is warm and welcoming. It's late enough that empty tables dot the room. Colorful photos of the food delight the eye.

Shared starters make inroads into our hunger. By the time we reach the mains, even Raine has thawed.

Dad looks a new man as he as he falls on the house specialty, filet mignon with a blueberry sauce, and blots his freshly shaved upper lip at intervals. "Raine, I understand your father is Michael Sheffield, the sculptor."

Around a mouthful of risotto con spinachi, she says, "Yes."

"A little outré for my taste, but his work is interesting. Did you ever notice any influence of Donatello?"

She laughs. "I don't think so, too modern."

"Hmmm," He drops the subject.

We move on. "Have you found out any more about the drawings?" I ask.

Raine narrows her eyes. "Drawings? What drawings?"

"You didn't tell her?" Dad's tone is accusatory.

"I told her that you went to visit a dealer and found him dead." I look over the dessert offerings to avoid their faces.

"Not about the drawings then?"

"No."

"A Florentine dealer, Guiseppe Parenti, contacted me some weeks about an exciting find. I arranged to meet him in Florence when Parliament wasn't sitting, which is now."

A little wine has spilled onto the table and dad is drawing a finger through it.

"These sorts of negotiations are delicate. They take time."

"Do you know what drawings the dealer was offering?" Raine asks.

After a long silence, Dad says, "Donatello. Supposedly of the bronze David and Judith and Holofernes. The dealer told me that they were removed from the Medici archive when the family were driven out of Florence along with a contract and receipts."

Pressing the wine-coated finger to his lips, he licked the moisture away. "According to him, the documents are currently in the possession of an old Florentine family who have decided, all these centuries later, to sell them for financial reasons. I was assured that the provenance was excellent."

"Did you actually meet?" The sharp hunger of the hunt in Raine's eyes startles me.

"Parenti and I had a coffee when I arrived. I demanded proofs and he promised them to me. But he didn't disclose the name of the seller. My impression was that the documents were in a safe place, presumably not his shop. He invited me to stop by the next day and he would show me some photos. But when I got there, he was dead."

Raine presses. "Why didn't he show you when you were having coffee? "

"They were locked in his safe. Parenti was a sly dog, with a shady reputation, but he was also cautious.

Bringing the proofs into a public place was out of the question.”

“Weren't you suspicious? No Donatello drawings are known.”

“Of course I was skeptical. As I said, he promised to show me proofs. But if there were any, the murderer took them. Nothing has been found in his shop according to the police. They are probably going to search my room.”

He drains the dregs of the cappuccino. “But we know he had to have made drawings for all of his works. Just because no one has found any doesn't mean that they don't exist.”

Impatient, I throw in my opinion, “I'll believe it when I see the actual works, and they're certified genuine.” *Perhaps they never existed.*

Raine

This statue is so natural in it vitality and delicacy that other artisans find it impossible to believe that the work is not moulded around a living body - Vasari

I'm mainlining caffeine and my exhaustion vanishes. When Lord Ravenscroft goes back to the hotel, we order another round of coffee and hold a council of war.

“Your dad is hiding something.”

"What?"

"Maybe he has already seen the proof. Maybe he knows where the cache is. Maybe he was trying to cut out the middleman."

"Why would he try to deceive us?"

"Because he's guilty?"

Graham's fist hits the table and cups crash to the floor. A waiter rushes over with a broom, another with a mop. "That's ridiculous," he hisses.

My knuckles beat a tattoo against the rustic wood tabletop. "Maybe we should go to the police. Find out for ourselves what's going on."

He's flushed and shaking with anger and doesn't answer right away. Instead, he scans the floor as if searching for stray fragments of crockery.

I signal a waiter, who brings him a glass of water. He gulps it down, coughing as too much liquid goes down the wrong way. Graham wipes his face with a napkin.

"All right. We can go first thing tomorrow. Dad said the Questura is right down the street. Not that I believe your crackbrained idea. But doesn't hurt to get another perspective."

"First thing tomorrow, if our luggage hasn't arrived, I am going clothes shopping. I only packed a few little extras in my carry-on."

"It will probably all be there when we get up."

"Or still in Lyon or Paris," I say, pessimistic to the core as I trudge off to bed, tossing and turning, my mind jumping like a squirrel collecting acorns.

In the morning, the desk clerk tells us that our luggage is promised for later in the day. After a buffet breakfast in the Sala Parliamento with its frescoed ceiling, we decamp to talk to the police.

Fruitless. The inspector sends us off with fleas in our ears.

A visit to the dealer's wife yielded nothing. She tells us, not so politely, that she knows nothing about her husband's business. Graham tries to bully her, but I drag him off, while she screams threats to call the carabiniere.

We even visit the Medici Library, on the off-chance that they have a record of the missing drawings and an idea of who might have taken them back in 1494. No trace of the records exists.

"This is a wild goose chase. I think I'll go back to my original plan and spend the morning at the Bargello." I contemplate going back to my room and huddling under the luxury duvet. The breakfast pastry is lump in my stomach. Communing with the plethora of Donatello sculptural delights in Florence might soothe my jangled nerves.

"Perfect," Graham says. "Maybe someone there has heard of this mysterious cache."

A fellow student and I had taken a trip to Florence while we were studying Renaissance art at the Courtauld Institute. The city had overstimulated every sense. Besides the heady mixture of medieval and Renaissance design jumbling the eye, the sounds, the smells, touching rough stone, an almost palpable taste to the air had made me dizzy.

Almost fifteen years later, vertigo hits again as we walk into the Bargello. As my heart beats rapidly and my mouth dries, my tongue feels swollen. Spots whirl in front of my eyes and I feel myself falling, but Graham manages to catch me before I topple to the floor.

A man rushes over to help. He's slender, middle-aged, medium height, with ink-black hair and dark eyes that shine with the heat of liquid lava. After he helps get me rebalanced, he takes my hand, pressing a light kiss against it. "Are you all right signorina?"

I gurgle.

"Forgive me. Perhaps I was rash." He edges a little way away. "I am Federico Cardini. I work as a consultant at the Bargello."

"Graham Spencer-Ross." Graham pauses "And fainting beauty here is Raine Sheffield."

I choke thank you. Neither reacts, so maybe the sound never got out.

Cardini's lips fold inward. Finally, he says, "Let me take you to a bar for coffee and a pastry. Perhaps that will help the signorina recover." He proffers his forearm and I hesitantly touch my fingers to the light wool fabric.

Ensconced at Scudieri, across from the Duomo, each of us with a demitasse of espresso and slices of velvety chocolate known as torta pistocchi, my curiosity roars back.

"This is very kind of you, Signore Cardini. Do you often pick up art-struck tourists?"

Cardini's smile shows off slightly uneven teeth that save his features being too perfect and my breath catches. He epitomizes everything in the romantic Italian male, even if he is at least ten years my senior. When you're already in your mid-thirties, the age difference isn't as daunting as it would have been ten years earlier.

"Not at all. I noticed how you were overcome by splendor of the museum. Since I am an expert on renaissance sculpture, I thought I would find out what appealed to you most."

My eyes widened. Graham's jaw dropped.

"How fortuitous," Graham says. "Dr. Sheffield is a specialist in Donatello."

Cardini runs a manicured nail down his smooth jaw, then taps his lips. "Are you really?" His voice has an insistent quality that makes me uneasy.

"Uh, yes." I don't volunteer that I am a lowly sixth-form teacher, not an exalted university lecturer.

A final slurp and he's puts empty his cup back in the saucer. He motions toward the gleaming espresso machine behind the counter. "I hope you would both like another coffee."

We nod and he snaps his fingers in the air. A server comes over to collect the cups. "Tre espresso doppio per favore," Cardini says.

Tenting his fingers under his chin, he leans back in

his chair. "Signore Spencer-Ross, I take it you are the son of Lord Ravenscroft."

I notice Graham's lack of surprise that Cardini knows who he is. After all, his father is a well-known art connoisseur and collector.

"And you, Signorina, are also the daughter of Michael Sheffield, the sculptor?"

"How did you know?" Unlike Graham, I am surprised. Dad's well-known, but there isn't anything obvious to connect us and Sheffield's a common name.

"I have met your father several times and you look very much like him."

Picturing dad's slightly squashed face and pugnacious jaw, I'm not sure whether to be flattered or offended.

Once the new drinks are deposited, Cardini continues. "I spoke to Lord Ravenscroft a few days ago. He told me that an art dealer approached him about some Donatello drawings. Perhaps that is why you are both in Florence?"

I bristle at the implication that we are a couple. Graham ignores that irrelevance.

"The dealer is dead," he says shortly.

"It was in the papers." Cardini says, drink the smalll glass of water that accompanies the coffee. I understand your father found the body and has been questioned. Does he know where the material is?"

"Not that I know of."

"Pity. Quite a coup to reveal it to the world, especially for a man of your father's reputation, Signore Spencer-Ross."

"Graham, please. All this formality is so cumbersome."

"True. You may call me Federico."

"You may use my first name as well," I break in.

"Thank you." He gives one of those funny little bows.

"Do you know anything?" we say in unison.

"Signore Parenti, the dealer entrusted with the sale, had made it known that he was looking for a buyer. When your father arrived in Florence, many of us assumed he was the purchaser."

His face droops. "A sad day for Italy if the documents go elsewhere."

"They seem to have vanished," Graham said. "If they ever existed."

Graham

Donatello's works were considered more like the distinguished works of the ancient Greeks and Romans than those of any artist who has ever existed - Vasari

Cardini offers to give us a tour of Florence, concentrating on Donatello. We would meet tomorrow morning at the statue of Donatello outside the Uffizi for convenience. Then he bids us arrivederci and heads back toward the Bargello.

"Dad will be meeting with the police again. No point in going back to the hotel."

I agree. Excitement or trepidation makes me shiver but per usual I can't tell difference. Collywobbles, goosebumps, and electric shocks were the same.

We walk down to the Ponte Vecchio, then spend time looking at Ghiberti's Baptistry doors, before heading back to the hotel to see if our luggage has been delivered.

When I see my battered lemon-colored behemoth on the luggage rack, I dance around the room singing "We Are the Champions."

Once I've put things away, I make a cup of tea and take a long soak in the hydromassage tub. Graham made a dinner reservation at Chianineria Trattoria dall'Oste, just down from the hotel but I should have time for quick nap.

Pounding on the door. I'm chilled. The water is cold. Must have fallen asleep.

Graham's voice is two octaves higher than normal.

"Raine, Raine. Open the bloody door."

Heart racing, I jump out of the still-bubbling water, barely rescuing the teetering tea mug on the edge from destruction. I grab a towel and wrap it haphazardly.

"Keep your shirt on. I'll be right there."

Graham's fist is up, ready to pummel the door once more as I pull it open.

Graham gapes. "What the ...?'

"I was in the bath." I look down at the slipping towel and hastily pull it up. "What do you want, you herbert?"

"Dad's disappeared." Graham looks forlorn, like a puppy that's just been kicked.

Graham

In the expression of Holofernes we can see the effects of wine, sleep and death in his limbs which look cold and limp - Vasari

While Raine's dressing, I decide to take up the matter with the desk attendant.

"Did you see Lord Ravenscroft leave the hotel?" The man reddensd. Clearing his throat, Giuseppe— that was the name on his badge—says, "Signore Cardini, from the Bargello, asked to see him. When he came down, they left together."

"Did they say where they were going?" My voice comes out as a whisper. The man strains to hear me and I repeat it. This time I'm too loud and he backs away.

"Perhaps they are having a coffee? But where? Who knows." He shrugs.

Grumbling with frustration, I go back upstairs to my room and check my email and messages. Nothing. I pace, look out the window, do some online browsing. An hour passes. With no word from Dad, stomach rumbling, I tap on Raine's door. "You want to go to dinner now?"

"Your dad turned up?" She opens the door, relief lighting up her face.

"No. But Dad's an adult, so no point worrying. I don't want to lose our reservation."

Raine frowns. "Does it matter where we eat?"

Philistine. "Of course it matters. This is a renowned steakhouse known for its bistecca Fiorentina."

"Fine." She manages to turn it into a hiss at the end, like a snake ready to strike.

Once down in the lobby, I ask once more at the desk after my father, but no dice. Then I try to take Raine's arm but she pulls away with a don't touch me glare, then walks stiffly out through the door.

Once we're seated, I mull over the menu. Raine sits back, scanning the other diners, paying no attention to the food choices. With a free hand, I decide to order for both of us.

The waiter comes over, straighten his bow tie and bowing to my 'date.' To get his attention, I clear my throat.

"Si, Signore?"

Can't help puffing out my chest a bit as I say, "We'll start with the Crostini misti and the Tartare con crema ai porcini e crumbled di Grana." Turning to Raine, I grin. "Hope you don't mind raw meat."

I can tell as she pastes on a worldly expression, that the idea of eating raw meat is totally alien to her. But she waves the comment away airily as if it's something she eats every day.

With our server poised for the rest of the order, I plump for the famous steak to share, endive salad, roast potatoes, and a bottle of Chianti Classico to fill out the meal.

A piece of crostini halfway between her plate and mouth, Raine says, "At least we know your father knows Cardini."

Already on my second G&T, I try unsuccessfully to submerge my irritation. "I don't know if they just met and I bloody well don't care. He's dragged us here and now he's being an arse, swanning off like that."

Then I take a savage bite of the typical Tuscan salt-free bread spread with tartare just as a voice says in my ear, "Signore, are you Graham Spencer-Ross, son of Lord Ravenscroft?"

Choking on the morsel I'd just shoved into my mouth, I turn my head sharply practically clocking the at the man leaning over my shoulder. He's short, dressed in a plain black suit and white shirt, with an expression that mixes suspicion and pity.

"Yes." I push the chair back and stand, looking down on the shorter man. "Why?'

"I am Vincente Monti of the Polizia di Stato. You will need to come with me."

I sit down and calmly smear more tartare on bread.

"What is all this in aid of?" He popped the bread in his mouth as if uninterested in the answer.

"Your father was found at the foot of the Ponte Vecchio about an hour ago."

"What? Is he all right?"

"I am sorry, Signore. He is dead."

A choking sound gave way to a shout. "I, I can't believe it."

"His identification was in his pocket. Whatever the motive of the assailant, it was not robbery. His wallet was intact and his wristwatch had not been touched."

Raine's fork, unheeded in her hand, clattered onto the plate.

"I am sorry to interrupt your evening," Monti said. "Please accompany me to the Questura, Signore. An officer will take the young lady back to your hotel."

Graham didn't move, but Raine obediently stood, slinging her bag over her shoulder. She tapped Graham's cheek gently and he staggered to his feet.

Dazed, he follows Monti out, forgetting to pay the bill. Raine, who was telling an officer where she was staying, handed over her credit card, hoping the uneaten meal wouldn't take her over the limit.

Graham

*As Henry Moore carved or modelled his sculpture
every day, he strove to surpass Donatello, and failed,
but woke the next morning elated for another try.-
Donald Hall*

Hours later, I am escorted back to the hotel. I've seen my father's body. He's looks different dead, robbed of the vitality that made him such a force. There was a noticeable ligature around his neck. Inspector Monti said he'd been garroted, piano wire deeply embedded in his neck.

All m airs and graces deserted me as I vomited over and over. Raine is sitting in the lobby tapping on her phone, eyes red from crying. I rub my face, feeling the rough five o'clock shadow.

She looks up, lower lip clamped between her teeth to keep her mouth from quivering.

"I have to call Mum." Instead of going up to my room, I sit in the armchair next to the sofa she's curled up on. Her presence is comforting, and I don't want to be alone.

The call goes to voicemail, and I leave a brief message. All she'll want to know is if he changed his will before he died.

"Why did he leave with Cardini? Do you think he found out something about the Donatello drawings?" Raine prods not-so-gently.

Hiccupping, I give her a hard stare. "Doesn't matter now, does it? We can just toddle back home so I can arrange the funeral."

"And be invested as the next Lord Ravenscroft. Well done you." The irony is Raine's voice isn't lost on me.

"My father had a life peerage. There is no title to inherit. I've no idea about the state of my father's affairs." With a head shake, I say, "I shall have to meet with the lawyers and bankers about all that."

"What about Cardini?" Raine asks again.

"What about him?"

"Wasn't he the last person to see your father alive?"

"Maybe he thought my father knew where the papers were." I lift a shoulder. "Doesn't matter now. My father's dead. Nothing will bring him back."

I can't think about anything but going home, making arrangements. A yawn overtakes me as Raine stalks away, climbing the stairs like they're Everest.

I sit in the lobby. Word must have gotten out. A barman comes over with a whisky.

"So sorry for your loss."

The voice isn't that of the man holding out the drink. Standing next to him is Federico Cardini.

"Graham, I just heard about your father."

"Bad news travels fast."

"Florence is a small town, really."

"Why are you here, Federico?"

"The bar stays open late, and I wanted a nightcap. I ran into a friend who works at the Questura, and she told me what happened. Bring your drink. We can sit in the bar."

At some point, Cardini helps me to my room.

Can't make it on my own.Not bothering to undress, I fall onto the bed.

***

Raine

The legs move, the arms are ready, the head alert, and the whole figure acts; by virtue of the character, the manner and form of the action presents to our eyes a valiant, invincible, and magnanimous soul. – Francesco Bocchi

The sun peeks weakly around the edges of the curtains. Early morning light or bad weather? The time on my phone shows six a.m.

Determined to keep the appointment at the Uffizi with Federico Cardini, I free myself from the covers. Simple outfit, walking shoes, a swipe of makeup. The buffet isn't open yet, so I leave Graham a note at the desk and get a recommendation for coffee.

Off to meet Cardini. I know you don't care, but I want to know if he has any connection to the drawings. Then I may wander the shops on the Ponte Vecchio.

After several espresso doppio macchiato and one too many cornetti con crema, I waddle and slosh to the Uffizi.

No sign of Cardini but I'm early so I stand in the portico near the statue of Donatello sculpted by Giovanni Bastianini and Girolamo Torrini in 1848.

I'm picking at the sores of the murder. I don't hear the elegant Italian approach.

"Buongiorno, Doctoressa Sheffield. I hope you were able to sleep well last night." Cardini stands so close I can smell the aroma of coffee and cigarettes on his breath.

"I suppose you didn't hear that Lord Ravenscroft was murdered last night?"

"Yes. It was in the morning paper. Such a pity. I am sorry for his son." His expression unreadable, he says, "I wonder if Ravenscroft told him anything more about the drawings."

Instead of rising to the bait, I to pry out the story of Cardini's meeting with Ravenscroft. "I understand that you might have been the last person to see him alive. Did he tell you anything?"

"Surely the murderer would have been the last person." Cardini says, smoothly.

"The desk clerk said that the two of you left together around six o'clock last night."

"Just for a coffee and a chat. Lord Ravenscroft told me he was planning to meet you and Graham for dinner. He never arrived?"

"No. We asked the desk clerk, who told us he'd gone out with you, so we left on our own."

"I hope you at least enjoyed your meal.'

"Hardly. The police came and took Graham to see his father's body before we finished dinner."

"That must have been painful."

Raine grimaced. "He seemed quite distressed when he returned to the hotel."

"I take it Graham won't be joining us this morning? Or do I call him Lord Ravenscroft now?"

"No, he has to make arrangements to get his father's body back to England and plan the funeral. If the police allow it, I imagine he'll leave Florence very soon."

"A shame for him to cut his visit short." Cardini looks out onto the Piazza della Signoria. "I looked forward to taking you both to the Orsanmichele to see the Donatello sculptures that decorate the exterior."

"Aren't they copies?"

"Of course, but seeing even the copies in situ gives a perspective that is valuable for understanding the works."

"I imagine Graham's gone off Donatello."

"But you will join me?" His expression is unreadable.

"Of course. Thank you."

"Before we visit Donatello, I have arranged a little treat for you."

He shows his uneven teeth again, but this time they remind me more of the Big, Bad Wolf than charm.

He takes my arm, and we turn toward the Arno in silence. I want to talk more about the stolen drawings and the murders but he walks quickly, making conversation impossible. When we finally stop near a cluster of small boats, I'm breathless.

Boats. My spirits lighten in spite of myself. "I had no idea that there was boating on the Arno. Not exactly Venice, but near enough."

"Do you prefer Venice, then, Raine? A pity."

"I have a preference for the Venetian painters," I admit. "The Bellinis, Carpaccio, Titian, Tintoretto. Their use of color appeals to me. But for sculpture, Florence is better."

"Perhaps a trip on the Arno will bring you around to a more Florentine cast of mind," he says. "The barchetti are traditional boats in Florence, a bit like gondolas."

I stop to stare at a few boats in the water. The shape is similar to a gondola but there is no read uniformity.

We walk down to the landing stage, and he hands me in. "Raine, this is my friend, Antonio. Tonio, this is Signorina Raine Sheffield from England."

"Piacere, Signorina."

The burly boatman wears a white T-shirt and jeans, a far cry from the gondolieri of Venice with their striped shirts, dark slacks, and straw hats. His gravelly voice is deep, his eyes small, hard pebbles in a mottled face and I am certain I wouldn't want to run into him in a dark alley. My skin prickles as he quickly assesses me.

"Tonio is one of the best Renaioli in Florence."

"And that is...?"

"A boatman. He's also known for his ability to find lost things."

"Lost things?" Could he mean the putative Donatello drawings?

The prickles are now icicles and I suspect the meeting at the Bargello was no chance encounter. He knew who they are, why they had come to Florence, and had engineered everything. And now, here I am, on a boat, in the middle of the river Arno, with a covetous, perhaps murderous, art expert and his sinister henchman.

Graham

Donatello does not allow himself to be confined to a formula of a few words, for his incomparable creative energy bursts into the figurative and moral problems of his time, creating a whole new mode and a new world of visions. In the figurative arts, he is the first man and the most audacious of that enormously complex and extremely rich event which, in irreplaceable terms, we call the Renaissance.—Giorgio Castelfranco

My head pounds like a drum corps has taken up residence. My mouth feels like a sewer. And I'm sure I'm late for something. The memory of an engagement hovers on the edges of consciousness. I gulp down glass after glass of water, hoping to dispel the taste and the fog.

My phone shows a message.

Hope you're okay. Meeting Cardini.

That's what I forgot. Cardini. Throwing on some clothes, I race down the corridor and knock on Raine's door but there was no answer. Of course she has. Pull it together.

In the lobby, the desk clerk calls my name. Impatient, I want to ignore him, but the urgency in his voice draws me over. The clerk mutely holds out a folded piece of paper.

Stupid girl. She always has to have the answers. If I don't care, why should she? With a curse, I send a text.

Where are you

No response. Two minutes later, heart pounding, I call Monti.

Raine

If it were as easy to do a thing as to judge it, my Christ would not look like a peasant; but take some wood yourself and make one. – Donatello

As soon as Tonio pulls out into the middle of the river, Cardini asks, "Do you know where Donatello's drawings are, Raine?"

"There aren't any."

His thin smile turns him from a mild scholar to a menacing thug. But his voice is deceptively mild. "What if there were? What if some had been found?"

"After close to five and half centuries?" I scoffed, but my stomach cries out a protest to remind me that

I've had too much coffee and that I should regret the second brioche.

Still conversationally, he says, "I believe Lord Ravenscroft found those drawings."

"Did he find them? He never said anything of the sort to me." I grope in my pocket, find a crumpled tissue and use it to mop my damp face . "You might speak with Graham."

"I spoke with him last night and he denied knowing anything."

Talked with him last night? When?

"How did you see him last night?"

"He was in the hotel lobby when I stopped at the bar there. We had a drink together." He shifts closer to me.

"Maybe a few drinks. He was definitely worse for wear when I left him."

Stricken, I realize that he is a much better actor than I gave him credit for. "If you spoke with Graham last night, you must have known then that his father was dead."

He sidesteps the comment. "When I spoke with Lord Ravenscroft, he denied having the documents and seemed to think that you might be the key to the secret—or at least your father might."

What? Dad? What a preposterous suggestion. "My father is a sculptor, but that is all he has in common with Donatello."

"Still, Ravenscroft planned to go back to England and consult him. He seemed to think that if Parenti knew he was in danger, he may have sent the drawings to your father. That's what he told me as we parted last evening."

"Why would Ravenscroft think that Parenti knew my father? I've never even heard his name."

"An artist, a dealer..." Cardini spread his hands out.

"You're mad." I start to rise. The boat lists to the side.

Tonio yells, "sit down you little bitch or you'll have us all in the water."

Cardini pulls me back down. "Fate has crossed our paths. I will accompany you to London and speak with your father. The drawings would be worth a fortune."

My eyes turn toward the bank, straining for a glimpse of Graham. He must be up by now. Searching for me. Unless he's too broken by his father's death to care.

"What about Graham?"

"He will have some amnesia, I'm afraid. The result of too much drink last night."

Frantically I search for something to say, picturing Graham lying senseless in some Florentine back alley. "No generous donation to the Bargello?"

"Hardly. I am a poor art historian. But I have no problem taking an offer from the Italian government."

"How would you explain your possession?"

"Once your father tells me where they are, I will explain that he thought they were worthless and gave them to me. After my authentication, I will sell to the highest bidder."

"Why should I collaborate with you? If my father has located them, we could just sell them ourselves."

"No, Doctoressa. I think this will persuade to become my confederate." Cardini reaches into a pocket and produces a Swiss mini gun, poking it into my side..

My body instinctively recoiled but he wraps his other arm around me like an iron band.

"Tonio, I think we need to take a little trip down the river to San Jacopo al Girone."

I gasp and try not to cry out, certain he won't hesitate to shoot me if I try to draw attention.

"You will be comfortable there, Raine, while we contact your father. I'm sure he will tell me about the drawings in return for your safety."

Graham

Donatello made his figures in such a way that in the room where he worked they did not look half as well as when they were put in their places.—Vasari

I meet Monti at the Uffizi where Monti is questioning a man.

"He's always here, hoping that the art lovers will give him some money. Sees who comes and goes."

The man looks about eighty but is probably much younger. His gray hair is grizzled, his face badly shaven.

He wears trousers that are too big, cinched with a belt, a faded t-shirt, and surprisingly new trainers.

"Did you see a man leave with a young woman this morning?" Monti sounds like this isn't first time he's asked.

A crafty expression. "Is there a reward?"

"The usual," Monti barks.

The man nods as if closing a deal. "A British lady met Dottore Cardini met here and walked down toward the Arno."

Monti and I race toward the river, a pack of officers on our heels. A motorboat is waiting. We jump in and take off down the river.

***

Raine

Donatello was so admirable in knowledge, in judgment, and in the practice of his art that he may be said to have been the first to illustrate the art of sculpture among the moderns; and he deserves the more commendation because in his time few antiquities had been uncovered.—Vasari

An oppressive silence has settled over the boat.

"Are the documents real?"

"Why not?" Cardini is dismissive.

"How do you know they exist?"

"Oh, they exist. I have the photostats from the dealer."

"So you..." I can't even say it.

He says nothing. But an air of satisfaction steals over him as he nods at his confederate.

"And Lord Ravenscroft?"

"We were walking together near the foot of the Ponte Santa Trinità when a man appeared. He slipped a piece of wire around Lord Ravenscroft's neck. Before I could cry out for help, Ravenscroft was dead and the man had vanished."

I gaze at him in horror, mouth open to scream. His arm tightens more and he prods me again with the gun.

"Remember, I will shoot you if you make a fuss."

Tonio's laughs is as raucous as a gull's cry. We move faster through the water as an amplified voice sounds from somewhere near by.

"Federico Cardini. This is Vincente Monti of the Policia di Stato. Pull your boat to the shore."

Cardini shouts, "Tonio, go faster."

Shots ring out, hitting the water just in front of the barchetto. When I look back, a motorboat is speeding in our direction.

Several men stand on the bow, one a sharpshooter. Inspector Monti beside him with the bullhorn in one fist. Behind them, Graham is just discernible.

The revolver makes a small splash as Cardini slips it into the river. Tonio stops rowing as the grappling irons are heaved into the boat and we are towed toward the bank. Their arms folded across their chests, neither man's face shows any emotion.

When we reach the docking point, they are cuffed and led away to a waiting police van.

Graham

I don't want to be at the mercy of my emotions. I want to use them, to enjoy them, and to dominate them. – Oscar Wilde

Relief pours out of me when we catch the gondola-like boat. A burly man stands in the stern, poling furiously but they can't outrun the police cruiser. My shirt, sweat-stained, sticks to me everywhere.

All I can think is that Dad is dead, but Raine is alive. My cheeks are wet. I swipe my eyes with back of hand and let out the breath I've been holding as we watch the ropes pull the boat closer.

After the grappling irons are set, two policemen jump over to it, like pirates boarding a prize ship. When I try to jump to the boat with them, Monti holds me back.

Raine

Little beginnings sometimes have great endings. – *Benvenuto Cellini*

Even though I feel awkward, I agree to go to the airport with Graham. He proposed last night—and I refused. He's a drowning man grabbing for me like a life raft. He'll regret the offer soon enough.

We stand at the check-in desk while the agent prints out his boarding pass and weighs and tags his pristine trunk. The plane is late, but it has finally arrived, and he'll be back in London in a few hours.

We watch the conveyor belt carry his suitcase away. Then he grabs the envelope and his passport from the agent's outstretched hand, shoulders his messenger bag, and starts toward the security area.

"Bye," I yell after him, waving as if he was marching off to war. "Safe travels." Then I pause and mischievously call out "your lordship."

He turns, a tiny smile on his too-perfect features. "Thanks." With a little royal wave, he disappears down the pathway to security.

Dragging my ugly yellow suitcase, I catch the Volainubus Airport Shuttle to the train station at Santa Maria Novella with plenty of time to catch my high-speed bullet train to Rome. Florence left a bad taste in my mouth, and I can't wait to be elsewhere.

When I get to Rome, there is a text message from the school to the staff to informed of Graham's father death and his resignation from Meryton Academy.

On the advice of my father, I switch my focus to contemporary Italian painters, flitting from Florence to Rome and Milan. The double murder, seasoned with art intrigue, catches the imagination of the world and I read daily reports in the local and international newspapers until newer thrills replace the story.

Tonio turns out to be a mafia enforcer and Cardini's cousin. He was doing him a favor.

When the police search Cardini's apartment, they find both drawings stolen over many years from the Uffizi and the Accademia. There are forgeries too. He had quite a side business going. They also found the photostats of the putative Donatello material. Experts are still looking at them, but suspect they are fakes from the nineteenth century.

The case won't come to trial for a year or more and I put it out of my mind.

By the end of the summer, I'm on my way back to London. I've had enough of Italy and long for the familiar Islington streets. Having abandoned sculpture, I'm immersed in the works of Roberto Ferri, Monica Berengo, Gugliermo Castelli, Daria Petrilli, and Enrico Robusti.

When we touch down at Heathrow I call a cab service. Traffic is heavy but when our familiar building hoves into view, something in me relaxes as if a coiled spring has sprung.

I smell fish and chips as I walk through the door of our shared flat. Dad's in the kitchen, unwrapping crispy fillet from grease-stained paper.

"Just got back from a meeting at the Cultural Institute of Radical Art about a new commission." He points at the counter. "Want some?"

"Greasy fish?" I laugh, breaking off a piece. My sigh of pleasure fills the whole space.

"'Bout time you got back." He kisses my cheek. "Did you have a good time chasing Donatello?"

I toe off my shoes and plop down on the sofa. Chew on a nail

Chasing Donatello. That's how Graham characterized his father's quest. A perfect description of the doomed venture.

"Dad, what do you know about the Donatello drawings that were supposedly found in Florence?"

"Funny you should ask. That mad collector, Lord Ravenscroft, asked me about them a few weeks ago. He just died I think..."

"And?"

"Told him a rather dodgy Florentine art dealer contacted me about some drawings, but I wasn't interested. Would have been fakes anyway. Everyone knows Donatello left no drawings or documents."

Historical Notes

Eric Estorick had a very prestigious art career and was at one time director of the Grosvenor Galley in London. He and his wife provided the core of the Estorick Collection and donated paintings by Chagall and Kandinsky to fund it. In 1964 he was able to arrange for the recovery of 1,564 Torah scrolls looted during the Second World War and they were eventually distributed to synagogues all over the world.

For more information on Estorick, click **here.**

· · ·

Donato di Niccolò di Betto Bardi (c. 1386 – 13 December 1466), was born Florence. Two of his best-known patrons were the Medici and Martelli families.

Vasari says that he owned some of Donatello's drawings but none have survived. "I have both nude and draped figures, various animals which astound anyone who sees them, and other beautiful things."

There are three drawings in France that the French government attributes to him, but art historians generally agree that his drawings haven't survived.

For more information on Donatello, click **here**.

LEAVING CLEVELAND

Author's Note

This is a bit of backstory about Detective Lane Fairchild of the Sherburne, Michigan, police department, from his time with the Cleveland police. He first appeared in *Dead in the Alley* (2022).

Jokes are from Scott Burroughs, chief of the Port Aransas Police Department, in the *Port Aransas South Jetty* (https://www.portasouthjetty.com/articles/garcie-inspires-corny-police-firefighter-jokes/).

"You're never home, Lane." Hands on hips, my wife Josie glares. I'm in the middle of a high-profile case and, much as I love her, I have no time to debate my lousy hours.

In the background, the TV news shows headshots of five dead women.

I can feel heat at the top of my head, a bright red beacon. "When you married me, you knew what life would be like, hooking up with a cop." Need to cool off. I grab a bottle of water from the coffee table and slosh it over my head. Icy liquid sluices under my collar, down my neck, back, and chest.

"That was before we had kids. Now..."

The news reader's voice cuts through Josie's complaint. "A serial killer stalks the streets of Cleveland."

Women are dying. Women named Hollie Mann. Or Holli. Holly. Even Holley. The killer doesn't discriminate. We've found five bodies so far, women between the ages of twenty-five and forty. Who knew there were so many of them? This is the sixth. If she's another Hollie.

"Police are stymied by the deaths of these five women. Anyone with knowledge of these crimes should call the Witness HotLine. A reward is available for information that leads to the apprehension of the murderer."

"You're not paying attention, Lane," Josie snaps, hitting the off button on the remote.

When my cell rings, she stomps out of the room.

I hear her down the hall of our one-story, two-bedroom house in the West Park neighborhood of Cleveland. "It's okay, boys. Go back to sleep. Your dad needs to go out."

"But Mom..."

"You'll see him in the morning."

She's probably qualifying that in her own head. How many times have I still been out on a call when they're on their way to school?

The interruption breaks the tension in the room, but hearing Josie's words to the boys, my body slumps and a headache colonizes the space behind my eyes.

I call up the stairs. "Have to go, Josie. Not sure what time I'll be back."

"What a surprise."

My spine tingles at the low growl that accompanies her response. I open the door and I'm flooded with feelings of love, and an ache that I can't just stay home and cuddle with my wife, read a story to my kids, be a normal husband and father. "Love you," I shout.

Her voice drifts down, tickling my ear. "Love you too."

As a homicide detective in the Division of Investigations of the Cleveland Division of Police, the call is an invitation I can't refuse—but the party will include police cruisers, an ambulance, yellow crime-scene tape to create the outer barrier and red to block off close to the scene.

Still stewing, I arrive at the site, slam on the brakes, and hop out of the car. My still-damp shirt sticks to my bare skin as the fabric dries and I pull at the itchy material. The Cuyahoga County Medical Examiner has just arrived and pulls his Cadillac in behind my Subaru Forester.

Dr. Malcolm Jones, the ME for the last fifteen years, has seen it all, but still sounds bright and eager, unlike me. "Another one, Fairchild?"

I shrug. "The call just said dead woman and the address. If she is another Holly Mann..." I pause, then casually observe, "The screwy part is that four of the five dead women changed their names."

"Changed their names? Why?"

With a shrug, I say, "Who knows? Maybe they liked the name better than the one their parents gave them. Or they wanted to pretend to be married to a big-deal football star."

"Glad I only deal with dead bodies." Doc chuckles.

As we walk up the narrow sidewalk to steps that

lead to the open front door, our shoulders bump and I drop back. Techs hand us shoe covers and gloves before we step over the doorsill. The body is on the floor between the kitchen and the living room. Nearby, a broken cup lies on its side, liquid soaking into the sculptured aqua carpeting.

Jones grabs one of the techs. "Make sure you collect some of that spillage."

"Already did. We used an eyedropper to get some." He holds up a stoppered test tube in a labeled plastic bag. "Then we used blotting paper to get more." Another plastic baggie was the second exhibit, both clearly labeled. There was a third baggie with carpet clippings. The evidence person would quickly remove and put them in a drying hood to avoid contamination.

Assuming this was the same killer, the "tea" will include water hemlock. Easily found growing in local wetlands, the highly poisonous weed is hard to kill. I have it in my own yard. A small amount kills quickly, but not painlessly.

The ME puts a hand on my shoulder as he brushes past me, then kneels to look at the dead woman. Her eyes are open, and her body contorted. Just like all the Hollies. He holds one wrist, then has a tech turn the body over to take her temperature. "Victim pronounced dead at ten-fifteen p.m."

Vomit is everywhere. Another tech gathers more samples. I squeeze past into the kitchen. A square cream envelope sits on the counter next to the sink.

Someone has positioned an open card with a teapot and cup on the front nearby, a torn tea packet lying on top. Available in boxes of fifty at any drugstore, the envelope has no stamp or postmark. The whole thing looks like a display, just for us.

Printed on the front is "Hollie Mann. Requested Free Tea Sample." Even though the Hollies don't all spell their first name the same, the killer is consistent. All the envelopes are from the same printer. Self-sealing. Hand delivered. The killer must wear gloves, probably nitrile, since the only fingerprints are those of the victim.

I would bet they were all done at the same time. If we could find them, we'd know how many killings the murderer planned. Nothing's that easy. A deep gust of air mixed with frustration bursts through my chest, tearing at my throat. The exhale blasts out just as the tech comes up.

"Sorry."

"No biggie, sir." He wipes a sleeve over his face, then grabs paper evidence bags for various items. Each will be taped, labeled, and signed across the seal.

Did the murderer come to each scene and arrange the evidence, like stage sets? The first two were before my boss assigned me to the case, so I only saw photos. But they are eerily alike, down to the china cups. They are a common pattern. A vision of Josie comes up. We have cups like these.

Once the ME's guys finish the examination of the immediate area, Jones tells them to bag the body and take it to the morgue. "See you at the autopsy." He gives a little wave and walks out to his car.

My phone beeps. Prepared for a text from my boss, Commander Nathan Ellis, it's from Josie.

JOSIE: Kids and I are going to mom and dad's house. Not sure when we'll be back.

ME: Please don't...

Then I'm interrupted but inadvertently hit send as I stuff the device back into my pocket, so I pull it back out. Maybe the two words will be enough. She doesn't respond.

"Hey, Lane. Come check this out." My counterpart in the district calls me over to the coffee table.

Even though officers mill around, the room looks drained now that Jones and the body are gone. Officer Grier Roosevelt stands near the taped body outline that is still on the floor. "Looks like someone else was here with her." He points to the coffee table, where another teacup and saucer sat.

"How would you explain it?"

"Maybe the killer couldn't clean up."

"Why this time? There was nothing like it at the other crime scenes."

"Panicked. Screwed up." He never moves beyond the obvious.

"Maybe this was the intended victim. The others might have been a blind. Seems like the killer stuck around to see her die."

"Why leave the cup?"

"If there aren't any prints or other physical

evidence, this could be the killer thumbing his or her nose at us."

"Must be a woman. Poison is a woman's MO."

"Seriously, Grier? There have been plenty of male poisoners—H. H. Holmes, Michael Swango, Graham Young, Neil Cream..."

Roosevelt gives a snort, the seams on his face seemingly a map of disgruntlement. "Okay, you made your point. You sure like to make things complicated." He rolls his eyes and stuffs his hands into pants pockets.

When the theme from "Hill Street Blues" rings out, I walk out onto the concrete steps and pull my phone back out. "Hey, Commander."

Ellis' gravelly voice comes over the line. "Another one, Lane?"

"Yeah."

"Is it the soap star?

"Nope. All we know so far is that she's Holli with just an 'i' and she lives on 18th Street."

"Crap. We can expect at least one more, then."

I don't agree, but I don't argue either. Ellis is convinced all these killings are just.

"Stop by in the morning and brief me."

"Eight a.m. okay?"

"Make it nine. Have to drop the kids at school tomorrow. Elaine's out of town."

"Sure. See you then." Phone back in my pocket, I force my steps back into the house and stared at the taped outline where the body had been. Fluids were soaked into the carpet, and I wish we could open the windows to vent the sour smell—vomit, urine, tea, and the indefinable odor of death.

Back in the house, men check every room, bagging up evidence, dusting for fingerprints. Sergeant Philips slouches over in my direction. "Everything's under control. Go home. Come at it fresh. We'll be hours yet."

Home. To my empty house. My car sits alone at the curb, so I walk out to keep it company.

Both the sheer curtains and the drapes are wide open, but no lights show in the house when I pull into the driveway. My finger wanders to the opener, but I pull back. No point in parking in the garage for the few hours before I head back to work. Wet grass soaks my shoes as I cut across the lawn. The key sticks in the lock and I wiggle it back and forth, endlessly fiddling, before it finally clicks. Josie's been on me for weeks to spray with WD40, but I never find the time. The honey-do list is long. One of the many sore points between us. Lately, she's been playing "Cat's in the Cradle" as soon as I open the door, to remind me I'm neglecting the boys. Much as I like Harry Chapin, not sure I'll ever willingly listen to that again.

When I switch on the hall light, a minor earthquake erupts in my chest. The living room, usually a scene out of a mass destruction movie, is pristine, reminding me of alien abduction. Not a toy in sight.

The dog's bed, MIA. Even though it's just been a couple of hours, the whole place smells of dust and discarded lives, as if the abandonment is months old.

Ribbed wet footprints are the only sign that someone lives here. I slip off my sloppy shoes and carry them to the mat in front of the door. Then I retrace my steps, as if my socks will sop up all the wetness.

In the kitchen, I shove a package of popcorn into the microwave, grab two bottles of Carling Black Label, and turn on the TV. TCM has "Witness for the Prosecution." I settle in with my snacks and fall asleep during the courtroom scene. When my phone jangles, I tumble off the couch and land on a sea of kernels. At least the rolling beer bottles are empty.

My eyes blur, lashes wet and sticky. I can't read the screen and the ringtone is just the regular one. "Yeah?" I ground out.

"Lane? It's Vera Donaldson."

Josie's mom? Clearing my throat, I force politeness into my voice. "Uh, hi, Vera." Then I remember that Josie and the boys are there. "Josie and the boys got in okay?"

"Nice of you to show some concern for your family." Her wintery tone makes my face sting like she's sandpapering my skin.

I run a hand over my scalp. When I started going bald, shaving my head seemed like a no brainer. Josie loves it. Well, she did. Now I don't know if she loves anything about me.

I start to respond. "Look…"

She cuts me off.

"We've told Josie she and the boys can have a home with us for as long as they want."

I hear the subtext. She wants Josie to divorce me. My solar plexus throbs like she socked me in the gut. Vera and Ken never approved of her marrying a cop, especially one from Cleveland. They've pushed for years to have us move to small-town Michigan and now's their chance to lure Josie home for good.

How soon can I get to their place in Sherburne? I stub on the enormous boulder of reality. I have a major murder case. Absently, I pick up one of the beer bottles and hurl it against a wall. The crack of the glass is so loud, even Vera hears it.

"What was that? Is someone shooting at you?" She sounds shaken, as if she might even care.

I ignore the question. "Put Josie on."

"She's asleep. And so are the boys. They were exhausted by the time they got here. We told her to come this morning, but she insisted on leaving last night. Six hours, over six." The accusation is sharp and bitter.

"Tell her to call me. I need to get to work."

"That's your whole life. Your family is like a flea on a dog in comparison."

Sweat collects on my back, dampening the clean shirt I've just finished buttoning. Her bitter tone and scolding words up my guilt-o-meter to a million.

I lash out in self-justification. "Six murders," I yell as she hangs up. It doesn't make me feel any better.

A new day, a new murder, but no new leads. Copies of *The Plain Dealer* and *The News-Herald* sit on my desk, trumpeting the failures of the police, of me. There is a certain amount of fear-mongering, although only women named Hollie Mann are being targeted.

I page through the latest report. The fingerprints on the cup are from the victim. The only new piece of evidence is a long blonde hair. We have a hair from one of the other murders, so the lab will do comparison microscopy to see if the two samples are from the same person. DNA tests would take months.

At nine a.m. sharp, I rap my knuckles against the chief's door.

"Don't stand on ceremony, Fairchild." He's leaning back in his chair, rolling back and forth, hands behind his head. I walk into a heat wave. The chief keeps his office at hot-yoga temperature. Drops of sweat roll from the top of my head down my neck.

I drop into the wooden chair on the other side of his fourth-hand wooden desk and stare at cracks and splinters that scar the surface to keep me from having to meet his eye.

"Round the clock surveillance started this morning on Hollie Mann."

I wince. Yeah, there were still many of these women, but I know this one is the wife of wide-receiver Jonathan Mann, a blazing comet in the NFL firmament. Her own career in the TV soap,

"Reaching the Shore," is pretty stellar too. But I'm not convinced.

Nathan's piercing blue eyes lock onto mine. "Look, she's the most high-profile of the women who are left."

"Eight women." I stick out my chin. "The next victim could be any of them."

"We can't offer surveillance on all of them. Besides, Jon called this morning to ask for protection for her."

"He can hire security. This makes us look bad."

With a snort, Nathan runs his fingers through thick, curly gray hair. "You don't turn down Jon Manning. The mayor decided. Live with it."

With a nod of resignation, I turn and walk back to my desk, piled high with initial reports, and dig into the backgrounds of the possible victims.

I stare at the Facebook page of Holly Mann #12 and a chill hits me. She's blonde, chunky, with blotchy skin. Definitely not the soap star, but her bio states that Jonathan Mann is her husband.

* * *

We detail two teams of cops to watch Jonathan Mann's wife. One follows her and the other keeps watch on the mansion they own in Edgewater, on the West Side of the city. Their six-bedroom Georgian is right on Lake Erie.

She calls to complain. The conversation is long, and tedious.

"I don't need the police trailing me around."

"Your husband asked us," I explain, yet again.

"I'll get him to call off the hounds."

But he doesn't.

By the end of the day, Hollie has gone out three times, once meeting friends for lunch, once going to a nursery for plants, and now out for dinner with her husband. No one suspicious has been anywhere near the house.

My concentration shot, I should go home, but I dread the emptiness. No calls or messages from Josie. After I toy with the idea of asking someone out for a drink, I realize I've grown away from my old friends and made no new ones. Shrugging on the sports jacket that has graced the back of my chair since early morning, I pat my pockets for keys. A heavy hand falls on my shoulder and I whirl to face the intruder.

Six foot five and built like a heavyweight wrestler, Damon Edwards is the happiest guy I know. His slow smile calms the jump in my chest. "Scared ya, huh?"

"Jeez, Dozer. Almost dropped dead right there." I point to a permanent stain on the floor we call the Death Spot, even though the reason is lost in the mists of time.

His chortle fills the room. "Don't worry, man. You got lots more years."

My spine slumps at the weight of the comment. Without Josie and the boys, all I've got is the job. Not sure that's enough anymore.

"Goin' to Zone Car, want to come?"

"Sure. Nothing else to do tonight."

The place is full of cops. Not surprising since the bar is really a social club for the Cleveland Police Patrolmen's Association. Golf outings, cigar and comedy nights. It's the go-to place for Cleveland law enforcement. Not a cop? Forget it unless you have a pal to bring you.

After a glance at the Black and White with the Bud Light sign shining over it, we mosey back to the red-topped bar and get a couple of beers. The noise level means no conversation, which keeps my brood going. Brief snips of conversation swirl around us. A sudden lull in the noise allows a strident voice to blare out, "if a bunch of smoke eaters get laid off, are they technically considered fired?" Appreciative laughter swirls around the room.

Dozer leans over and puts his mouth to my ear. "Being a fireman is the only profession where you have to wake up to go home."

I snort.

"That's it, Kid, smile."

I wince at the unfortunate nickname. In school, I was Strong Arm for my pitching prowess. I went to Ohio State on a baseball scholarship but never made it to the majors. As one of the youngest detectives, I got rechristened Kid, and it stuck.

Beers downed, we have a second round, then move out of the crowd into the cool evening air. In the distance, sirens cry out from fire trucks, ambulances, and cop cars. The usual mix of violence, arson, and emergency medical events.

Under a streetlamp, I catch Dozer eying me. "Want some dinner?" He asks.

Now I'm suspicious. Does he somehow know that Josie took off for Michigan with the kids? I haven't told anyone. My stomach growls.

"Yeah, sure. I could use some food."

We head over to XYZ Tavern for a quieter venue, both opting for the brisket-laden Cleveland Cheesesteak with homemade potato chips. Their beer selection is extensive. Dozer decides on draft Fat Tire, and I go for a bottle of North Coast Old Russian Imperial Stout. We clink glass to bottle and take deep swallows.

"Spill, Kid," he says after his second mouthful slides down.

"Spill what?"

"Somethin's wrong. You're walkin' around with your chin dragging the floor." His keen, almost black eyes rake over me.

"Just the Hollie case." Not a lie, just half the truth. The case is smothering me like a wet, weighted blanket.

"Being reluctant to go home is never tied to a case. What else, man?"

Shit. Dozer proves again that he's one of the smartest detectives on the force. My mind spins around several other explanations before I collapse like a punctured balloon.

"Josie took the kids up to Michigan."

"To see her folks?"

I scratch my head. "Yeah."

Eyes narrowed, he finishes his beer and waves a hand at the bartender. "Two more," he tells him. A few minutes of silence later, my second bottle and his new glass are set down. I draw my finger through some spilled beer before the guy's back, handing me a couple of napkins and wiping the table.

"You told me once that she didn't like living here."

"Josie'd like to move back to Sherburne. Safer, she thinks, and a small-town environment for the boys. Her parents have been pushing for it, too. Don't like that she's married to a big city cop."

"Lookin' around?"

I shake my head no. "Not so far, but she's not leaving me much choice if I want to have a marriage."

"My advice..."

I know all about his three marriages and two divorces. With a growl, I hold up my hand. "No advice. I'll figure it out."

We eat our sandwiches and swill the beer. Then he drops me off at my car and I make the lonely drive home.

Next day starts out quiet. My primary activity outside paperwork is walking back and forth for coffee and donuts. Mostly, I wait for Josie to get in touch. Mid-afternoon, my phone rings with her number on the screen. Heart pounding, I swipe to accept.

"Dad?" Mike's five-year-old treble comes over the line.

"Hi big guy. Did your mom call for you?"

"Nah. Her phone was on the counter, and I just asked Siri to call you."

"Smart aleck." Not sure how Josie will feel about him calling me, though. "You and Jamie okay?"

"Yeah, but we miss you."

"I miss you too. Your mom say anything about coming home soon?"

"Nah. And grandma and grandpa keep saying they hope we'll stay here forever."

That's bad. I clear my throat. "Do you want to stay there?"

"Not if you're not here."

"What if I was?"

"That would be cool."

Jaw clenched to keep from shouting, I stay silent.

"Da-a-a-d…"

"Buck up, kiddo." I pause, uncertain about my next move. But when Josie's voice replaces Mike's, she's in control.

"Lane? I can't believe you called."

"I didn't." My protest falls on deaf ears.

"Then why are you on the phone with Mike?"

"Mom, mom, I called." I can picture him pulling at her sleeve. "Don't be mad."

I hear a catch in her throat. "It's okay, Mikey. Just let me talk to your dad."

Mike yells, voice fading as he moves away. "Tell him to come here. We miss him."

"Is that an option?" I can't seem to speak above a whisper.

"You mean for a visit, or permanently?"

"What are you thinking, Josie? Are you asking me to find a job up there?"

Silence.

"Josie?"

"Sorry. I was nodding. Guess you can't see that." Her laugh sounds nervous and self-conscious.

I smile, even though she can't see it. "It's too hard to do this on the phone."

"Come for the weekend." Her soft voice hits me in the chest, sounding wistful with longing.

"I can't..."

She breaks in, voice sour as a lemon. "Work. I know."

"Leave the boys with your folks and come down here."

I sound like a whiny asshole. When did I become that guy?

"No, you need to come here."

"Josie, I have a case with six murders. Can't just drop it and run up to Michigan."

"Of course not." Sudden silence. She's hung up.

Footsteps sound. When I look up, Chief Ellis leans on my desk, a scowl darkening his face.

"Just got a call from Hollie Mann. Let's go."

Two black and whites rumble as they wait for us. I

climb into one and the chief takes the other. They tear out of the lot, sirens howling like demented wolves.

Fifteen minutes later, we walk into Jonathan and Hollie Mann's mansion. Three cars, blue lights rotating, sit at the curb. Someone parked a black Tesla at an angle in the driveway. A visitor. Hollie drives a white Beemer. Jon has a Maserati. Red, of course.

Floodlights eliminate the shadows and heighten the drama of the scene.

As Nate and I walk toward the open doorway, my gut clenches. Maybe he was right after all.

***

The chief hangs in the doorway, talking to a couple of the guys, while I walk into the scene. I expect a repeat of all those other times. What meets our eyes is totally different.

Hollie Mann perches on a gold brocade couch, droplets of blood spattered over a silky white blouse. Her sleeves are shredded, scratch marks on her arms, but no cat is in sight. She screeches out some kind of guttural accusation, but her words are unintelligible.

Another woman slumps on the matching settee across the room, face resting in her hands. The sergeant nods in her direction. "Holly Mann."

The blonde on the couch snarls. "I'm Hollie Mann. That bitch just says she is."

My eyes widen in disbelief as I take in the disheveled woman, brown hair hanging loose from what's left of an updo. Dressed in an oversized long-sleeved aqua T-shirt that says "I Run for Life" and black nylon track pants, she seems almost comatose. Instead of scratches, she has several rents in the shirt with blood seeping through. They may be from the serrated knife lying near her blood-spattered Nikes.

"Did you separate them when you entered, or were they already sitting down?"

My sergeant frowns. "They were rolling on the floor, trying to control the knife, screaming, pulling hair. We pried them apart, but we had to go after them twice more when they went at each other again."

"Why is the knife still there?"

"Last place it landed. We're waiting for the CSI."

"Did you take pictures?"

"Yeah." He holds up his phone.

"Home-invading bitch." Blonde Hollie spits at her visitor. Brunette Holly doesn't respond.

Nathan walks in and states the obvious. "One must be the intended victim and the other the murderer."

Both women raise their heads and shakily point to each other.

On the coffee table midway between them are two cups, both overturned, liquid still dripping onto the Persian rug that covers much of the golden oak hardwood floor.

A square envelope is ripped open, but I can see the typed words "Hollie Mann. Requested free tea sample." The edges of the envelope and the accompanying card are wet on the edges, where the puddle of liquid has wicked into the paper.

Dark Holly keens, the whine plucking at my nerves like untuned guitar strings. I want to yell "shut it," but the thrum of a high-powered engine adds to the external noise. Light Hollie stiffens, then, one vertebra at a time softens into a relaxed posture. Dark Holly tenses and swivels her head, poised for the next threat.

A deep baritone growl reverberates through the room. "Get out of my way." A massive six-five and about 230 pounds, Jon Mann, face red and contorted, shoulders past the officers and pounds over to his wife. "What the hell is going on?" The refrigerator-sized wide receiver collapses onto the couch and snakes an arm around his trembling blonde wife, nuzzling her neck and whispering softly.

"It's okay. No one's going to hurt you now."

Gone is the relaxed posture of a few seconds ago. Shoulders tight, rapidly reddening face, like Mount Etna ready to blow. Tears leak from her eyes, lower lip pinned between impossibly white, even teeth, suddenly stained by a droplet of red.

Jon pulls her closer. "What happened, baby girl?" He strokes her golden blonde head. I can't help wondering if it's natural or a great dye job.

Before she can say anything, his glare spikes into us. A grunt rises from his broad chest. "Fucking assholes. You guys were supposed to protect her. Should've hired some professionals rather than trust you bunch of incompetents. The city should fire you all." He swings his free arm around, fist clenched like he wants to land a punch. "Where the hell were you when this maniac attacked my Hollie? Sleeping or out eating donuts? Sure as hell not doing your job."

Several EMTs rush into the room. Mann has to be pried away from his wife's side so the medics can check her out. Neither woman wants to be taken to the ER, but EMTs clean and bandage wounds, then dole out painkillers. Dark Holly pulls her hair into a neater bun. Light Hollie makes no effort to remedy her disheveled appearance, like she wants to prove she's the victim, not the aggressor.

Nathan moves closer, arms folded across his chest. "We need to take this to the station. Put them in separate cars."

The CSI walks in and establishes authority over the scene. "Okay guys. Move out. I need to take some photos." She turns to Nathan. "Chief, are you taking the women to the station now?"

"Yeah." He strides out but I wait until both Hollies, cuffed and accompanied by an officer, are out. I walk with Jon Mann. "You can ride with me unless you want to take your car and follow us."

"I'll do that. Easier to get Hollie home once we're done."

Where does he get that overblown confidence? The assurance that everything will go his way? This guy is positive that his wife will come home with him. That his fame, and maybe hers, will protect them from any consequences. Maybe it will.

Neighbors line the sidewalk and the street, the comments of the crowd swelling into a wave of noise. A couple of women try to rush up to Hollie, or maybe Holly, but our guys hold them back while we put them into separate cars.

Once each is in the backseat of a vehicle, I climb into a squad car, and we make a procession down to the District 1 station to the sound of yells and catcalls. Once there, each is placed in a separate interrogation room. Nathan and I go to his office to drink coffee and talk strategy.

Our shoes click against the tiled hallway as we move into the small space. We're in an eight-by-ten sound-proofed room. A rectangular table has three chairs. Holly sits on one side, her chair bolted to the floor. Cuffs are attached to the front legs, but we aren't using them. The floor is sealed concrete for easy cleanup.

Nathan and I face her, close to glowering. She shifts uncomfortably. Perfect. The two cameras and the microphone are high on the walls, almost hugging the ceiling, out of viewing range of seated suspects.

"This interview is being recorded." Each word drops from my mouth like a stone.

"Nine-o-one p.m. Present are Commander Nathan Ellis, Detective Lane Fairchild investigating officers."

I'm the lead. "Please state your full name."

"Holly Mann."

"No middle name?'

She shakes her head no.

"Please speak your response for the recording."

"No middle name," she says, breath whistling on a wheeze.

"Please spell it."

"H-o-l-l-y M-a-n-n."

"Is that your legal name?"

Her face creases. "Yeah, why?"

"Did you change it from something else?"

Now she glares. "No. You can check my birth certificate. I've always been Holly Mann."

Nathan asks, "Have you ever claimed to be the wife of Jon Mann?"

Defiantly she crosses her arms. "What if I did? It was just a joke. A friend dared me to put it on Facebook."

Once we collect the rest of the personal info, Nathan says, "In your own words, tell us what happened."

Holly leans forward, elbows on the tabletop, chin resting on fists. This makes her mumble.

"Please speak clearly for the recording," I tell her.

She straightens with a groan. A film obscures her reddened eyes. "About five-thirty, just as I was pulling things out of the fridge for dinner, the phone rang. Unknown number. Usually I just ignore those, but for some reason I answered. She said she was Hollie Mann, and I recognized her voice from the TV." A sniffle interrupts. "Do you have some tissues?"

I open the door and ask the cop at the door to get some. He's back in less than a minute with a newly opened box and a small plastic trashcan. I put them both on the table and push them close to her.

"Thanks." She blows her nose and squeezes the tissue in her fist. Then she rubs a cuff over her swollen orbs. "Anyway, she told me she was scared about being the next victim and that she was reaching out. I was surprised when she invited me over. I guess I was the random Holly that she found. When I got there, we sat and talked for a while, then she offered to make tea."

Holly looks toward the door like she's afraid someone will walk in. I think about snapping my fingers to get her attention, but she blinks, then leans even farther over the table. Her voice is low, confiding. "That's when I got suspicious. She put one cup down and handed me the other. I wondered why she was being so particular if both held the same drink. So I put it on the table next to the other cup and asked her about a picture on the wall. When she looked over at it, I switched the cups."

Nathan nods encouragingly. "Then what?"

She swallows a couple of times. "I think she must have noticed because she didn't pick up her cup. Then she accused me of putting something in her tea. I told her I didn't, but she started cursing and came at me with a knife that she must have hidden between the couch cushions. All I had were my fingernails. Amazing how the fabric shredded. I thought silk was a tough fabric, but this came apart like tissue paper." She gave a nervous giggle. "I have long nails." She displayed claw-like appendages. "Then I just fought as hard as I could to get the knife."

Reaching for another tissue, she says, "The police outside must have heard the shouting because they stormed in. By then I had several cuts and she had scratches all over her arms and face." Reaction sets in, and she starts to shake with sobs.

"Interview concluded at nine-thirty p.m." I turn off the recorder. "We're going to have your statement typed up, Holly. Do you want water while you wait?"

With a gulp, she gets control back. "That would be great. Thanks."

Outside the room, I find someone to bring her a bottle.

"That was quite the tale," Nathan says. "Now let's hear the other side of the story."

The scene in the interview room down the hall contrasts in every way from the one we just left. I'm surprised that Hollie has still made no attempt to neaten up. You'd think being a TV star would make her want to look good. The marks on her face are livid against pale skin. Her mouth twists into a snarl as we enter and go through the same rigamarole that we did with Holly.

"Did you arrest the bitch? Is she locked away?" Her screech is like a murder of crows, scratching my last nerve.

"You are both here for statements. No arrests have been made." Nathan seems calm, except for the tell-tale twitch in his cheek. "Tell us what happened when Holly arrived at your house."

"What, no Miranda?" Her voice is scratchy.

"You haven't been arrested," Nathan says mildly.

"I want my lawyer."

"Again, you haven't been arrested. But you can have a lawyer if you want."

"I want Jon," she shouts.

"Sorry, but he'll be waiting to see you once we have your statement of what happened."

"Where's your notebook?"

"We're recording the interview," I tell her.

Hollie starts to get up, but the chair is too close to the table and the wall, no way for her to move. "Can't sit," she whines. "I need to move around."

"The sooner we get this over with, the sooner you can move." Nathan, rigid on the ladder-back wooden chair, drums his fingers on the table.

"Describe what happened."

'My doorbell rang, and this woman walked in."

"You let her in?"

"The door wasn't locked. She just came in."

Interesting. With cops at the door, unlikely.

"Didn't say a word. Stalked into my living room, plunked herself down on a chair, and ..."

"And what?"

"She waved an envelope around. 'I have your free tea sample,' she said. I told her I hadn't requested any tea. Then she tried to hand me the envelope, but I wouldn't take it, even though my name was typed on the front. She threw it in my face, then sat back down." Twisting her fingers together, she looked every inch the television diva, emoting like her life depended on it.

"Who do you think you are? she said." Hollie wrings her hands. "My jaw dropped. She's some stranger, sitting in my house, asking me who I am. WHO I AM." She gives a weird little laugh.

"What did you say?" I ask.

"Hollie Mann. I'm Hollie Mann."

"No, she says, I'm Holly Mann. You're just a wannabe." Her throat works. "Get out of my house, I screamed. But she just came for me with some kind of bread knife she had in her purse."

"So the serrated knife was hers."

"Of course."

"What about the tea?"

"Oh, that. I guess I forgot. When she first came in and sat down, she handed me the envelope and suggested we taste the tea together. If I liked it, she'd take my order. When I came back, she started haranguing me. Threw the cup and accused me of trying to poison her. While I tried to pick up the broken pieces, she came at me with the knife. Eventually, your officers arrived and broke up the fight. And then you came."

With so many changes in her story, we went back over the details. Hollie's retellings became more and more confused. Finally, we left the room, leaving her alternately making threats and crying for her husband.

"I think we need to go back in there and tell her we know she's the murderer. See how she reacts." Nathan's drooping jowls and the crinkled lines in his forehead signal his distress. He had been so sure.

"Yeah, all topsy-turvy,

"Yeah, I know. Obvious for sure. Maybe we should talk to the husband before going back in there."

"He's pretty sore, but if we can get him to think about her behavior over the last few weeks, there might be some clues. A wedge to open her up.

Jon overwhelms the interview room, both with his size and a whiff of the locker room, that covers the usual smell of disinfectant. We decide to take him up to Nathan's office where there's more air.

The chief turns on the recording equipment and we're off to the races.

Before we can ask him anything, he says, "wife is perfectly normal."

"Did she express any fears about all these murders?"

"Not really. She might have said something once or twice about how weird it was, but she didn't seem worried."

"So you didn't have any conversations?"

"I'm not home all that much, but no."

"And you weren't concerned that a killer might target your wife?"

Jon Mann glowered, his eyes like coals under

shaggy brows. "Can't imagine anyone wanting to hurt that sweet girl."

"So no worries at all."

"Me and Hollie, uh, we have kind of an open marriage. I pay the bills and she looks good on my arm. We don't have a lot of heart to hearts."

"Why did you ask for police surveillance if you weren't worried?"

"Isn't that what a husband is supposed to do?"

We have an officer walk him to the lounge.

Nathan turns to me in disgust. "Crap. This is becoming a French farce."

Nathan's doctorate in English is showing. In the privacy of the office, I drop into comfortable banter. "Hey, don't throw that fancy education at me."

"Should have made you read that stuff when you were in my academy class." He smirks.

He turns serious. "Charge them both with assault." Then he waves me out and slams the door.

Both women are out on bail when we get an early morning call. It's Jon Mann. He's so choked up that I can hardly understand him.

"She's dead. You need to come to the house."

When we get to the Edgewater estate, the scene is much like the last visit. Jon Mann sits on the couch, head in his hands. A dark-haired woman lies on the floor, eyes open, in a pool of blood. There is a bullet hole in her forehead.

"Where's your wife, Mr. Mann?'

He looks at me through spread fingers. "Somewhere in the house. Not sure." His voice is thick and slow.

"Did she shoot Ms. Mann?"

"Guess so. I wasn't here."

"Where were you?"

"Out drinking with some guys. We picked up a couple of ladies. Was out all night. Got home to find this." He gestures at the dead woman.

The door between the kitchen and the living room slams against the wall. Hollie Mann, dressed in a slinky dress, hair artfully curled, face in full war paint, faces us with a Glock held stiffly in front of her. It's like an old-time western gunfight, except it's taking place in a swanky living room, with a dead woman on the floor.

"I told you not to call the cops." The blond woman's high-pitched shriek could shatter glass.

"How did you get her to come back here?" I ask.

"You guys really cramped my style, with all that blue around. Had to think of something else. Her face morphs into a slow, satisfied smile. "I told her that you two were back and needed to see both of us. She was so stupid that she believed me. I shot her from the kitchen door when she moved into the living room."

She had lowered the gun and now she snaps it up, finger on the trigger. "I grew up in Louisiana and my mamma taught me to shoot, after she shot my daddy."

I open my mouth to say something, but Nathan shakes his head.

Out of the corner of my eye, I see the sergeant pull out his service weapon. He's fast, but she's faster. By the time he's squeezed off a shot, she's gotten off two. The sounds could be from anywhere. I feel searing pain and warm liquid oozing down my arm. Hollie Mann has crumpled to the floor, dead. Jon Mann, a surprised expression on his face, has a bullet hole in his chest. As I watch, he topples forward, head hitting the glass-topped coffee table.

Everything is slo-mo video until I black out.

Josie's holding my hand when I open my eyes.

"Can't believe you're here." I croak like an old-guy frog.

"Dozer called and told me what happened."

"Are you back?"

"Just for now. I'm leaving Cleveland."

The pain that hits me is worse than being shot. "No hope, then?"

The pain in her eyes rips into me, but her words are a surprise. "There's always hope."

The door to the room is open and I hear whispering in the hall. Then the pounding of feet, along with shrill cries.

"Dad, dad." Mike and Jamie run up to the bed.

"No jumping." Josie's tone is firm, but I hear a smile underneath.

"Mom says we're leaving Cleveland." Mike is the self-appointed spokesman.

I push a button on the remote lying by my right hand. The bed raises up while I gaze at the wide eyes of my two precious boys. Once I'm sitting up, I put the solemn question.

"How do you feel about leaving? Do you want to live in Michigan?"

They look at each other, silently communicating.

Mike puffs out his chest. "You're going too, right?"

I look at Josie and she shrugs.

"Do you want me?" I mouth the words just to her.

"If you'll leave Cleveland, yes."

"Guess we're moving, boys."

Their cheers bring tears to my eyes, and I leave Cleveland, putting eight dead Hollie Manns behind me.

Vanishing Trees

Bay

I look out of the kitchen window on a late September afternoon and see scraped, empty ground where trees should parade their autumn colors. Instead, landscape scarred from building a new house, stretches back to overgrown acres nearby and reminds me of what our property used to look like.

The faint track of the unpaved road that leads from the wilderness glimmers in the fading sunshine toward the highway and I turn from the naked yard to check the stew simmering in the crockpot.

Ring, ring.

Greg? Calling to say he'd be late? I wipe my hands on the dish towel tucked into my apron and move to the cell phone that sits next to the deep stone sink.

Unknown number.

Being married to a former cop, I always answer. Never know when bad news might arrive.

"Hello?"

"Mrs. Musgrave?"

The gruff, gravelly voice sounds familiar. An echo from the past? Not surprising in the small town of Shelburne, Michigan. Where I grew up. Turned my back on. And had now returned.

"This is Ms. Bishop, Bay Bishop."

"M'kay. Forgot you didn't change your name." Somehow disapproval. seeps through the silence that follows.

Irritation makes my skin prickle. "And you are?"

"Quint Wrightman. Your husband home?"

High school memories flood in. Quint, a weaselly looking kid, aspired to lead the bike team. Not that he had a chance with Greg Musgrave, superstar cyclist, on the team.

He'd pursued his dream with the tenacity of Wile E. Coyote. Several times, he and his brother Marcus tried to force Greg off the road during races. Greg was as crafty as Roadrunner and always eluded danger in those days.

Why was he calling? If it was about bikes, he could have called the shop. "I remember you. From school."

No comment. Maybe I'm not even a distant memory. Obliterated after I turned him down for prom and went with Greg.

Returning my attention to the phone, I say, "No. He's at the shop. Can I give him a message? Or do you want to call him at WonderWheels?"

"We have everything he wants in stock."

"I don't know what you're talking about."

"Trees. Shrubs. For your new palace."

I glance out the window at the raw land. With a cafe to run at WonderWheels and a wine bar at Alleyn's Bistro, I've left this to Greg.

The spectacular view from the front showcases the lake. But the ground is bare. We could wait for volunteer beach grass and trees to take hold, but Greg doesn't want to wait.

When I argue for letting the land come back on its own, he says, "Developers are buying up land around us. I want to set boundaries and ensure our privacy before developers build more houses."

Trees, shrubs, grass. After having owned a restaurant, being swindled by my late husband, and starting my life over again, I realize we can do this.

My watch says four p.m. Greg should be back by five-thirty.

"Six?"

Key taps to convey he's a busy man. "Sure. You live on Stoney End Road, right?"

"Right at the end. Only house there. See you."

In the ensuing silence, I say, "Siri. Call Greg."

"Hey, Greg. Quint Wrightman is coming over at 5:30. Don't be late."

Greg

Cycling up the steep drive, I see Bay's car. Even with a bumper barrier in place, she avoids parking in the garage ever since she hit the back wall a month ago. I bring the bike up on the porch and lean it against the wall.

Silence as I rattle the doorknob. No click of dog nails against the hardwood. No 80s rock seeping out from the stereo as I unlock and push open the door. No bright voice to welcome me.

My cop instincts kick in. Even though I may have taken ridiculously early retirement from the force after injuring my knee in a takedown last year, my cop instincts are still ingrained. I reach for a nonexistent gun as I edge forward.

My hand gropes for a nonexistent holster. Internal laughter shakes my shoulders. Don't even own a gun anymore. Toyed with keeping it, but Bay didn't want guns in the house. She had a point. If I locked it up in a gun safe, getting it in an emergency wasn't practical. And I don't go to the range very often these days.

A checklist runs through my head. No signs of a break-in. No unfamiliar vehicles. Front door locked. Logical answer—Bay has taken Ace for a run. I go inside. Ace's leash hangs on the coat rack, but if they're running, Bay wouldn't bother.

My stomach growls, reminding me I missed lunch, and a cheese sandwich sounds good. With Quint coming in half an hour, she won't be long.

When they get back a few minutes later, a little wet and very sandy, Bay sits on the porch steps, pouring little heaps out of her shoes, watching me munch from a plate of cheese and crackers. Ace circles, panting, his soft brown eyes begging for a treat.

"Want some?" I hand Bay the plate and dig into my pocket for his ever-present biscuits.

"Just get home?" She asks, eyeing the caked mud guards on my bike.

"Few minutes ago. Figured you and Ace were running."

She pops a cracker in her mouth, then raises a brow. "Quint Wrightman? Why didn't you tell me you'd hired him?"

"Does it matter? Doubted you'd even remember who he was. And dad said he has the best selection of trees in the area."

She looks at Ace, who rubs against her knees, creating little heaps of sand. "Why didn't he check things out?"

"No time. I couldn't be here. And letting him wander around the property alone, well, no. I just gave him measurements and a general idea, listed the trees and bushes we wanted, took some photos, and shot the whole thing off in an e-mail."

Bay runs up the stairs, Ace on her heels. You'd think he was her dog, not mine.

The doorbell chimes.

When I open the door, Quint's sour face greets me before he resets into a smile. Marcus, the perpetual shadow, hovers behind him.

I grin. "Hey Quint, Marcus, great to see you."

He looks as far from a successful designer as I can imagine, with his dirt-stained plaid shirt, grimy overalls, and mud-clogged work boots. A sweat stained Detroit Tigers cap, brim to the back, has created an angry red line in his forehead.

Marcus is his carbon image.

"Slip your shoes off and come in."

We take seats in the living room.

Ace trots in, sniffs at Quint's pant legs, then moves to Marcus. Inspection done, he stretches, and lies down at my feet.

"What kinda mutt is it?" Marcus asks.

"Portuguese Water Dog." I reach down and fondle his ears.

"Fancy pure bred, huh? Not into that myself." Quint doesn't hide his scorn.

"He was a rescue," I say, listening for Bay's footsteps.

A minute later, she walks in, a glass of water in her hand.

"Hi Quint, Marcus. You two don't look that different. Still Tweedledee and Tweedledum."

Marcus laughs. "Twenty years, forty pounds."

With a shrug, my beautiful wife seats herself in her favorite armchair. "Tell us about the trees."

Bay

My eyes run over Quint, from the toes showing through his socks to the hair sticking out the back of his cap. He hasn't shaved in a few days and his stubble looks more unkempt than fashionable. Marcus is his doppelgänger.

As the spokesperson, Quint clears his throat, once, twice, three times.

"Need some water?"

"Nah. Just warming up."

A sly grin curves his lips, and his eyes run up and down my body like I'm for sale.

"Did you get the trees I wanted?" Greg taps his leg with the long fingers I've always loved.

"Copper beech, purple beech, black and red oaks, white and paper birch, jack pine, green ash, silver maple—"

Greg holds up a hand. "The varieties of Japanese maples?"

Marcus frowns. "Decorative but, well..."

"We like them. Glorious colors. Being shorter, they're great for proximity to the house. Live a long time."

Greg shifts back and forth. "Back to the matter at hand. The shrubs for the front—Harry Lauder's Walking Stick, coral bark willows, and the red dogwood shrub?"

Quint sighs. "Yeah, some of each. And ten varieties of Japanese maple, different colors, grow fifteen to twenty feet."

I break in. "How many trees altogether?"

Quint looks down at the tablet on his knee. "Thirty-five trees, ten each of the shrubs, except the twisted hazel. Only two of those."

"And the cost?"

"Including labor?"

"Yeah, the total," Greg says with a growl.

"Trees, except for the Japanese maples, are all about ten feet. We're looking at $37,500 for the trees, but I'm giving you a fifteen percent discount for volume, so $31, 875 plus six percent tax."

"And the shrubs?"

"Total minus discount, plus tax is $2860."

Greg and I look at each other. Who knew land-scaping would cost so much?

"M'kay," Greg says. "When can you start?"

Marcus must be the scheduler, because now he consults his pad. "Tomorrow's Friday, and we have a big job next week. How about the following Monday?"

"And how many days?"

"Shouldn't take longer than a week to complete the prep, mulching, and planting."

Marcus taps a finger on his tablet. "What are your plans for watering? We can put in water troughs around each one."

"Is that extra? I ask.

"Ten bucks apiece."

"Fine," Greg says.

Marcus makes a note.

"Do we give you a down payment now?" I ask.

Quint looks up. "Half now, half when the job's done. If you have an air printer, I can run the contract and you can write a $16,500 check to Wrightman Landscaping.

"You should be able to connect from your tablet." I'd turned off the password protection. As soon as I hear the printer finish, I finger the app and reset it.

While Greg pulls out the checkbook from his shirt pocket and unclips the pen, I go into the office and grab the printed contract. Greg's signature is clear, mine a wavy line with a couple of bumps.

Quint and Marcus' eyes gleam with satisfaction. A

frisson runs through me. I almost hear a whisper of "sucker." Did they overcharge us? Greg didn't get any estimates, so who knows?

I hear their voices mix with laughter as Greg walks them to the door. The truck revs and gravel sprays as they leave. Only then does my husband shut the door and snick the lock.

"That's a lot of money." My voice shakes.

"Worth it," Greg says. "That bare ground is an insult to the house. And it will keep the wild area behind from encroaching. We just have to plan the party."

Two Mondays later, a truck full of equipment and a big land mover show up to level the ground and prepare the sandy soil. By the following Friday, all the trees and other plantings are in green plastic water wells around them. The landscaping softens the property and removes the rawness of a new build.

The Saturday spread in the Sherburne Gazette features photos of our front and back yards, showcasing the new planting. Quint and Marcus are marketers.

Townspeople come by. When Greg gets home from the shop, gawkers are everywhere. The entire town knows about our tree preserve. I'd never had time to message him to expect company.

With a wry smile, he says, "Beach barbecue, everyone? The festivities continue until early Sunday morning, resulting in a late brunch.

Bay

Monday afternoon, Greg is at the shop when Marcus arrives to pick up the second check. He'd balked when I suggested he wait until Greg got home.

"Sorry, I'm busy later."

"Can't I send it to you? Or drop it by the office tomorrow morning?"

Silence and I'm talking to dead air. He hung up on me.

An engine roar heralds his arrival forty minutes later. No truck today. Marcus pulls up in a fancy red sports car. I hear his tires scrape the gravel.

I open the door a crack, the check dangling from my fingers. He pushes against the heavy carved wood and opens the aperture as wide as he can while pulling the slip from my fingers.

"Great advertising for us."

"The world was here on Saturday."

"Phone's been ringing off the hook, people wanting appointments."

With a grin, he surveys me from my toes to my face, lingering on my torso for far too long.

"Still think you're in high school?"

"Nah, my tastes have matured, and you've ripened."

I give him a level stare, my tone flat. "Tell your brother we're happy with the look of the landscaping."

"Quint said to ask you to put up a review on our website."

"I'm sure Greg will be glad to do it."

Then I step back and shut the door in his face, turn the lock, and lean back against the solid wood, taking deep breaths to calm my racing heart.

Standing on the porch, he yells. "You look a lot better than you did in high school. Couldn't imagine what Quint saw in you then. But if you ever decide that Greg's not man enough, call me. I'm between girls at the moment."

His boots clump down the walk and I hurry to the back porch, ready to replace his sleazy innuendo and seek serenity amid Japanese maples.

Greg

I check the new plantings each afternoon, feeling a thrill every time I see the stunning array. The new plantings need careful attention. On Wednesday, my jaw drops. Three black holes gape, water wells crushed, stakes cracked, hessian straps cut off.

Heart beating like a kettle drum, I shout. "Bay."

Ace barks, dancing around my feet.

"What's the matter?"

I point to where a purple beech and two red maples had been.

"Looks like we have a tree thief. Bring my camera. I need to take some photos."

Minutes later, Bay comes down the deck stairs and gives me the camera.

I fiddle with the settings while she asks, "Why steal trees?"

"Big business. National forests are the most common target. Thieves chop them down, cut them up, and sell the wood for timber. Especially desirable specimens for furniture and carved objects go for the most money. Lately, reports of trees being dug up and carted away are increasing. Steal a tree, sell it to someone else. Pure profit."

Ace strolls over to the holes, curious.

I take pictures of him by near the empty spaces.

"Hey, Acey. Come here." His head comes up. I snap my fingers, and he jogs back to the porch. I take pictures of the paw prints.

"Good boy. Don't want you contaminating the scene," I tell him as he crunches on a biscuit.

Bay calls from the doorway. "I notified the police. They're sending someone out."

My only thought is becoming a laughingstock to the Sherburne PD and enduring endless jokes.

"Unbe-leaf-able."

"When did he twig to it?"

Sirens herald several blue and whites. Bay and I stand in the drive as I reach the end of this self-created litany.

Newly promoted sergeant Macie Collier snickers as she comes over.

"Is this the crime scene? Don't see any gravediggers out here."

"In the back." I start around the house, stopping at the deck.

Contemplating the empty holes where trees had been, she says, "Can't believe they could do this without someone hearing."

"Both at work."

"Macie?" Lane Fairchild bawls from inside. "You out there?"

"Yeah. Looking at the scene."

"CSI will be here in a few."

"Doubt they'll need to do much." Macie laughs as Lane walks out, stretches his neck, and stares.

"Looks like the scene's already compromised."

"Ace. Couldn't stop him when he came out with me."

"I think Falynne will be able to distinguish between paw prints and human footprints." Lane's matter-of-fact demeanor belies the laughter in his eyes.

"We'll need your shoes for comparison." Macie's tone is snarky, like she thinks someone has one-upped me.

"Haven't been out there, but I'll change into another pair. Want to come with and supervise? You can bag them as evidence."

She scowls. "I'll send a patrolman."

Lane winks at me.

"And why are you here, Lane?" Her voice swings between a whine and a growl.

"Checking up on my old pal, Greg."

Another car crunches up the drive. A door slams, and my dad comes puffing around the side of the house. Must have been listening to his police scanner. After a quick glance, he says, "Think it's a prank?"

"You mean my cop friends could have done this?"

With a wince at Lane's scowl, Dad backtracks. "No, of course not. Maybe one of the bike clubs?"

"I can picture a line of riders balancing ten-foot trees on road bikes."

Lane interrupts. "No security back here?"

"I have security for the house. And lights in the yard. Now I'll have to put in cameras," I grumble.

Another vehicle grinds on the gravel. Falynne's here. She may only be about five feet and look like she's twelve, but her competence is frightening and when she takes control, every cop on the force is her willing slave.

She hauls a big case of forensic gear. "Good thing you have a big driveway, Greg."

Braids swinging, she stands, hands on hips, scanning the scene. "What's behind the property?"

"A strip of uncleared land with an access road to the beach lot, then the highway."

"People parking in the lot can reach your place via the access road?"

I shake my head. "No. There's a fence, and the gate locks. Anyone going to the beach has to walk down the beach access road."

"How did the landscapers get in?"

"Gave them a key." So stupid.

Moving toward the gaping holes, Falynne says, "Okay, guys. I'm going to start taking photos. You may as well go inside. I'll give a shout if I need anything."

A little later, she comes in, knocking mud off her boots before slipping them off on the mat. "Lots of tire tracks in the wooded area behind your property. I'm taking casts, but they're pretty muddled."

"The landscapers had their equipment back there."

"Who'd you have?" Lane asks.

"Quint and Marcus Wrightman."

Lane turns to his sergeant. "Macie, take a couple of guys to Wrightman Landscaping and get casts of their tires. Their work boots. If there's mud, take samples. That okay with you, Falynne?"

"Yup. Thanks."

Bay

After the weekend spread, this is big news in Sherburne and the story fills the front page of the Gazette. The Detroit Free Press and the Chicago Sun-Times pick it up as their joke story of the day. Soon our stolen trees are on Twitter, Instagram, and dancing on TikTok.

Letters to the editor claim there is a tree mafia or offer wacky advice like bear traps, surrounding the trunks with flypaper, or painting the trees with glue.

The police make no progress in the three days

following the theft. Greg broods over the holes in the yard. He's stayed out of the shop, working on some bike designs at home when Quint calls.

Greg turns on the speaker. His face clouds as we listen.

"You get in touch with your insurance company?"

"Nothing much will happen until the investigation either comes to a dead end or the police charge someone. Just in case the trees are recovered."

"You want me to replace them?" Quint's voice quivers with glee.

"Pay for them all over again?"

"Yeah, but when the insurance pays out, you'll get all that money back. We can't plant much longer this season."

I start to protest, but Greg says, "Okay. Let's do it."

Quint and I gaze at the new trees.

"You takin' precautions?" He asks, taking a handkerchief out of his back pocket to wipe his face.

"I called a forester to get the trees marked, but he can't come until next week. We're having cameras installed, too. They'll be in by next Friday."

Three more trees vanish the following night.

***

Greg

Falynne's back, peering at the empty holes. Evidence collected, she slips off the nitrile gloves and her shoes before coming into the house. Lane, Macie, Bay, and I guzzle lemonade, pretending we aren't eager for the results.

"The footprints appear to match the previous theft. The tire tracks from the truck too. We'll check them for a match. Since they're new, we can disentangle them from the landscapers' truck."

"But they were back to replace the missing trees."

My heart sinks. "No other evidence?"

She gives me a bright smile and holds up a coin envelope. "Fibers left on one of the trees near the truck. We also know there are two perpetrators. The depth of the prints tells me that the two individuals, probably men, have similar weight and build."

Two men, with marked similarities. I glance over at Bay. She stares back, an idea dawning on her face.

"Do you think..." she blurts as I say, "I wonder if..."

"Okay, let's have your new harebrained idea." Lane's grin belies the insult.

"What if Quint and Marcus Wrightman..."

Bay, excited, breaks in. "Just what I was thinking."

"Why would they?" Macie frowns, unconvinced.

"I can think of two good reasons," I counter.

"First, they know about the trees..."

"So did everyone in town," Macie interjects.

I favor her with a glare. "And they have means. They used the back access road.

"What would they do with them?"

"Either sell them to someone else or resell them to us."

"And the other reason?" Macie resists this solution.

"Quint and I were rivals in school over the bike club. He wanted to date Bay, but she was already with me."

"We know how that turned out," Bay says, sotto voce.

I ignore the reminder of how I drove us apart. "Maybe he's been nursing a grudge. Seizes the opportunity for payback."

Lane rubs the top of his bald head, then moves his hand down to his neck. "Could be you're the latest victim."

"There've been other tree thefts?"

"A few. One offs and no clues to the perpetrators. If it's them, they're moving into the big time."

"We need a plan to catch them in the act."

Greg

No surprise Quint offers to plant more trees the day after the theft. I tell him I want to wait a few days to decide because, though the insurance company would reimburse me, the immediate effect would drain my bank account.

"Let me know. The season is ending soon. We've sold most of the trees."

Two nights have gone by since the last theft.

Two nights of staking out the backyard. The cop cars are out of sight. We positioned two guys where we expect the thieves will park. Their task is to observe and then tail the thieves, but not to confront them if they appear.

Lane, Macie, and I huddle in the darkness of the unlit porch.

Temperatures have dipped and the enclosed porch harbors a deep chill. The moon's a sliver, not bright enough to bathe the yard in light.

Bay made us a thermos of coffee and I've just refilled the mugs when we hear muffled footsteps through the mulch. Voices whisper out of the darkness.

A couple of shots ring out and the lights in the yard die. Everything is silent with expectation.

"Must be out," a voice whispers.

"Told you, there's a night bike ride from WonderWheels."

Two LED lanterns cast a glow on the ground. With a clatter, a shovel hits one of them.

"Be careful," a gravelly voice cautions.

All we hear is the sound of shovels scraping against the earth.

A whisper comes out of the dark. "How many are we taking tonight?"

"Five. I already have a buyer for the specimen birches. I'll just tell Greg I can't get any more this season."

Grunting ensues.

A faint cry drifts on the wind, owl-like rather than human. "Don't let it crash."

Straining to see in the poor light, I watch a tree being lowered to the ground.

"Good idea to plant them so they're easy to dig up again."

"I know what I'm doing. This ain't our first rodeo."

Cackle. Snort.

"Go," Lane yells, pulling his Glock.

We run forward as other cops run up from the back.

Macie and a patrolman cuff them, using the element of surprise to their advantage.

Quint and Marcus spew epithets all the way to the squad cars.

At the arraignment, the brothers face charges of grand larceny.

A prank, Quint claims. Swears they would have returned the trees. Meanwhile, the police investigate similar thefts spanning a decade. As evidence pours in, they aren't talking.

Can't wait to see them in court.

Dead in the Alley (a sample)

Sherburne, Michigan

Derrick Anderson walked out the back door of the restaurant kitchen, pulling out a pack of cigarettes and his lighter. His wife, Bay, didn't like him smoking but he definitely needed one, or three, to be the genial host this evening.

He didn't mind that his day started at 3:00 a.m. The quiet in the restaurant soothed him and he forgot everything while he baked all the bread and prepared the desserts for the evening, maybe even try out a new idea or two. Then he'd take a nap before helping Bay set up the tables for the dinner service.

Today had been fraught. When he got back late in the day, he'd had it out with Vince about the missing cases of wine and, despite the man's protestations of innocence, gave him his notice. Then he had a call from Wally Volker, their financial backer. Derrick needed to break Wally's stranglehold on his balls before he left for a new life in the Maldives. A friend there had offered him the chance to manage the four themed restaurants at a new luxury resort. Besides the career boost, diving and surfing made the whole package irresistible. Why had he thought that Michigan would be a good place to escape his New York problems?

Just now, he'd had an argument with the sous chef, Ellen Paschen, and needed to cool off. He dropped the cigarette butt and ground it viciously with his toe when he heard the roar of a motorcycle revving up...

Bay

The back door had slammed on the suffocating kitchen atmosphere. Derrick going out to the alley for a smoke, even though he knew I wanted him to stop. Ellen, our sous chef, glowered over a lemon sauce. Vince, our sommelier, leaned sulkily against the back door. Leaving them to brood on their own, I did a last-minute check of the fifteen tables for the first dinner service. We were booked for both seatings.

As the only fine-dining establishment in Sherburne, we realized early on that having set dining times worked better than a constant stream of customers. People from all over the area, both locals and tourists, had embraced the concept and our restaurant over the last two years. Our dream of creating a destination restaurant in my Northern Michigan hometown had become a reality.

We renovated a disused 1889 brewery located on the edge of town, close to the highway, creating the perfect space for our upscale restaurant. The venture cost more money than we planned, so we found a guy in Detroit who specialized in funding start-ups.

Rubbing my back as I straightened up for the last time, I looked with pride at the dining room. We had wanted an upscale but rustic feel. Snowy white tablecloths were covered with Inox hammered stainless-steel silverware; the handles designed to look like twigs. Handmade pottery that looked like the lakeshore in blues, greens, purple, and sand, came from Claybanks Pottery, down the road in New Era. Deep forest green napkins were folded into double stars, part of our signature look. In a few short years, Derrick and I had managed to make a success of our move from the frenzy of the New York City restaurant scene to my hometown of Sherburne, Michigan.

Above the dark paneled wainscoting, we had exposed brick darkened from years of brewing. Rough hardwood flooring stained black, and a pressed-tin ceiling enhanced the antique look. We festooned one exposed brick wall with enormous prints. Derrick matched his brilliance as a pastry chef with a natural gift for photography. His award-winning pictures illustrated our cookbook, *Sherburne Bistro: American Classics.*

Breathing deeply, I drank in the scent of grouse that permeated the space. Today marked the opening of grouse season in Michigan and our special prix fixe menu featured a British-themed dinner for tonight. Derrick's friend, Jason, and my brother, Toby, went out hunting a couple of days ago, giving me time to hang them before plucking and cleaning them. I had brined them using a mixture of hard apple cider, fresh orange juice and peel, herbs, and spices for four hours. Then I put a sprinkling of bay leaves into the pan, giggling a little while I brushed olive oil over their fragrant flesh. My parents loved trees in the laurel family and named the three of us girls Laurel, Bay, and Olivia—guess they couldn't stomach Olive. They told us that they expected all their children to be crowned with success, but maybe my capricious fairy godmother thought with a name like Bay, fate meant me to be a chef.

Looking at the array of oysters heaped up, ready to be opened, I reached for one and rubbed my thumb over the shell, admiring the geologic pattern. Then I picked up the curved oyster knife sitting nearby. Prying it open, I examined the flesh clinging to the pearlescent interior, then lowered my nose to inhale the scent of the ocean, briny and enticing. I loosened the flesh and slid the mollusk into my mouth, savoring the salty, mineral flavor. I had to walk away, before I ate them all.

We'd had a special menu printed up for the dinner, which I laid carefully on top of each plate, planning to offer it once a week through the end of the year.

Sherburne Bistro
The Glorious Grouse Dinner

Basket of Breads

Starter

Oysters with champagne mignonette

Rhode Island Moonstone 🦪 Maine Glidden Point 🦪 Belon 🦪 Pemaquid 🦪 Chesapeake Bay Olde Salt 🦪 Washington State Shigoku 🦪 Kumamoto 🦪 California Pacific Gold

Salad

Frisée with foie gras, pear, and cherries dressed with oil and sherry vinegar

Main Course

Whole roasted grouse napped with a wild cranberry game sauce

Pilaf of rice and mixed mushrooms garnished with chopped hazelnuts

Sweet and sour red cabbage

Dessert Selection

Nigella Lawson's Chocolate Guinness Cake
Cambridge Burnt Creme
Sticky Toffee Pudding
Cranachan
Treacle tart

Cheese Plate

White Stilton with mango and ginger

Colton Bassett Stilton
Montgomery's Farmhouse Cheddar
Parmigiano Reggiano DOP
Water biscuits made in-house

Hearing Ellen's bad-tempered instructions to the prep cook, I went back into the open kitchen with its Wolf range and two freestanding ovens—a deck oven for breads and a convection oven for pastry. When I heard the sound of a motorcycle revving up outside over Ellen's harangue, I saw the door to the alley propped open. Vince must have gone out to join Derrick in a last cigarette.

The skid, the scream, and the sound of breaking glass got my attention. Vince barreled through the door and grabbed me by the shoulders. "You don't want to go out there, Bay."

I tried to push around him. "Why not?"

"Oh my God. Derrick," he choked out, eyes rolling. "It's...it's hit-and-run. Call 911."

"An ambulance?"

He shook his head. "Too late for that. Just have the police come."

Vince dropped heavily to a chair and clutched the sides of his head with shaking hands. When he finally looked up at me, rivulets ran down his cheeks. He kept clearing his throat, but no words came out.

I stumbled across the room to the phone at the reservation stand and dialed 911 and gave them the small amount of information I had. They told me to stay on the phone until someone arrived. Only a few minutes elapsed before I heard the sirens. I informed the dispatcher, hung up, then went back to Vince. He watched as a team of police officers exited the two squad cars. An ambulance pulled up behind them.

Putting a hand on his shoulder, I tried to shake him to attention.

When he turned to look at me, tears still dripped from his red-rimmed, swollen eyes. "Hit by a motorcycle. When I got out there, the rider peeled out. Left him there, surrounded by trash, broken and bleeding. I rushed over but he... he... died. Never said a word."

Tremors hit me. I sank to my knees as the sound of screaming enveloped me. "Dead, dead, no, no, no." I wanted the voice to shut up, leave me to mourn. My voice. And I couldn't stop the screaming or the tears as I curled on the floor in a ball of despair.

I don't know how long I lay there, helpless to do anything more than cry. By the time the police swarmed in, Vince had helped me to my feet and got me into a chair. With the backdoor open, late afternoon sun lit the scene, but my vantage point didn't allow me to see Derrick.

I looked down and my watch glinted back at me. We were supposed to open in a little over an hour. Vince hovered in the corner. I called out. "Vince, could you put a sign on the door and start calling people with reservations? Tell them we're closed."

He nodded and walked toward the reservation stand.

"Mrs. Anderson?" A policewoman stood in the doorway.

"Bishop," I croaked.

She checked me out, her lips pursed, eyes narrowed. "O-kay, Ms. Bishop." Her arms were folded across her chest. "I'm sorry for your loss."

Fresh tears welled but I wiped them away as I sniffled a few times. "Thanks." I could barely push the word out.

"Did you see anything?"

My head bobbed a negative.

"I wouldn't let her see, Macie," Vince yelled from the dining room, sounding both protective and belligerent.

My head snapped up and I stared at her. Macie Collier had gone to school with my younger sister, Livvy. Even though I had been back for more than two years, I didn't realize that Macie had joined the police force here. And how the hell did Vince know her?

"I thought you moved to Detroit."

She flinched at my tone. "Didn't like the big city life. I came back about a year ago. Guess you didn't notice." Hands on hips, she said, "You came back too."

"Livvy didn't say anything."

She shrugged. "We don't hang out much these days. Our lives kind of moved on different tracks after she went to Pratt." She cleared her throat.

"Are you going to question me now?"

"Just waiting for Detective Fairchild. He'll be in charge of the case."

I stood and rolled my shoulders. "Do I need to ID the body?"

"Not necessary. The scene is pretty gruesome. Just as well that Vince kept you from looking."

Gruesome. What did that mean? I slumped back into the chair, my lungs working hard to get in any air.

"I'm sure the detective will explain everything," she said.

Macie leaned against the open kitchen door watching us, occasionally turning her head to look out as the police team scoured the alley for evidence. Then a man in a plaid sports jacket loomed up behind her. "Excuse me, Officer Collier." She stepped aside. "Ms. Bishop? I'm Detective Fairchild."

I looked past Macie as she moved to let Fairchild pass through. A few inches taller than my five five, shaven head, dark eyes, and stubble dotting his jaw. He closed the door, scratched his cheek, and leaned against the big worktable.

"Not a typical hit-and-run. Your husband looked like he might have been targeted. Whoever hit him deliberately ran over the body a couple of times."

I could picture Derrick, lying in the alley, his body mangled, blood everywhere. My gag reflex kicked in, along with my overactive imagination, and I barely made it to the large commercial sink, pushing the dishwasher as I doubled over. When I wobbled to my feet, Ellen handed me a glass of water. Swishing warm water around cleared out the sour taste in my mouth.

I put down the glass and stared at the floor, my

mind a whirl of conflicting ideas. I couldn't understand why anyone would want him dead. True, he could be prickly, but that didn't get you killed. People came to the restaurant for his desserts. None of that added up to being murdered by motorcycle.

"Could it have been mistaken identity?"

Macie snorted. "He's dressed in his chef clothes, minus the tall hat."

"Toque," I said absently. Fairchild glared and Marcie's mouth snapped shut.

I stared at the grouse and began putting plastic wrap over the pans. Seeing my sous chef, slack-eyed, leaning against a counter, I called out, "Ellen. Start putting these back in the cooler." She jerked to attention, then robotically came over and picked up the pan, immediately dropping it on the floor.

"S-S-Sorry." Her face drooped, a study in misery.

I motioned to the commis. "Just get it cleaned up." Then I went back to covering the birds. Ellen picked up another pan and shoved it in the refrigerator.

Fairchild cleared his throat as he gazed around the kitchen at the small audience.

"Do you have an office?"

As we walked out of the kitchen and down a short corridor, he said, "Are you contacting your customers?"

I looked over at the edge of the desk, then nodded.

"Don't give out any information. Just say unforeseen circumstances."

"I'll go tell Vince. He's making the calls."

When I got back, Fairchild sat behind the desk, fingers tented under his chin.

I bristled at the way he had co-opted my space. Then reality socked me in the eye. I collapsed into the chair.

"Did your husband have any enemies you know of?"

My lips pursed while I thought over his question. Derrick fit in surprisingly well for a big-city boy, learning to fish and hunt. He hung out with my brother and his friends. Joined Rotary and went to the lunches.

"Not here. We moved from New York to open the restaurant, but I don't think he had any enemies who would have followed him."

"Why did you choose Sherburne?" He leaned the chair back, his tone conversational.

"I'm from here. We wanted to open our own place, and Northern Michigan is much less expensive than New York. Less competition for fine dining too. We could see a better future."

Fairchild's phone beeped and he gave me a look that said get out. "Excuse me, but I need to take this."

I walked out the door, leaving it slightly ajar, and leaned against the wall. He mumbled something, but I couldn't catch the words.

Then he called out. "Ms. Bishop, you can come back in."

He started to speak as I crossed the threshold. "The ambulance is going to take him now."

Then the office door slammed against the wall as my dad walked in and glared at Fairchild. "Bay. You okay?"

"Dad?"

"Why are you here, Mr. Bishop?" Fairchild asked with icy politeness.

"Vince called me. I'm going to take you home, Bay. You can find her at the Bishop Inn, Detective Fairchild."

I almost laughed at that description. Bishop Inn hadn't been my home for almost two decades. Even though I'd agreed to move back to Sherburne, our uneasy truce kept me on edge. My parents fell in love with Derrick; I felt like the outsider. My dad arriving on the scene threw me.

Fairchild's lips twisted at my dad's pronouncement, but he managed to say, "Fine. We're still working the scene, and the medical examiner has to look at the body. I'll be at the Inn sometime in the next few hours. In the meantime, may I use your office, Ms. Bishop? I'll let you know if we need to remove anything."

My eyes searched the office, but I didn't see anything incriminating. "What would you need to remove?"

"We'll need to go through your business records and check the computer. I'll need the password. I can have an officer work here, but we'd rather take everything back to the station."

"Get it later, Fairchild. Can't you see she's in no state to talk to you?" Fairchild brushed past my dad. I tried to stand up again, but my legs wouldn't hold me and I dropped back to the chair. Dad leaned down and kissed my cheek, then pulled out a handkerchief to mop my face. Deciding that today, my family could be my refuge, I stood and let him put his arm around me. "Let's go, kiddo. Let your staff close the place up."

I scanned the dining room. The kitchen had emptied out and everyone stood around, looking at me. My eye caught on one of the special grouse dinner menus. I picked it up, tore it into pieces and watched the tiny scraps flutter to the floor like snow. Ellen, our sous chef, made shooing motions. "Go home with your dad, Bay. We've got this."

I threw her a grateful look as my dad led me out.

A siren stuttered, then blared. The ambulance. I swallowed down the bile that rose in my throat as I thought of Derrick, encased in a body bag, being loaded into the meat wagon. We'd been together for ten years, married for six. We were a team. I couldn't imagine how I would be able to go on without him.

At the Ready (a sample)

Chapter 1

One secret of success in life is for a man to be ready for his opportunity when it comes.—Benjamin Disraeli

Chicago, February 2014
Micki

Today's the day. Best suit. Flawless hair and makeup. Every inch the polished senior associate. No four-inch heels. Frederick Lanscombe, managing partner, is a little sensitive about his height. At five seven, stilettos bring me close to six feet. I tower over him. Not a good look since this meeting is the crucial first step in the campaign to be the next partner at Miller, Lanscombe, Baker, Francis, Masters, and Hargrove.

The door to the small conference room is wide open, an open box from Do-Rite gracing the polished mahogany in the middle of the room. Three partners sitting in judgment. Fred at the head of the table, eats a maple-bacon donut. My mentor, Rebecca Masters, smiles and gives me a small thumbs-up. Tyler Miller, associate managing partner, nods to acknowledge I'm here.

I'm more than here. After a hundred years, this firm is still a boys' club, but I'm determined to crack into the top echelon and become the second woman to make partner.

Hayden Forbes-Cartwright barrels into me. I fly through the door and end up on hands and knees. When I look up, Fred's mouth and donut haven't met. Rebecca's hand is over her eyes.

"What an entrance, Micki." Tyler's mocking laugh pricks my balloon of confidence.

A snigger erupts from Hayden as his big hand reaches down to pull me up. "So sorry, Micki. Couldn't put the brakes on in time."

Upright, my ankles wobbly as I balance on my low-heeled shoes, my glare has the heat of the Milky Way. Not that Hayden pays any attention. His bogus concern is yet one more layer of deceit.

Points to him. I'm the klutz and he's the chivalric hero. "Have a seat, Micki, Hayden." Fred gives us each a once-over. Dressing well is one of the unspoken rules. Hayden's navy-blue pinstripe is comparable to my silver-gray jacket and matching pencil skirt—points even on wardrobe. My phone in my lap, I pull up my spreadsheet. I've kept score since the first time we met. The advantage has seesawed back and forth, but we're competing for the pinnacle in the stakes race, so I'll have to up my game.

Hayden and I were adversaries from the get-go. We started here, on the same day eight years ago. Me half an hour early. Hayden fifteen minutes late, strolling in with his uncle. All my muscles clenched when he looked me over with his trademark devil-may-care smile.

"I know you both received the memo. With Sonny Philips' retirement, the firm will promote one associate to partner this year. As the two seniors, you will be the leading candidates."

Hayden stops fiddling with his Chicago Yacht Club tie. "Does that mean you'll consider other associates?"

"Technically, yes, but in reality, you are the only ones qualified right now. The partners will evaluate you on several criteria besides the competencies you've shown in your time here."

He pauses.

Hayden rushes into the momentary silence. "Does every partner vote?"

"You know they do," Tyler chides his nephew impatiently.

"Are some votes weighted more heavily than others? Like seniority?"

"No. Please go on, Fred." Rebecca's eye roll should send a message.

When I glance toward Hayden, he shows no embarrassment, not even a slight flush. Most lawyers learn early to put on a neutral face. I permit myself a tiny smile. Minus five to Hayden.

Fred looks at the sheet in front of him, then from Tyler to Rebecca. He positions reading glasses firmly at the end of his long, narrow nose. "The criteria includes enthusiasm, treatment of others, the opinion of your mentor."

He places a finger on page, then clears his throat, glances around. "Also, maintaining personal control, commitment, successful building and protection of your reputation and that of the firm." Another pause.

Tyler breaks in. "We're looking for consistent hard work, always available, constant improvement, and most important— being perceived as trustworthy." He gives an oily smile, staring at me as if he doesn't trust me at all.

Hayden's eyes dart like tiny silverfish, his tell when he's calculating his chances for winning. I put in the long hours and never turn down a request. Hayden skates by, taking credit for the work of junior associates. He boasts about staying late when he disappears in the middle of the day.

When your uncle's name is on the door, you have an extra pass. Tyler Miller will definitely push for Hayden to be the next partner.

Fred is still talking, and I wrench my attention back to his droning monotone. "Besides the formal evaluation, the other piece is assisting Rebecca with a high-profile insider trading case. It's more than usually sensitive because our client is a candidate for a Senate seat. He says it's a setup. Not necessarily a strong or provable defense. You'll be combing emails, social media, accounts, and documents to find evidence."

I suppress a shiver. The sensation of a bucket of night

crawlers being dumped down my spine short circuits my thoughts. Then I remember what Mom used to say when I lost confidence. "Be your own cheerleader." *Rah, rah.*

But I'm beaten to the punch. "What a great opportunity for us to show what we're made of." Hayden's wide smile and crackling delivery are as phony as a carny barker's come-on.

Our managing partner nods his head approvingly. Hayden is his favored candidate too. Fred and Tyler have some kind of mutual admiration society and Hayden benefits.

Yeah, he's a suck-up.

My turn. *Say something but avoid the gush.* I clear my throat as quietly as I can. "This is an amazing challenge. I really appreciate the chance to work on a case so important to the future and reputation of the firm and, potentially beyond, Fred."

Kind of stiff. Fingers crossed I've hit the right note. The knot in my chest loosens when Rebecca winks.

As we walk out, she stops me. "Micki, I have a lunch appointment, but let's have a drink after work." She looks around. Tyler's just going into his office, not paying any attention to us. "We haven't had a good chat for a while."

"Great, Rebecca. Just come by my office when you're ready to leave."

Then I cancel my date for the evening. Work comes first, always.

After-work drinks have replaced the three-martini lunch, unless you're Hayden Forbes-Cartwright. He indulges in both. An unwind is just what I need along with a heads-up on what I can expect in the next few months as we grind through the promotion process.

The Gage is lively at five thirty. A millinery shop in the early twentieth century, the transformation into a happening bar and restaurant on Michigan Avenue in the twenty-first includes historic framed ads for hats.

Rebecca pushes through the crowded room after the hostess, who seats us at a quiet table in a corner near the tile fireplace. We won't have to shout and have less likelihood of being overheard.

Our waiter arrives in classic server attire, pristine white shirt and black slacks. His curly red hair is a Raggedy-Andy mop.

"One Paris Rose, one Jabberwock, fried pickles, and a cheese board." Rebecca hands back the menus and lets out a breath.

Then she pulls out a legal pad. "Thought we could go over some strategies for the work. You can work on the emails, social media, anything online, and whatever documents we can upload. That way, while you're traveling, you'll have plenty of material to access."

"Great. I've been anxious about being away at such a crucial point in my career."

The pencil between Rebecca's fingers moves up and down like a seesaw. "Thanks to technology. Years ago, we were tied to the office, the library. I'm glad you can go to the awards ceremony. Kind of like the Oscars for authors."

"Yeah. Still, five working days away..."

"I'll make sure you're front of mind for all the partners. As far as the work, our new legal research assistant is already busy organizing everything as documentation comes in."

The barman puts the flute containing the Paris Rose cocktail in front of Rebecca. She hurriedly pushes her legal pad to the side, but not before a few drops splash onto the paper, leaving a light pink trail. She takes a sip just as the server deposits the cheese board in the middle of the table, along with a basket of fried pickles. Meanwhile, the barman has brought my Jabberwock in its coupe.

No time for lunch and my stomach growls. Cheese is a magnet for me. Hence my passion for pizza. With grabby fingers, I snatch some almost before the server gets the platter on the table. "Sorry," I mumble my apology through a mouthful of cheese. "Starving."

Rebecca nibbles on a pickle. "Simon Greenberg is an attorney with Talcott, Maier, a state legislator, and the front-running Republican candidate for Senate from Illinois. We went to law school together and have faced each other in court many times."

She places cheese on a couple of pickles and pops them, one after the other, into her mouth, then sighs with satisfaction. "The SEC received a tip claiming he made use of private information to trade stocks from several companies he represents. After an investigation, the Commission decided on civil charges. Unfortunately, because his candidacy has made him a public figure, criminal charges are pending as well. There may well be some questions about election finance, too."

"Wait. Shouldn't Hayden be here?" Not that I want him, but if we're a team, he deserves the same explanations.

"Hayden has already been briefed."

Be professional. In control. Pretend it doesn't matter.

"Oh. I see." But I don't. Not at all.

Rebecca takes a huge swallow of the pink liquid. "Not by me. After our meeting, Tyler and Fred took Hayden to lunch and briefed him there."

How does she know? Or is this an assumption? My heated protest escapes before I can rein it in. "But it's your case."

She waves the comment away. "He was so full of himself when he got back. Swanned into my office. 'Simon Greenberg, huh? I wondered after the rumors flying around. Good for us.' Then he laughed and walked out."

Her scowl could freeze the Chicago River. "I was sure Tyler at least would make sure he's up to speed, and I wanted to put you in the loop right away. Fred and Tyler are bound to give Hayden some instruction on how to handle things, and he will take advantage of the time you are away in April."

My cocktail beckons and I chug it down, sputtering slightly as the potent alcohol burns the back of my throat. "Should I cancel the trip?"

She ignores that. "You'll meet the client tomorrow, so make a powerful first impression. Wear good jewelry and heels are fine. Simon is tall, so he won't mind. Red lipstick if you have it. He respects women who can stand up for themselves—usually."

Mindlessly curling my hair around a finger, I muse about wardrobe when I should be concentrating on the facts of the case. Rebecca has moved on and I hurriedly refocus.

"You'll have plenty of work to do while you're out of the office. Have a tech set up your laptop with VPN. It will be your lifeline to the firm. Video meetings will help too. Make sure you can report on progress every day. You need to maintain a firm, visible presence while you're in Paris."

We see the waiter in the distance and Rebecca catches his attention. Once we have refills, she takes a sip, then leans forward. "Show you're dedicated to the firm and the case and you can work without supervision. I'll try to schedule the meetings first thing in the morning to mitigate the seven-hour time difference."

"And the other complications?"

"Hayden is one, as I'm sure you've guessed. More in terms of your selection as partner. The bad news is the partners decide long before the case ends. But he'll try for every plum he can pluck. The other is, because of the election cycle, Greenberg is pushing to clear it up or bury it quickly. News of the pending charges will hit the papers tomorrow."

Why haven't they leaked already?

Rebecca must be a mind reader. "The papers are planning front-page splashes with stories, commentary, and reactions on at least two inside pages."

I can picture the *Tribune*. Huge headline and photos on their broadsheet front page. Stories about the investigation, the campaign, lots of background on the candidate, a piece where the rest of the field comments. Then an editorial on the op-ed pages. Maybe a political cartoon. The *Sun-Times* tabloid format will be just as comprehensive in a more compact form. "Collusion?"

"Cooperation." Her forehead wrinkles, brows touching. The corners of her mouth turn down.

"Keeping him from making incendiary comments is going to be a job in itself. We want as little coverage as possible while we work on clearing him—if we can. The damage to his reputation is a gift to the other contenders. He's been the front runner, the poster boy for the party."

In two swallows, the Jabberwock has disappeared. I order another, then, still hungry, I pop more bread and cheese into my mouth.

"Hey, guys. Didn't get the memo." Hayden pushes into the tufted leather booth and reaches for a pickle, almost knocking me to the floor. "Uncle Tyler thought you might be here, Rebecca. Said it's your usual watering hole." His stress on "uncle" makes my blood feel like ice water.

"A casual afterwork drink." Rebecca's voice is flat.

Hayden reaches over and taps her legal pad. "Sure you aren't strategizing?" The twinkle in his eye shows malice, not amusement. "By the way, I met Laney this afternoon. She's a cutie."

"Laney?" The name is unfamiliar.

With a leer, he says, "Our legal researcher. Fresh out of her paralegal program."

The server comes by with my third drink.

"Are you running a tab?"

Rebecca nods.

"Two Satan's Whiskers. Need to play catch up with these two." His smirk makes my skin crawl.

"How appropriate."

He snickers. My snarky comment bounces off his crocodile hide.

Before the drinks guy can take off, I hold up a hand. "I'd like to order something to go, please."

Pad out, he looks a bit like a bird, head to the side.

"Shrimp cocktail with no sauce, and the apple salad. Just put the shrimp on top of the salad with the dressing on the side."

"You got it."

Hayden puffs out his chest like a pouter pigeon. "Me, I have a date as soon as I finish these truly spectacular drinks."

"Drinks named just for you."

He grins. "You know it. Scary but seductive. And I have some seducing on tap."

Probably with our new researcher. I push the sour feelings back. "Have fun."

"Oh, I intend to."

Rebecca's warning look doesn't make any impression either. She grabs her coat off the empty seat. "Off to have dinner with my hubby. He's cooking tonight."

I trudge to the office, take-out container in hand, ready for a little research of my own.

Chapter 2

Smell is something that attracts me instantly. So if the guy smells nice, there is an instant attraction.—Alia Bhatt

March 2014
Micki

JL Martin, a new friend I'd like to know better, asked me out several times in the last month. Good thing he's persistent because getting up to speed on the insider trading case is kicking my butt big time. Today is Sunday and I'm giving myself the evening off. I worked for five hours earlier, but tonight's the night.

Except for a few dinners at my parents' house, I spend every waking hour at my office. Just hours of research, meetings with the client, too much time with Hayden, and at least one meeting a day with our team of seven. We've added a legal secretary, a file clerk, and a first-year associate.

No friends, no hockey either at the arena or on TV. All my meals are delivery, or just bowls of cereal. Three boxes of Chocolate Chex stashed in my credenza help with sudden hunger attacks.

JL is just my type. Not breathtakingly handsome like my friend Cress' boyfriend, Max. I don't need movie star good looks. He's got that craggy jawed, French-Canadian hockey-player aura. He's well-muscled but not muscle bound. No visible tattoos. Cropped brown hair, sprinkled with gray. Deep brown, almost black eyes, like pools of dark chocolate, complete the package. My heart stutters every time I see him. *Take a deep breath.* Then snort as water goes up my nose.

I met JL last December. He's a security specialist. His company, WatchDog, Inc., supplied bodyguards to protect my best friend. A narcissistic lunatic, someone we went to school with, tried to destroy Cress' life and career. Still entangled with my now-former boyfriend, the immediate attraction unsettled me, and I buried it deep. Now that Sam is an ex, I dig it up. JL can be the safety valve to relieve the pressure of work.

Water drips down my long hair into my face. My eyes are squeezed shut to keep errant drops from seeping in. The slick, soapy granite surface means one hand stays flat against the marble cladding, so I don't slip and fall. I fumble to find the knobs that shut off the multiple sprays. When the hot water stops, the immediate sensation is ice coating my skin. Shivers run through me while I grope for a towel. Any old piece of cloth in a storm would help at this point.

Where the fuck is it? I know I put it in easy reach. But this master bath is so much bigger than the normal-sized room in my former condo that I feel spatially challenged. The walk-in power shower is at least three times the size of anything I've ever used before. Too many months alone, my mind wanders in sexy directions. If things move along well, JL and I might have fun in here.

That's all I want. Some fun. After the shit show that is Sam Beamer, I deserve a bit of no-strings happy.

My feet start to slide, and I grab on to the edge of the glass with my left hand, grope with the right, and dislodge a soft French terry textile that I catch just before it hits the floor. I wipe my eyes, then rub the cloth against my dripping hair. So what if it's the bath sheet. At this point a washcloth would do. I wrap the cotton fabric around me and notice, my eyes now open and dry, the hand towel is right where I put it for a quick pick up.

Bending over, I use the newly rediscovered hand towel to wrap my hair in a makeshift turban, tighten the bath towel around my quivering body, and step out into my slippers. At least they're where I expect them to be.

The frustration that made my heart pound leaks

away now I've reestablished control. The weakness in my limbs subsides and I don't need the wall to prop me up. The generous bath sheet starts to slip, and I readjust it once more before walking into the bedroom. That's when I hear shouts. Not screams of distress or pain. More like the insistent howl of an angry predator spewing pure vitriol.

"I know you're in there, you fat slut. Show yourself, bitch. I have things to say to you." A drawl. How does he do that? Howl with a Southern accent?

Sam. Can't believe he found me. Goosebumps march up my arms and across my chest, the good-old-boy accent sending me into high alert. I force myself to keep my hands down so I can't put my fingers in my ears, then slip behind the edge of a long curtain, craning my neck to peek out the window.

Dancing in rage on the narrow sidewalk, Sam's hand curls around something, but from this distance, no glasses or contacts, I can't make out what it is until the former baseball wannabe does a wind up and lets the object fly.

The condo I'm subletting is on the top floor, and he throws like a girl. That's why he's a wannabe. No way that missile is going to reach me. When the projectile hits the wall two stories below, I see it's a small rock. Not only is he incompetent in throwing, but he didn't even use something that would cause much damage.

"Where are you, shyster? Stop cowering and show yourself, you filthy cow." His invective might make a passerby think he was harassing his lawyer instead of his former girlfriend.

I edge away from the window, flop onto the king-size bed, let the towel drop to the floor, and wrap myself in the royal blue velour bedcover. The velvety feel is comforting as I try to ignore the epithets and relax into the luxurious warmth. The memory of our next-to-last encounter sweeps over me.

A cold, sunny December day and we've had an early adjournment, so I decide to surprise Sam with a lunch date. Opening the door, I hear loud noises. "Sam," I call out, wondering if he's sick. When I walk inside... Surprise.

Sam's not alone. His companion's red hair splays out against the deep plum of my new couch.

Startled, I scream, and he lifts his head, a bald spot outlined by the straggly, shoulder-length hair. Hazy eyes stare into mine. His thick, gravel tone is accusatory. "What the hell you doin' here, Micki? Shouldn't you be at work?"

"Yeah. Who are you?" The redhead's voice is high and nasal.

I straighten to my full five foot seven and, with a glare so hot it could set the furniture on fire, I tell her, "I am the owner of this condo. Until just now, I was also the partner of this douche."

"I live here, baby." He stares as if daring me to contradict him.

With a swallow and a deep breath, I summon all the flair I use in the courtroom, snapping, "You don't live here anymore, you bastard. Out." My forefinger points to the still ajar front door.

"But, Micki, darlin', I need to…" He grabs for the bib of his overalls, voice a combination of whine and wheedle.

"Scram. All you need to do is leave and never come back."

He scrambles up and faces me. He's trying to pull up his boxers with no success. "Back off and let me explain." He gives a menacing growl.

I step forward, my stilettos pushing down into the denim of the overalls that pool on the floor, and shove farther into his personal space. The bright red nail of that same forefinger pokes at his chest. "You need to leave. Right now."

He backs up, and a ripping sound makes his face redden. "You tore my pants, bimbo,. These are fucking expensive," he snivels. "Prada."

My disbelieving gasp turns into a laugh. "How the hell do you afford Prada? Save up from all the meals I've paid for? The rent you've saved living here? A wealthy patron you never mentioned? Certainly not from the mediocre art you produce." My eyes narrow. "Oh, I know, they're knockoffs. Should be more careful with your money, Sammy."

His enraged growl makes me expect he'll shake his raised fist at me, but he hauls off and punches me in the face. Shocked, I put a hand on the arm of the couch to keep my balance, taste blood as my bottom lip catches between my teeth, and don't make a sound.

"You'll be sorry," he yells as I slam the door on his fingers. He yelps and steps back, so I close the door, set the deadbolt, and sink onto the floor, trying to block out his banging fist against the wood.

I shudder with frustration as they clatter down the stairs of the six-flat building. That's when I realize he still has a key, but I'm too discombobulated to deal with it now. Instead, I call my best friend, Cress. She promises to come right over.

I drop my head into my hands. Can't hold back the tears and I start to bawl.

The visions dissolve as I hear Sam, still screaming like a banshee. A hail of pebbles smash into the building. Then another rock hits, this one bigger. I pray he hasn't caused any major damage. I crack open the window and yell. "What did you expect? You cheated on me and ruined my couch, you fucker." Pulling the window back down, I reach for my cellphone and dial 911.

JL

When the woman you lust after agrees to a first date, you feel you've won the World Cup. Micki and I met last December when Max's girlfriend, Cress, faced accusations of plagiarism, a threat that could have destroyed her writing career, and eventually escalated to physical violence. Cress' best friend came as part of the package. She was a magnetic field that drew me in, although she had a longtime boyfriend, Sam.

Our uneasy relationship, built on mutual friends and embarrassing circumstances, has been tentative, even after Sam turned out to be a total douche. The day she found him having sex on her couch, she threw him out, but not before he hit her. Despite her reluctance, Max and I convinced her that a trip to the emergency room had to happen. Her belligerent attitude made the staff happy to see the back of her. Since then, I've given her space but, three months later, I'm ready to try for a goal.

Last month, standing in front of Max's Gold Coast mansion, she was a vision in a chic emerald-green wool coat, unbuttoned so I could admire the stunning blue silk wrap dress with the deep neckline that matched her Pacific-blue eyes. Her long, straight, honey-colored hair curved below her shoulders, swinging slightly when she moved. Short enough to fit under my chin, I itched to hold her gentle curves.

Heat rose from my feet to my face. Instead of repeating the greeting, what popped out was, "Micki, ma chère, I want to take you out sometime." At least it wasn't what I'd been thinking. *I want to take you to bed, right now.*

She blinked. Then blinked again. "Uh, yeah, sure." Sparkly nails in some kind of graduated blues pushed back flying silken strands. Her words were so tentative, I followed up with the inane, "Really? You're sure?"

"Sorry. You surprised me. But yes, I'm sure."

That's when I screamed victory, waving my arms in the air like a madman, only slightly constricted by the stiff leather of the new jacket Maman sent me for my birthday. No butter-soft hide for her. It's rich, dark-brown, textured like tree bark. The look sharp. It would wear into suppleness eventually, but not for a few years at least. I would never tell her I would have preferred something more pliant. Pre-ruined, a term a friend coined.

Micki's reaction was adorable. Shock, delight, and amusement flitted across her face in rapid succession. Her eyes sparkled as she tossed her head, silky tresses flying in all directions. In the end, we both doubled over laughing.

Moaning, she held her side. "Damn it. I have a stitch. Laughter shouldn't hurt."

I tried to nod and straighten up at the same time, gasping from the pain. "Calisse," I grunted. My face was wet. Never believed cry laughing was real until then.

"Just so you know, I'm planning on karaoke." I crossed my fingers, hoping one of my favorite things appealed to her, too.

A mischievous grin touched her lips. Then, fists raised, she screamed, "Score!" And we dissolved into new paroxysms of laughter.

A door slammed, and Max ran down the steps. No

coat. He started shivering as soon as he stopped. "Bloody hell." He rubbed his arms. "What the fuck do you maniacs think you're doing? I'm sure people can hear you all the way to South Shore."

Micki giggled. "Bit of an exaggeration, Max."

His chest made a rumbling sound. "Come in out of the cold. Cress has rum hot toddies ready."

"Not whisky?" Max's impressive collection of rare whiskies impressed the select few allowed to share the treasured elixirs.

"None of my single malt is going to be wasted like that." He turned and ran up the stairs as if Jack Frost was nipping at his nose.

All this flashes through my mind as my new Italian beauty, an Aprilia RSV4 motorcycle, idles at a red light. I can see the drivers around me staring at its sexy shape. It is a heavy bike, and not as fast as some of its competitors, but the four-cylinder engine produces a sound that makes your neck hair stand on end. It's compact, so it works well on city streets. My chest thrums with pleasure, seeing the desire and envy of the surrounding drivers.

The vibrations keep me in a constant state of physical awareness at this very long red light. So long I count with the longest swear I know under my breath, "Osti de tabarnak de sacrament, de câlice de ciboire de crisse de marde!" Finally, after what seems like infinity but is only five times through the litany, the light changes. I rev the engine, producing an operatic peal, bob and weave past the slow-moving buses clogging Inner Lakeshore Drive, crawl through several intersections, and head toward the Gold Coast.

The Drive has more traffic than I expect and I'm running late. When I turn onto her street, I can see the impressive Parisian-inspired condo building just down at the corner. Micki rents a condo with an option to buy.

As I reach the intersection of Goethe and Stone, a fracas erupts just outside the building entrance. The concierge tries to tackle someone throwing stones at the façade. I roar up, tires squealing, tear off my helmet, and run toward the combatants. Behind me, the bike is on the ground, writhing from the throbbing engine. In the distance, sirens wail as I pull the two men apart.

The concierge steps back, uniform looking the worse for wear. The other man is Micki's cheater ex-boyfriend, Sam Beaton, in his usual country hayseed outfit of sloppy, tattered overalls and a red-checked shirt with frayed collar and cuffs. Both are paint splattered. He's a "naïve" painter, although I think he's just bad. The fake good 'ole boy persona is part and parcel of the presentation.

Sam looks me over and drawls, "Weel, if it ain't the Frenchy."

"French Canadian, tonton." It means boob, which amuses me.

He glares and takes a swing. Unprepared, I end up

on the pavement at the wrong end of a punch on the nose. Sam cackles. "Serves ya right, ya filthy Canuck."

I ignore the pain, push myself up, and slug him in the jaw. He tumbles to his knees like garbage down a chute. I push him onto his back with my foot. Only then, with my foot resting on his chest, do I pull out some tissues to sop up the blood I can feel dribbling out of my nose and trickling down from my lip to my chin.

The police surround us. One latches on to my arm and moves me away. The other pulls Sam to his feet. One officer, hands on his hips, says, "We got a 911 call from this location. What's going on?"

Sam opens his mouth. I know he is going to blame me. But before he gets a word out, the concierge takes charge. "Officer, this man." He points a shaky finger toward the slob, who adjusts the bib straps on the overalls. The concierge quivers with rage, his voice rising to falsetto. "This man came into the building asking about one of our residents. When I refused to give him any information, he ran out and threw rocks at the windows. Screaming obscenities. I was trying to stop him when this gentleman arrived and subdued him."

"You made the call?"

"No. I don't know who called. Probably a resident."

Just then, Micki, feet bare, runs out the door. Her hair is half up, face bare of makeup, allowing a stunning flush to show through.

"Thank God you're here," she shouts at the officers. She points at Sam. "This jerk has been stalking and harassing me. I even have an order of protection out against him, but he just ignores it. Mostly he yells at me from a distance, but attacking the building, well..." We all look where Sam had been throwing rocks. A pile, like a miniature cairn, sits on the edge of the lawn. The concierge winces at the sight of the pockmarks in the lintel over the door and fine cracks in the ornate fanlight.

Micki turns toward me, recoiling at the sight of my damaged nose. "Sam, you dirtbag. I hope you go to jail for assault and vandalism. Maybe you'll learn a lesson." She moves closer and dabs my nose with her right forefinger.

"I'm so sorry," she whispers to me, standing on tiptoe to kiss the side of my cheek.

"All better." I grin.

"Yh, ri-" Sam jeers, his words blurry from his broken jaw. "I knkd oo dn, sshoe."

Micki looks down at her bare feet and frowns. "If I had my stilettos on, I'd make you sorry, Sam."

He tries to snicker, but a groan of pain is all that comes out. Mighty struggles don't make any difference since he can't squirm out of the grip of the cop holding his left arm. Now cuffed, the cop hangs on to him.

"That was a tap. No harm done." I see worry clouding her eyes. "Don't worry. His jaw is worse off than my nose."

"Jus' way. Oo'l paaa." Can't tell whether Sam's unintelligible mumble is a threat or a complaint.

I hold my body still and bite my inner cheek. Micki takes no prisoners. She walks up to the balding man with the beer belly hanging over his belt and pokes him in the gut. "Shut up, jerk."

"Ore," Sam spits out. Then groans.

"Pot, kettle." Micki sends back a sizzler.

Wailing sirens distract all of us as two ambulances skid to a stop, tires squealing in counterpoint.

"We're transporting him to emergency to have his jaw checked out before we charge him." The senior cop loosens his grip as the EMT comes over. He focuses on my nose and the contusions on my cheek. "You need to be checked out, too?"

When I remove the tissue, the bleeding has stopped. "Can't tell till the swelling goes down, but I think it will be fine. I'll have a doctor check if something crops up."

They wrestle Sam into the ambulance. The cop turns back to me. "We'll need a statement from you. Meet us at the Eighteenth Precinct on Larrabee. Check in with the desk sergeant and tell him you're there. See me, Sergeant Lam. He'll know to expect you."

I call after him, "Fine. I'll be right behind you." Crisse, this messes up my plans.

"Have Max and Cress pick you up," I yell to Micki as I race for my bike. "I'll meet you at the bar when I'm done."

"I'll take an Uber." Her arms are tight across her chest.

"Please." My sad hound expression must work because her arms drop, and her stony face softens.

"Okay. Just because you asked nicely."

I give her a thumbs-up, then follow the blue and white down the street toward the police station. In my rearview mirror, Micki dwindles into the distance.

The building that houses the Eighteenth Precinct is fairly new and I stop by the long, raised counter inside the door, helmet under my arm. A woman in uniform leans over a partition and I let her know I'm here to see Sergeant Lam. She points me to the waiting room, chilly in the cold March evening. A cup of coffee would be welcome, but the pot has been sitting too long, smells burnt, and when I try to pour out the inky black liquid, it's almost congealed. With a small twitch of my shoulders, I put the foam cup down on the table.

I alternate between sitting in one of the vinyl chairs and pacing back and forth, the heels of my boots clacking against the beige linoleum tile flooring. Two groups huddle in different corners of the room, ignoring me but occasionally looking over to stare at each other. Several of the women have swollen eyes and tear-streaked cheeks, mascara melted into blotches. The men keep their distance from the women, forming several smaller groupings close by. All I hear are occasional swear words and some sobs. I wonder if there was some incident they were all involved in. Yelling comes from the hallway, in some language I don't know. It gets louder, then gradually fades.

When Lam calls me in, my body floods with relief. This is a crap way to have a first date. I stand, find I'm stiff, and stretch out my back before following him back to an interview room. The other guy is already there, a notebook out. "I thought you recorded these things now," I say.

"We do. But sometimes I want to make a note." He taps the ballpoint against the stiff green cardboard cover.

I didn't see Sam when I came in and when I ask, they tell me he's still at the hospital. "You wouldn't have seen him, anyway. We take suspects through a different entrance."

Knowing I won't find out any more from them, I finger my nose, trying to decide if it's broken or bruised. It feels swollen but not too disfigured. Breathing is laborious. I tell them my story, then wait for them to produce a statement. I sign and rush out the door. Before I go to Stanley's Kitchen & Tap, I have to go home. I can easily wipe the blood off my jacket, but I need to change. I like tie-dye, but a blood-spattered shirtfront is not the look I'm going for.

ALSO BY THE AUTHOR

Global Security Unlimited Series
At First Sight
At the Crossroads
"Code Silver" (short story)
"Toucan Laugh" (short story)

Murder in the North Country
Dead in the Alley

Grant Family
"It's Just a Guise"
"A Heartfelt Christmas"
"Partridges and Gold Rings"
"Unsocial Media"

Anthologies
"Colonel Fitzwilliam Meets His Match" in *Austen Tea Party*

"Aegean Persuasion," in *Tales from the Golden State of Mind*

"Melting the Iceman," *in Second Time's A Charm: A Second Chance Contemporary Romance Anthology*

"Medway Meeting," in *Tea with Austen*

"A Heart for the Guy," in *Light My Fire*

"Off the Bench," in *Well Played*

"Two Minutes for Holding," in *Love, Lattes, and Holiday Tales*

Sharon Michalove writes romantic suspense and traditional mystery.

After growing up in suburban Chicago, she attended the University Illinois where she received four degrees because she didn't have the gumption to go anywhere else. Then she spent her career at the university, working in departmental administration, publishing and libraries. Her specialties are 15th-16th century European history, polar exploration, and food history.

In graduate school, she met and married the love of her life. They shared a love of music, theater, travel and cats. He died in 2013.

After spending most of her life in a medium-sized

university town she moved back to Chicago in 2017 so she could go to more Blackhawks games and spend quality time at Eataly. Sharon frequently uses her knowledge of music, history, and food to enrich her novels. She also loves hockey, reading, cooking, writing, and various less elevated activities like eating eclairs and sampling gins and single malts.

She is a member of Sisters in Crime, Mystery Writers of America, and Chicago-North Romance Writers, Historical Novel Society, and Regency Writers. Currently, she is president of the Sisters in Crime Chicagoland Chapter and an at-large board member of MWA Midwest. Her Global Security Unlimited series was a finalist for the 2024 Chanticleer International Book Award for Genre Series.

Website: http://coffeeandeclairs.com

Newsletter: https://coffeeandeclairs.com/subscribe

Amazon author page: http://amazon.com/author/sdm_romance_and_more

Goodreads https://www.goodreads.com/author/show/2128144.Sharon_D_Michalove?from_search=true&from_srp=true

BookBub: https://www.bookbub.com/profile/sharon-michalove

www.ingramcontent.com/pod-product-compliance
Lightning Source LLC
Chambersburg PA
CBHW061339310726
48974CB00001B/115